BUT NOT FOR VENGEANCE

A CLINT WOLF NOVEL
(BOOK 23)

BY

BJ BOURG

WWW.BJBOURG.COM

TITLES BY BJ BOURG

LONDON CARTER MYSTERY SERIES

James 516
Proving Grounds
Silent Trigger
Bullet Drop
Elevation
Blood Rise

CLINT WOLF MYSTERY SERIES

But Not Forgotten
But Not Forgiven
But Not Forsaken
But Not Forever
But Not For Naught
But Not Forbidden
But Not Forlorn
But Not Formidable
But Not For Love
But Not Forborne
But Not Forewarned
But Not Foreboding
But Not Forespoken
But Not For Blood
But Not Foreknown
But Not Fortuitous
But Not For Fear
But Not Foreseen
But Not For Lust
But Not Forspent
But Not Forsworn
But Not Foregone
But Not For Vengeance

BUT NOT FOR VENGEANCE
A Clint Wolf Novel by BJ Bourg

Cover design by Christine Savoie of Bayou Cover Designs

PUBLISHED IN THE UNITED STATES OF AMERICA

CHAPTER 1

Friday, February 25
Mechant Loup, Louisiana

Cole Peterson loved Mardi Gras. It was his favorite time of the year. Since he was a member of the fire department, he was able to participate in the town's night parade, which always ran the Friday before Fat Tuesday. Although he wasn't a practicing Catholic, this parade always reminded him that Ash Wednesday was fast approaching, and with it, the beginning of Lent. He didn't believe in depriving his body of anything it wanted, so the tradition meant nothing to him. Well, except for one thing: it was crawfish season!

"Hey, Cole, how's it going?"

Cole swiveled his head around to see a dark Tahoe slowing to a stop at the back of the procession. It was Detective Clint Wolf and his large German shepherd, Achilles.

"Detective Clint!" Cole hurried from his position near the barricade and approached the Tahoe. He stopped a few feet from the passenger window, which was down. "You think he still remembers me? Or will he take my arm off?"

"If you call me Detective Clint again, I'll have him jump from the window and tear both your legs off."

Sirens and music were blaring up and down the line of floats, and it was hard for Cole to hear everything Detective Clint was saying, but that last part was loud and clear.

"Wait…what?" Cole had stopped dead in his tracks. "He would do that?"

Detective Clint's face, which had appeared serious, now cracked into a smile and he started laughing. "Hell to the no! He remembers you. Just stop calling me Detective Clint. We're friends."

Cole sighed and continued toward the window. He rubbed Achilles' head and then shook hands with the chief of detectives.

"You staying dry?" Detective Clint asked.

"Yes, sir, now that the rain has stopped." Cole flipped the rain suit hood back and rubbed a few beads of moisture from his dark face. "I was worried the parade would be cancelled."

The town had been lucky in years past to always have beautiful weather for the night parade, but today had been different. It had rained nonstop for most of the day, which made the seventy-one-degree temperature feel more like the early fifties, but the krewe members would not be denied. They showed up wearing a wide array of rain gear—from professional suits like Cole was wearing to plastic garbage bags with cut-outs for their arms and heads—and loaded their throws onto the floats.

"The mayor would never let that happen. She loves Carnival season as much as anyone." Clint grunted. "Me, I would've cancelled this shit. I'd rather be home watching Gracie herd the dogs with her Barbie Jeep than riding around in this cold mess."

"It ain't cold, Detective—I mean, Clint. Winter's long over with. It's almost summertime now."

"Give me the nineties any day of the week," Clint said, glancing in his rearview mirror. "Well, kid, it looks like I need to pull off. That float behind me looks like it wants to move."

"Before you go," Cole said, shifting his feet, "I wanted to ask about Takecia. I heard she doesn't have a boyfriend anymore."

Clint sighed. "Yeah, her boyfriend really put a stranglehold on their relationship, so she's a free woman again."

"You think you could put in a good word for me?"

Cole shifted his feet again as Clint studied him. To Cole, Takecia Gayle was a goddess. If he could have even the slightest chance with someone like her, he would be in Heaven on earth.

"I'll tell her you're interested and see if I can convince her to take you to lunch," Clint said with a sigh, "but I can't promise anything. You're a bit younger than she is. She'd probably feel like she's robbing the cradle."

"Shit, she can rob the cradle, the grave, and my mom's bank account." Cole could feel his face beaming. "If she went to lunch with me and I died the next day, I'd die a happy man."

Clint laughed and waved to Cole as he drove away.

Cole returned to his post along Main Street between Lacy Court and Kate Drive, and smiled down at a group of kids who were eagerly awaiting the approaching float.

One of the boys was looking up in awe at his black and yellow rain suit. The boy pointed to the radio mic clipped to his shoulder and asked, "Are you a cop?"

"No, I'm a firefighter," Cole said with a sense of pride. It had been his childhood dream to become a fireman when he grew up and, directly out of high school, he had realized that dream. "We get to help out with the parades."

"Wow!" said the kid. "You must be brave. I want to be a fireman, too, but I'm afraid of the dark."

Cole squatted on his heels to look the kid in the eyes. The float had reached them, and the riders were throwing candy, stuffed animals, and footballs all around them, but the kid was transfixed on Cole.

"When I was your age, I was afraid of the dark, too," he explained loudly, trying to be heard over the Mardi Gras Mambo that blared overhead. "But you know what?"

"What?" asked the wide-eyed boy, who couldn't be older than seven.

"When you grow up, the fear of the dark automatically disappears," he explained. "You're only afraid of the dark when you're little. Big kids aren't."

The boy beamed. "For real?"

"Yep."

"You think I can be a firefighter when I get big?"

"Absolutely! Just do like I did. Study real hard in school, read a bunch of books on being a firefighter, and ask your mom and dad to bring you to the fire department. When y'all get there, ask for me. My name's Cole. I can show you around and let you meet the fire chief. I'll even let you get in the big fire truck."

"Really?" The boy turned toward a man and woman who were standing close by looking down at them. The woman's eyes were glistening and the man was smiling warmly. "Mom, dad, can we go to the fire department?"

They both nodded and the little boy screeched. He whirled around and threw his short arms around Cole's neck. Although he was small, he had a strong grip and he hugged Cole like a python squeezing its prey.

Cole put an arm on the boy's back and smiled awkwardly up at the parents. He hadn't expected this reaction from the boy, but it made him feel good to make the kid happy.

Once the boy had released him, Cole turned back to watching the crowd. His job was to ensure that no kids—the small variety or the grownup variety—ran out in front of the floats. Every year across Louisiana, at least a few people were run over and killed by floats or the tractors and vehicles pulling them, so the police department partnered with the fire department each year to get as many bodies as possible along the parade route to help keep its citizens safe.

Cole nodded thoughtfully as he watched the last float approaching. Public safety was a rewarding job. While most of his calls for service were for brush fires or chemical spills, he did get to respond to a dozen or so traffic crashes each year and a house fire every few years. He was glad there weren't more tragedies in this small town, but he did feel an itch to do more.

He glanced toward his right, where Detective Clint had long ago disappeared. Clint Wolf and Takecia Gayle got to help people every day. If they weren't arresting bad guys, they were doing other things to help keep the public safe. He suddenly wondered if he could become a cop.

"Officer Cole Peterson," he said aloud, knowing no one could hear him over the noise from the last float that was creeping by, "how can I help you?"

The young man smiled sheepishly to himself and nodded. Yeah, he liked the sound of it. He would apply for the police department first thing next Monday and try to get in on the action. He might even be able to go out on the water with Lieutenant Melvin Saltzman and save people from drowning or help find overdue boaters—

A piercing siren suddenly snapped him from his thoughts. He had been watching the kids to his right as the last float ambled away, and he hadn't noticed the police car approaching from his left, which marked the end of the parade. He looked in that direction now and saw that it was the woman of his dreams—Sergeant Takecia Gayle.

CHAPTER 2

Cole Peterson stood frozen. He simply smiled and waved at Takecia Gayle, but the goddess of a woman waved him over. He looked around to see if she was signaling to someone else. Surely, she couldn't be summoning him. But everyone was gathering up their folding chairs and loot and heading for their cars to beat the mad rush that usually followed the end of the parade.

With a gulp, Cole approached Takecia's patrol cruiser, walking as though picking his way through a mine field. Usually very smooth and talkative, he was suddenly at a loss for words. He smiled nervously and tried to say hello, but only a croak spilled from his lips.

Takecia held up her cell phone. "Clint said you wanted to take me out to lunch."

Cole could feel his throat constricting, threatening to cut off his oxygen. He nodded.

"How old are you?"

"Um, I'm about to be twenty-three, ma'am."

"You can't call me ma'am."

"Yes, ma'am." Cole winced. "I mean, okay."

Takecia was thoughtful. "Twenty-three, huh?"

"Yeah." Cole realized he could still talk, and decided he had to act now, or he would forever lose this opportunity. "I'm twenty-three going on thirty. Mom always said I was wise and mature beyond my years, and I never argue with Mom."

"Respect for your mother is a plus in my book." Takecia studied him for a long moment. After a while, she nodded. "Okay, I'm free tomorrow for lunch. Do you know where I live?"

Cole swallowed hard and shook his head. "No, ma'am."

"Call me that again and it's off." Takecia fixed him with her dark and mysterious eyes before snatching a sticky note from her console and scribbling on it. She handed him the paper. "This is my address. Pick me up at eleven. This is not a date. It's only lunch. Do you understand?"

Cole nodded as he reached inside his rain suit and placed the sticky note in the breast pocket of his BDUs, right next to his heart.

"I need to hear you say it," Takecia said.

"It's not a date."

Although she tried to fight it, Cole could see a smile tugging at the corners of her mouth.

"See you tomorrow," she said, and then drove away.

Cole felt as though he was floating on air as he followed the crowd south along the Main Street. His vehicle was parked at the fire station, which was several blocks in the opposite direction, but he wanted to make his way toward the barricades that were blocking traffic on the southern end of town. As soon as Chief Susan Wolf announced that everything was clear, he would help the other firefighters remove the barricades and allow the traffic to once again flow through town.

Several cars that had previously been parked along the shoulder of the road were now lining up to follow the back of the parade toward the northern end of town and make their escape over the bridge as soon as those barricades were removed.

As he walked past M & P Grill and heard someone blow a horn, Cole shook his head at the impatience of some people. There was no use getting in a hurry. Traffic was insane before, during, and after a Mardi Gras parade. If people would only accept that and settle in for the long haul, there would be a lot less road rage.

The sound of Takecia's siren had faded to a low wail, and he felt his face heat up at the remembrance of their date tomorrow. He couldn't believe it was happening. Clint had really come through for him. What if Takecia actually liked him and they started dating? So what if she was a few years older than him? He'd heard of older women marrying younger men. Hell, hadn't Demi Moore married Ashton Kutcher? He thought he remembered reading that he was in his twenties and she was in her forties when they'd hooked up. If that was okay, then there should be no problems at all with him and Takecia, because they were both still in their twenties.

Cole was reminding himself to check on the status of the Moore-

Kutcher relationship when he heard the revving of an engine, screeching tires, and screams fill the air behind him. He whirled around in time to see a truck slam into a man and woman. The impact sent the man hurling through the air and into a nearby ditch, while the woman was trapped beneath the vehicle. As he watched in horror, the truck jostled roughly as it drove over the woman's body.

"No!" Cole bellowed. Wishing he had a gun, he sprang forward, racing toward the scene. The truck plowed forward into the confused crowd, heading south onto Main Street with no regard for the safety of anyone.

As Cole's legs pumped as fast as he could make them go, his hand reached for the radio mic. He needed to call it in. He needed law enforcement and he needed EMS on the scene immediately.

"Dispatch, we need help!" he hollered into the radio. "Near M & P Grill! We've got multiple casualties!"

People were aware of what was happening now and were scattering out of the path of the oncoming truck, which was picking up speed as it headed south, but a few more people got hit. Cole was only a dozen feet from the front of the truck when he heard a woman scream from his left. He glanced in that direction and saw a lady sprawled out on the western shoulder of Main Street, her arms reaching toward the road as she cried out in terror.

The truck hadn't reached her yet, so Cole quickly surmised that she had been trampled by the panicked crowd. His eyes followed hers and he let out his own terrified screech. There, standing frozen on the highway and staring directly into the bright lights of the oncoming truck, was the young boy from earlier.

Without an ounce of hesitation and without slowing down, Cole dove directly into the path of the killer truck and shoved the little boy as hard as he could.

What happened next was a blur. Cole felt the hard metal of the truck make contact with the right side of his torso. His ribcage immediately exploded in pain, even as his body was pitched forward and slammed to the hard blacktop. Before he could even think about moving, the truck was once again upon him. He felt his bones crunch and his flesh tear as the tires rumbled over him. The weight of the vehicle crushing down against his back was unbearable. Something burst within him, sending a wave of pain through his body. His brain was working in high gear, trying to assess the damage and manage the pain, but it was an impossible situation. He knew he was already dead.

As the rear tires raced over him, he felt his body jostling around like a rag doll and new levels of pain attacked his receptors. When he finally lay still, he was left gasping and wheezing for air. He could hear himself struggling for life. Through a whirl of pain, he thought that he sounded like his great grandfather had, there at the end, when he had died of emphysema.

People were still screaming all around Cole. He heard someone crying and begging God for help. Someone stood over him and told him not to move. Sirens were approaching now. At least, he thought the sounds were sirens. What if they were the sounds of trumpets calling from Heaven? He hoped he was going to Heaven. He wondered if he should've gone to church more. His mom had wanted him to, but he had been too busy.

Above all the chaos and pain, a whimpering sound suddenly emerged. Unable to move more than his eyeballs, Cole shifted his gaze toward the sound. Had he been able to do so, he would've smiled. The little boy he had spoken with earlier—the same one he had thrown so violently out of the roadway—was kneeling before him, crying. Cole wanted to tell him not to cry, that everything would be okay. It was certainly okay for Cole, because the little boy had survived. His death hadn't been in vain, and his life now had true meaning. He suddenly felt completely at peace.

Cole closed his eyes and allowed the darkness to wrap its ugly arms around his consciousness. As he faded into nothingness, the pain started to subside. With the last flicker of life within him, he found himself hoping that there would be light at the end of this tunnel, and he reflected on the only regret of his short existence—he would never get to go on that date with Takecia Gayle.

CHAPTER 3

"Clint, did you hear that radio traffic?"

I was sandwiched between both crowded sidewalks along Washington Avenue, and there were floats in front of me and behind me.

"Ten-four, some of it," I called out to Susan over my police radio. "It was from the fire department channel, and it sounded like someone said there were multiple casualties."

"What's the location?" Melvin asked. "Anybody got eyes on the area?"

I had instantly known the sound of the voice on the fire department radio. It had been Cole Peterson, and it sounded like he was running. His mic had been keyed up for only a second, but I hadn't heard any gunshots in the background. There were only some screams from the crowd and a vehicle revving its engine.

A million thoughts swam through my mind. I blew my siren as I approached Seventh Street. It was a cross street that extended the width of town. If I could access it, I could return to where I'd last seen Cole, but the going would be slow, because every street was crowded with pedestrians. Some of them were rushing to catch the parade one last time, while others were trying to make it to their cars and get a head start on hitting the roads once the parade was over and the barricades were lifted.

No one reacted to my siren, but then I didn't really expect them to. Every police cruiser and emergency vehicle that had driven by had been blaring a siren. Thus, I began honking my horn and waving my arm out of the window, imploring people to get out of the way.

An undercover narcotics agent from the sheriff office, who had been working the crowd in search of illegal drug activity, noticed what I was trying to do and leapt into action.

"Get back!" I heard him shout. "We've got an emergency!"

After pushing the crowd away from the opening to Seventh Street, he removed the barricade and stood aside while I drove through. I gave him a wave and crept forward, careful not to hit anyone as I made my way across town. When I reached Coconut Lane, the foot traffic thinned out a bit and I was able to make better time. I was soon merging onto Main Street near Orange Way and heading south toward Lacy Court.

My heart jumped to my throat when I made my approach to the scene. It looked like a battlefield. Bodies seemed to be everywhere. People were screaming and running around. Someone was pointing toward the south, declaring that the suspect had fled in that direction.

I was numb. As though working on automatic pilot, I told Achilles to stay in the Tahoe and, leaving it running with the windows partially down, I stepped out of my SUV. While the carnage was all around me, I was fixated on one lifeless figure lying in the middle of the roadway. I recognized the rain suit, but that was about it. The body of Cole Peterson had been twisted into an unrecognizable and lifeless human pretzel. Even before I reached his side, I knew there would be no fixing him. He was gone. There was no way he could've survived whatever it was that had happened to him.

I dropped to my knees beside him. A man, woman, and small boy were standing nearby crying.

"He…he saved Benny," the woman said. "He jumped in front of that truck and saved my boy!"

I immediately snapped out of my trance. I would have time to feel bad about Cole later. Right now, I needed to relay information to the other officers in town.

"What did the truck look like?" I asked, holding my police radio poised to make a call.

"I…I don't know," the woman said, still visibly traumatized by what she had witnessed. She turned to her husband, but he was of no help. He only shook his head and stared blankly at me, his face frozen into terror.

"We…we got separated," he finally said. "I didn't see anything."

A woman tugged at my arm and screamed for me to help her little girl. I called on the radio as I followed her, letting dispatch know that a truck had plowed through the crowd and injured at least a dozen people. I gave the direction of travel and said I would report back more as I learned it. I heard Takecia call out and say that she had made her way to Back Street and was heading toward the southern end of town.

"Shots fired," Officer Baylor Rice called out in a calm voice. "A truck hit three pedestrians and broke through the barricade. I fired three shots at it, but it escaped, heading south toward Old Blackbird Highway. It's a Chevy pickup, jacked up with large tires and a dull black primer paint job. It's also got bullet holes in the windshield. I need a medic ASAP. I've got one with life-threatening injuries."

"Are you in pursuit?" I heard Takecia ask.

"Negative, I'm rendering aid to the injured."

I wanted so bad to jump in my Tahoe and race across town to chase down the bastard who had killed Cole, but I was being pulled by the arm to where a small girl was sprawled out beside a ditch. There was a cut on her forehead and her dress was stained from being dragged through the grass.

I cursed silently as I dropped to my knees and checked her pulse. With a sigh of relief, I told the mom that she had a heartbeat. I put my ear to her mouth and could feel air.

"She's unconscious, but she's alive," I told the woman. "Stay with her while I check on the others, but don't move her."

The woman nodded and sat beside her daughter. She reached out with both arms to scoop her daughter into her lap, but I grabbed roughly at her arm.

"For the love of God, ma'am, don't move her!" The words had come out meaner than I'd meant for them to, but I was in a hurry. "She could have a neck or back injury. If you move her, it could make things worse. Do you understand me?"

She gulped and nodded, dropping her arms to her side.

I whirled around and searched for someone who could use my help. Everywhere I looked, people were screaming and agonizing over what they had just witnessed, but there were also others who had jumped into action. Every victim I saw had at least two people tending to them, with the exception of two bodies located near the M & P Grill parking lot. It was obvious the bodies were of a woman and man. One—the man—was in the ditch in front of the restaurant, and the other—the woman—was in the middle of the parking lot. There were muddy shoe impressions leading down into the ditch, so someone must've checked on him and figured him for dead. Everyone was steering clear of the woman, too, so they must've surmised the same about her.

I pulled out my radio one more time as I counted the injured on my approach to the downed couple.

"Headquarters, we've got approximately eighteen down in the area of M & P Grill, with three who appear to be Code 1," I radioed. "See if we can get air med in here to transport some of the victims."

"Ten-four," came the reply.

I shook my head in anger as I pocketed my portable radio. Counting the three Baylor had called about, we now had twenty-one victims in all. Hopefully, that would be it, but this was already shaping up to be among the worst tragedies this town had ever seen.

What I didn't like one bit was that we had no idea what—or who—we were dealing with. Was this a terrorist attack? Or maybe the work of some drunk asshole who was out of control? Or what about someone suffering from a severe medical condition? I'd heard of drivers slipping into a diabetic coma and being involved in a car crash, but this seemed the least likely of all the scenarios I could come up with. Passing out and getting into a crash was one thing. This suspect had held his or her foot on the accelerator and mowed the victims down.

When I reached the woman in the middle of the parking lot, I squatted beside her and checked for a pulse. Her body was mangled worse than Cole's and she didn't have a heartbeat. Her head was twisted oddly to the side, with a mane of dark brown hair covering her face. The light from a nearby lamppost illuminated her figure and I got the sense I knew her. I carefully brushed back her hair and sighed when her face came into view. It was Malory, the manager for M & P Grill.

"Damn it," I said with a growl. "What in the hell is going on around here?"

Getting wearily to my feet, I carefully approached the man in the ditch. It had rained all day, so the grass was slick and the ditch muddy. There were deep shoe impressions in the mud that led up to the body and into the ditch. My own boots sank to the ankle when I reached the man. Like Malory, he didn't have a pulse, and, also like Malory, I recognized him. I'd only met him a few times, but I knew I was looking down at Malory's husband. The poor girl had gone through a lot of boyfriends before she had finally met Wesley Chouest. They eloped and got married after only dating for a few weeks, but they seemed genuinely happy.

I had just made my way out of the ditch when Susan's Tahoe appeared from the same direction I had come. The look of concern was readily apparent on her face when I approached her.

"What in God's name happened out here, Clint?" she asked.

I shook my head slowly, glancing first at Malory and then toward M & P Grill. There were burnout marks that began in a parking spot near the building. The marks extended from that spot, directly over the location of Malory's body, and out of the lot onto Main Street.

"It looks like someone peeled-out of that spot and just plowed right over everyone," I said. "But I have no clue why someone would want to do something like that."

Susan surveyed the scene before us. Thankfully, more personnel from the fire department had arrived on foot and were helping tend to the wounded. They were much more skilled at life-saving measures than either Susan or me, and we were both damned glad to see them.

"What can I do to help?" Susan finally asked.

I pointed to some of the bystanders who were milling about, seemingly too shocked to leave but not knowing what they should be doing. "Can you start getting names and contact information from those people before they scatter? If any of them are eyewitnesses, make them wait across the street. As for the victims and their families, we can get their information at the hospital later."

My wife nodded. "What're you planning on doing?"

"I'll string up some tape and then call Buck for some extra hands." I frowned."Whatever happened, it began right here and stretched all the way to where Baylor is, so this entire parking lot and that stretch of highway is part of a giant crime scene. Amy and I won't be able to process this alone, and there's no way the three of us can clear everybody out of here."

CHAPTER 4

After taping off the scene, I quickly photographed the bodies of Malory, Cole, and Wesley, and then begged three blankets off of the fire department. With the fire chief's help, I used the blankets to cover the bodies. Typically, I wouldn't have altered the crime scene in any way until it had been thoroughly processed, but the scene and bodies were wide open to the public, and a family member of one of the decedents might stumble upon the scene at any moment. In a small town like Mechant Loup, news travelled fast, and it wouldn't be long before word got out about who had been struck down by the killer in the truck.

Once the bodies were covered, I asked the fire chief to stand beside Cole's body to protect it. Next, I moved to the entrance of the parking lot to preserve that part of the scene. This was when I called Sheriff Buck Turner. He had been the sheriff of Chateau Parish for almost seven years now. Since almost the moment he had won the job, our two departments had enjoyed a close working relationship, and I considered him a friend. Now, more than ever, I would need his help.

"I heard what happened," Turner said when he picked up the phone. "If you need anything at all, just say the word."

I thanked him and asked if he could send his crime scene unit to town. "We've got a lot of area to cover," I explained. "I've got the parking lot secured, but the crime scene stretches for almost a mile. I'll need half a dozen bodies to help process it."

"I'll get Tuttle to put a team together and have them head down there right away," Buck said. "Anything else?"

"I could also use some detectives at the hospital. We've got eighteen injured. Some of them will be transported to Chateau General, but others will be airlifted out of here. If you could lend me some detectives to track them down and interview them and their families wherever they go, that'll be a huge help."

"Done. Anything else?"

"That's it for now."

Buck paused for a second. "How many dead?"

"Three that we know about right now," I explained. "Some of the other victims are critically injured. I pray we don't lose any more."

"It'll be a miracle if you don't. The death toll always rises in a situation like this."

He was right, but I didn't want to admit it. When I didn't say anything more, he asked the million-dollar question.

"Are you thinking terrorist attack?"

I hesitated, not liking to put a label on the case so early in the investigation. We hadn't even identified most of the victims and hadn't conducted a full interview yet, so we knew next to nothing.

"I don't know, Sheriff," I finally said. "I really don't know."

"My money's on it being a terrorist." Buck spoke with a finality that was not uncommon for him. "When someone randomly drives a vehicle through a crowd, killing and maiming almost two dozen people, there can't be any other explanation."

"Well, I'd appreciate it if we don't label this case until I start gathering some facts," I warned. "You know how the media runs with this kind of shit, so we need to be careful about what we release."

"Sure thing, Clint. I'll make sure that nothing leaves my office. If anyone calls for comment, I'll redirect them to you."

I thanked him and ended the call just as Mayor Pauline Cain pulled up. She parked her car a block south of the crime scene and stepped out on shaky legs. Even from that distance, I could see the look of utter shock on her face as she walked toward me and took in the scene around her.

Detective Amy Cooke, who was the sole detective working under my command in Mechant Loup, arrived next, and she was followed shortly afterward by Officer Regan Steed. Moments earlier, I had heard Takecia, Officer Shade Rankin, and Melvin call out on the radio to say they were heading south in search of the suspect's vehicle. A second later, Baylor had announced over the radio that members of the fire department had arrived at his location to care for the injured, and he said he was heading south to join in on the search.

I wanted to go speak with Mayor Cain, but a young man and woman were approaching the yellow tape, so I turned my attention to them. The man wore a long-sleeved shirt, but it didn't hide all of his tattoos. Even in the darkness, I could see tattoos on his hands and neck. He nodded a head toward the parking lot.

"Can we get our car out real quick?" he asked.

"Which one's yours?" I already knew I wouldn't let a single car be moved until we had processed the scene for evidence, but I wanted to know where it was located.

"The red one near the building."

I turned toward the restaurant. The new owners had announced that they would keep the parking lot open for townsfolk during parades, but the ten spots against the building would be reserved for employees and the owner's family members, just like in previous years. Since it was from one of these spots that the killer's vehicle had launched, I began to wonder if the killer worked here or was a family member. Of course, it was always possible that someone had parked there without permission.

"Do you work here?" I asked.

"No." He shook his head. "My mom and dad own the place. They let us park here for the parade."

"What's your name?"

"Miles."

"Miles Griffin?" I asked, knowing that the newest owners of M & P Grill were Victor and Faith Griffin.

He nodded and shifted his feet. He seemed to be in a hurry.

"Did you see what happened?" I asked.

"No, sir. We caught the parade by the bridge." He turned to look at the activities taking place on the street. "One of my friends told us some people got run over, and my wife's real upset about the whole thing. We just want to go home. We've got a newborn with a babysitter and we promised we'd be home before ten."

Cole's radio traffic had come through at nine-thirty-two. It was almost ten now, so this couple would definitely be late to pick up their baby. I explained that it was a crime scene and they would have to wait a while to retrieve their vehicle, but I promised I'd let them out as soon as I could. They didn't like it, but Miles said he understood, and they moved to a spot where there wasn't much movement taking place.

"Oh, no, Clint!" Pauline said when she reached the crime scene tape. She was staring in shock at her surroundings. "Who did this? And why?"

I told her what we knew so far. As I talked, I glanced north along Main Street, where several patrol deputies from the sheriff's office were escorting a convoy of ambulances into town. Members of the fire department had already placed six of the victims onto spine boards, and Susan began waving the ambulances in their direction.

Four more of the victims had been treated for minor injuries. They now stood with Amy, providing whatever information they possessed. Regan walked over to assist Amy, and I knew they would arrange to conduct more detailed interviews later. At the moment, we needed to know what happened and we needed someone to tell us the identity of the suspect—and I needed the crime scene unit to get here so I could start helping with the interviews.

"Is…um…is that Malory over there on the ground?" the mayor asked softly. "Someone told me Malory had gotten hit."

I scowled. Pauline and her late husband used to own M & P Grill back before she became mayor, so she was very familiar with Malory.

"Yeah, that's Malory," I finally said. "The fellow in the ditch was standing next to her when the truck sped out of the parking spot. It hit both of them."

"Are you sure?" Pauline glanced at the blanket that covered Malory's body for only a second, and then looked toward the ditch. "How can you tell he was standing next to her?"

"His left shoe is on the ground near the crook of Malory's right arm," I explained. "It looks like they were walking toward the restaurant when the truck sped out of that empty parking spot and hit them. That's when the truck continued out of the lot, turned south on Main Street, and left the area."

Pauline put a hand over her mouth. Even though the flashing lights from the emergency vehicles distorted her face, I could still see that she lost a shade or two of color. "So, is…is that Wesley in the ditch?"

"I haven't touched him other than to check for vitals, but it certainly looks like him." I indicated Malory. "And they were walking side-by-side back to the restaurant, so I'm pretty positive it's going to be him."

While Pauline stood there in shock, I turned toward the sky. I could hear the chopping of helicopter blades overhead. I glanced across the street and saw that three firefighters had cleared out a parking lot for the chopper to land, and they were guiding the bird down with large spotlights.

The sheriff's deputies who'd responded had gone to work and

quickly moved the stunned crowd back to both shoulders of the road and cleared the travel lanes. Within minutes of their arrival, two of the ambulances were already turning to transport victims to the hospital. As one backed in my direction, I looked through the windows on the rear doors and saw two victims strapped to gurneys. Neither of them appeared to be alert, and there was a sense of urgency in the movements of the medics.

"God help them," I whispered.

CHAPTER 5

After the two ambulances had left and Mayor Cain had wandered off, I slipped under the crime scene tape and stood on the eastern shoulder of Main Street. I began waving people over and asking if they saw anything. If they didn't, I asked them to move toward their vehicles and leave if they could. If they were blocked in, I asked them to remain near their vehicles until the road opened up.

Ten minutes later, I was still working to clear my side of the street while simultaneously keeping the crime scene secure when movement and a scream from the north caught my eye. I turned to see a young woman running for all she was worth, her eyes focused like lasers on the parking lot of M & P Grill.

I quickly turned from the group of people I'd been addressing and made my way to the far corner of the parking lot entrance. The woman didn't seem to notice me, as she continued charging full-speed ahead. When she crossed under the nearest light post, I recognized her as one of the waitresses from the restaurant. She had never waited on me and I didn't know her name, but I knew instantly that this would be tough. From the look on her face, she had heard about Malory and it had destroyed her.

"Ma'am," I called when she was still about thirty feet away, "can you hold up? This is a crime scene."

Her roving eyes had located the blanket under which Malory's body rested, and she was heading straight for it. She didn't even give me a glance. It was as though I was invisible to her.

"Malory!" she screamed, pumping her arms and legs as far and as fast as she could. "Oh, my God! *Malory!*"

The young lady was about five-four and she must've only weighed about 122, but she was curvy and solid. When I stepped in front of her to stop her from entering the crime scene, she nearly knocked me over. Luckily, I had prepared for the impact. The instant my arms wrapped around her torso, I rotated my hips and allowed her forward momentum to carry us in a semi-circle.

Once she came to a stop, she began swinging her balled-up fists and screaming at me to let her go. In a flash, Regan and Susan were upon us, and they took control of her arms, all the while speaking soothingly with her to try and calm her down.

"Is that Malory?" she demanded repeatedly. "Is that Malory?"

While Susan and Regan held her, I stood directly in front of her and blocked her view of the body.

"Yes, ma'am," I said softly. "I'm sorry, but it is Malory."

She let out a gut-wrenching wail and collapsed. She would've crashed to the ground had Susan and Regan not been holding on to her. They eased her to a seated position, and we all got to our knees with her. None of us said a word as she cried and cursed and begged God to trade her life for Malory's. I glanced up occasionally to make sure no one else was attempting to breach the line of flimsy tape that secured the scene, but the crowd was thinning considerably.

It was taking some time to get the young woman under control, so I stood and waved Amy over.

When we were out of earshot of Susan, Regan, and the woman, I asked Amy if she learned anything useful.

"A few people witnessed different parts of the incident, but no one saw the same thing." She pointed toward the opposite side of the street. "The parade had finished passing and this one lady was picking up her folding chair when she heard tires screech. She described it as a peeling-out sound, but she described it as coming from up Main Street, and not from across the street. I asked her if she saw the vehicle hit anyone in the crowd, but she said no. She said there were people standing and moving around in front of her, so she couldn't see the road. She's a short lady and probably couldn't see over a four-foot wooden fence, so it's understandable."

I nodded and waited for more.

"Next, we've got a young couple whose kid—a little boy named Benny—was about to be killed when Cole Peterson jumped in front of the truck and saved Benny's life," she said. "When the truck first started barreling down the street and people started getting hit, the crowd scattered in all directions. The dad was paving a path through the crowd to safety and dragging the mom behind him, while she was dragging Benny. They had almost made it out of the roadway when a group of teenagers rushed right past them and knocked her down. She lost her grip on her husband and on Benny. She fell on the shoulder and Benny fell in the middle of the road. She said Benny stood and stared at the oncoming truck, apparently too afraid to move. She said that's when Cole dove right in front of the truck and pushed Benny."

I pursed my lips and nodded. "I spoke to that woman earlier. She said Cole sacrificed his life for her son."

"He did." Amy frowned. "Cole was a good kid."

I nodded my agreement. Had it not been for Cole, Melvin would've died a little more than four years ago after being stabbed in the chest. Cole was only seventeen or eighteen at the time, but he had sprung into action and saved my friend. It seemed like he had once again leapt into action to save someone, but this time it cost him his own life.

"And get this," Amy continued. "Benny's mom said Cole had spoken to her son earlier in the night."

"Really?"

"Yeah, the boy mentioned to Cole that he was afraid of the dark, and Cole got down on his level and explained how he was also afraid of the dark when he was little, and that the fear would disappear as he grew older." Amy smiled. "The mom said she's never seen her son so happy. Cole also invited them to the fire department to meet the fire chief and sit in the fire trucks."

I smiled to myself. I could almost hear Cole talking to the kid like a big brother, making all of his fears melt away.

"Was Benny's mom or dad able to give you anything more?" I asked. "When I spoke with them, they said they didn't see the truck that hit Cole."

"Nah, they couldn't give me any more than that." Amy paused and glanced down at her notes. "One man did say he saw a truck fly by and hit a little girl. He said the side mirror hit her on the head and killed her, because she fell next to a ditch and didn't move after she fell."

CHAPTER 6

My heart dropped to my combat boots when Amy mentioned a girl getting hit on the head and killed. In the darkness and chaos surrounding the scene, it was quite possible we'd missed a body.

"Did he say where she ended up?" I asked, already scanning our surroundings.

Amy pointed to an area beside the street. "He said she fell right over there."

I let out a long sigh. "I checked on that girl."

"Was she dead?"

"No." I was relieved to see that the little girl and her mom were gone, because that meant they had made it into an ambulance. "She was unconscious, but she was alive."

"I asked the man if he checked on her, but he said he didn't." Amy shook her head. "He admitted to being scared out of his mind and running away like a little bitch."

"Did he get a look at the driver before he ran away?"

"He said it happened so fast that everything seemed like a blur. In fact, that's the way most of the witnesses described it—a blur."

"How many of them were drunk?"

"Most of them," Amy said with a grunt. "Even some whose kids were with them."

I had expected as much. Carnival season was all about drinking and having a good time, and I was not opposed if others wanted to drink themselves into oblivion. For personal reasons, I chose not to drink anymore, but I didn't care if others did it—as long as they didn't get behind the wheel.

"Anything else?" I asked.

"No, but I've got more people to interview."

I thanked her and turned to my wife and Regan. They seemed to have the woman under control. She had stopped screaming a minute earlier, and they were just helping her to her feet. She brushed off her jeans and straightened her blouse. When she looked up, her eyes found mine. She frowned.

"I'm sorry," she said when I approached them. "I…I was just…I don't know what I was thinking."

I told her not to worry about it. "I would've done the same thing in your shoes. I recognize you from the restaurant. You worked with Malory, right?"

She nodded.

"I'm sorry about your friend," I said. "In all the times I've eaten here, I never got your name."

"I'm Rebecca Theriot." Her voice still quivered and a few tears continued to stream down her face. "They made me the head waitress when Malory moved up to manager. She and I are…are…were really close. I…I was her maid of honor when she got married. It was a small wedding by design, so there weren't many people who went."

I nodded as she talked, waiting patiently while she described the wedding. I needed to ask some questions, but if it made her feel better to talk about the wedding, then I was willing to listen. I needed her calm.

"So, were you at the parade tonight?" I asked.

"No, sir. I was home and someone called me to say that there had been some kind of accident, and they thought Malory had gotten killed."

"Who called you?"

"Ivy."

I cocked my head to the side. "Who's Ivy?"

"She's married to Miles Griffin," Rebecca explained. "Her in-laws own the restaurant."

"Gotcha." I indicated the front of the restaurant. "Do you recognize any of those vehicles?"

Of the ten spots, only nine vehicles remained, which left me to wonder if the vehicle that had sped out of here belonged to a worker or a member of the Griffin family.

Rebecca studied the cars and nodded. "Some of them. The two vans on the far left are our delivery vans. They stay parked here unless there's a delivery to be made. The red car next to the vans belongs to Miles. I don't know the next two cars. I'm sure they didn't have permission to be here. Although we put up signs, it happens every year. The last owners had threatened to put a gate at the entrance and block off the whole parking lot during parades, but Mr. Griffin said he wouldn't do that."

I nodded and asked her to continue.

"The next one that's to the right of the empty spot, I don't know it either," she said. "The next car's for one of our cooks. The last two are for two of our waitresses. They're both single and they've got kids who love parades, so they usually meet here and then try to catch the parade multiple times. I know they go to where the parade starts, and then they come here, before going to the end of the parade and catching it one last time. One of their moms lives in town, so they go there after the parade and eat supper. They should've been back by now, unless…unless something happened to them."

I glanced at Susan. "Do we have names of all of the victims?"

"Not yet." Susan then turned to Rebecca. "Do you want to try and reach them by phone to make sure they're okay? If you can't get through to them, I can call the sheriff's detectives at the hospital."

Rebecca nodded and pulled out her phone. She paced back and forth in front of us as she held the phone to her ear. After a second, she stopped suddenly and blurted, "Thank God, Jen! Are y'all okay?"

She talked excitedly for a moment and then told Jen that she had to go.

"They're okay," she said breathlessly. "They heard about what happened and they decided to stay at her mom's house until things clear up."

I was barely paying attention to what she was saying as I scanned the lot some more. "Look, you identified all the vehicles parked against the building, but none of them belong to Malory. So, where's her car?"

"I didn't see her car." Rebecca tucked her cell phone away and looked over the rest of the parking lot. Suddenly, there seemed to be a flicker of hope in her eyes. "It's nowhere in the lot. Hey, are you sure that's her on the ground? If her car isn't here, that must mean she didn't come to the parade, so it can't be her in the parking lot. Can I see under the blanket? I bet it's not even her!"

"I know Malory, and it's definitely her," I said softly. I looked around the lot. "What about her husband? Do you know what he drives?"

"He's got a truck, but I don't see it." After a moment of surveying the parking lot again, she pointed to the empty spot.

"That's usually the spot where Malory parks…"

Rebecca's voice trailed off as she turned and surveyed the lot again, as though still searching for the missing vehicle. She then returned her gaze to the empty parking spot and a puzzled expression fell across her face. "Huh, that's weird."

"What kind of truck does Wesley have?" I asked, my curiosity thoroughly aroused.

"It's a black Chevy truck. He's got big mud tires and those running boards and it's high off the ground."

"Is the paintjob bright and shiny?" I asked.

"No," she said with a grimace. "It's an ugly dull black. I think it's called primer black?"

There was a collective gasp between Susan, Regan, and me. I turned to the burnout marks leading from the parking spot and then back to Rebecca.

"How sure are you about that description?" I asked.

"I'm positive," Rebecca said, staring from Susan to Regan and then back to me. "Why? What's going on?"

"I think Wesley and Malory were run over by Wesley's own truck," I said. "It's the only logical explanation."

CHAPTER 7

South of Town

As soon as members of the fire department had arrived to render aid to the wounded pedestrians on the southern end of town, Baylor had jumped into his patrol car and sped off to try and catch up with the rest of his crew. He was angry with himself. He had fired three bullets at the rapidly approaching truck and, while all three shots had impacted the windshield of the pickup, not one had hit the driver.

"What if I could've gotten off *one* more shot before jumping out of the way?" he asked himself aloud as he now raced south along Old Blackbird Highway. "Maybe that one might've gotten the suspect and we'd have him in custody."

As was customary anytime there was a parade in town, there was a long line of vehicles waiting to enter Mechant Loup. He had peeled off from the back of the parade to man the barricade on the south end of town until the parade would end, at which time he would've removed the barricade and allowed the traffic to flow through. Now that this maniac had barreled through town and killed some people, there was a good chance traffic would be backed up until well after midnight.

Baylor had two thoughts as he was rapidly approaching Rooster Drive. First, had he not jumped out of the way of the speeding truck when he did, there was a very good chance he might've become yet another victim. He could still feel the rush of wind as the truck shot past him, and he remembered thinking how close it had been. He nodded his head affirmatively. Yeah, had he taken the time to fire one more shot, he'd be dead—and Amy would've killed him for dying.

His second thought was about the fleeing vehicle. What if it hadn't continued south but, rather, had ducked into one of the neighborhoods along the way? If it were him, he wouldn't stay on the main highway. That would just be begging to get caught. No, he would turn down some street and park in the driveway of an abandoned house or under a carport—anyplace that would make him seem like a random vehicle that belonged in the neighborhood.

His mind made up, Baylor slowed when he reached Rooster Drive. Before turning into the neighborhood to search it, he exited his marked patrol car and approached the line of cars still waiting to pass through town. The first vehicle he came to was occupied by a family of four—a dad, a mom, and two little girls in the back seat—and they appeared frustrated.

"Hello, officer," the driver began, "do you know how long it'll be? We thought the parade was supposed to end at nine or nine-thirty."

"It was." Baylor smiled at the kids in the back seat, but they didn't smile back. They appeared grumpy. "I apologize for the delay, but we had an incident in town."

"Really?" asked the mom, who leaned closer to the open window. "What kind of incident?"

"A truck was speeding through town and hit a few pedestrians," Baylor explained. "I was wondering if you all saw a dull black Chevy truck drive by here and turn into this neighborhood. It's got a lift kit and large mud tires."

"Is that what all the cop cars were about?"

Baylor nodded, but didn't elaborate. "Did you all see a truck turn down this street?"

The man scowled. "I mean, we saw a few vehicles turn down the street, but we weren't really paying attention. I guess a truck like that could've turned down there and we didn't notice, but the cop would've seen it."

"Come again?"

"One of the cop cars turned down the street," the lady said, leaning even closer to the open window. "It was down there for a while, and then it left and headed down the bayou."

Baylor sighed. Someone from his department had already thought of that possibility. He hesitated, but decided to check on it anyway, just in case the suspect had been hiding down there and now thought the coast was clear.

After thanking the family and checking with a few other drivers, Baylor made a quick run through the neighborhood. There were hundreds of vehicles along the three main streets and more than a dozen cross streets that made up the neighborhood, but he didn't see a truck that matched the description of the one he was hunting.

Upon leaving Rooster Drive, Baylor called Takecia on her cell phone.

"Any luck?" he asked.

"None so far," she said. "I made it down halfway to the coast and haven't seen anything yet. Shade jumped onto Cypress Highway in case the suspect doubled back, and Melvin's going through every street and neighborhood along the Old Blackbird."

Baylor nodded to himself and slowed his vehicle. At this point, both highways were getting plenty enough attention. He decided to start checking the more remote areas south of town. He was about to end the call when Takecia stopped him.

"Bay, did you find out who got hit from the fire department?"

Baylor detected a hint of somberness in her voice that surprised him.

"Yeah, I heard one of the firefighters mention the name," he said slowly. "It was Cole Peterson."

Takecia let out a gasp.

"What is it?" Baylor asked. "Were you friends with him?"

Baylor knew she wasn't related to anyone around here, because her mom and dad had immigrated to the United States from Jamaica and they had no other family members in the country.

After a moment of silence and a long sigh, Takecia said, "He asked me out on a date."

"Wait…what?" Baylor was genuinely surprised. He had met Cole a few times and knew the kid was infatuated with Takecia—hell, he told everyone in the world about it—but he was quite a few years younger than Takecia and he always seemed nervous when he was around her. "He actually got up the nerve to ask you out?"

"Yeah, well, Clint mentioned he liked me and wanted to take me out, so I kind of initiated the conversation," Takecia admitted.

"What'd you tell him?"

"I told him yes, of course." Her voice betrayed the sadness she felt. "I wouldn't have brought it up to him and then turned him down, you know? So, I told him to pick me up tomorrow for lunch. I told him it wasn't a date, but I don't think he even heard that part."

Baylor thought back to when he was young and really liked a particular girl. The fear of rejection was probably the worst of all his adolescent fears, and he remembered how overjoyed he felt when the girl of his dreams said yes when he asked her out. Of course, she turned out to be a nightmare, but that was a topic for a different day. Now, he felt sorry for Cole's death, but happy that he got to experience that small victory before he died.

"Look, Takecia, it sucks to all hell that Cole got killed, but you've got to know that he died a very happy young man." Baylor was speaking with pure confidence. "He's been telling everyone who'll listen how much he loves you, so for you to accept his request for a date is huge. You made his last moments the most memorable and exciting of his young life."

There was a long moment of silence on the other end of the phone, and Baylor began to wonder if Takecia liked Cole as much as Cole liked her. Her last relationship had ended in disastrous fashion, but Amy said Takecia had rolled with those punches and just kept on going. Baylor worked with Takecia on a regular basis, and she never brought up Jeremiah Baker's name and she never seemed sad, so he knew Amy was right. Tonight, though, she seemed bothered by what had happened. It made sense, because Cole was genuinely a good fellow.

"How'd it happen?" Takecia finally asked.

"He jumped in front of the truck to save a small boy," Baylor said. "At least, that's what one of the other firefighters told me."

"That sounds like something Cole would do," Takecia said quietly. And then, without uttering another word, she ended the call.

CHAPTER 8

M & P Grill

It was almost ten thirty in the evening when members of the sheriff's office crime scene unit arrived to process the scene. By then, Main Street was completely clear of people and the entire strip of highway between M & P Grill and the barricades on the southern end of town had been cordoned off. We had enlisted the help of the state police to divert traffic from Old Blackbird Highway to Back Street and then up Market Street, where it intersected with Main Street to the north of the crime scene.

Earlier, Susan had taken Achilles from my Tahoe and brought him home, where her mom was watching Grace. Normally, Grace would've ridden with one of us during the parade, but the weather had been too ugly throughout the day, so we had left her home with Lisa Wilson. For that small miracle, I was eternally grateful.

At my request, Sheriff Turner had placed his drug task force unit on the northern end of town to monitor every vehicle that left the area, hoping to ensnare the suspect's vehicle.

So far, none of our units to the south had been able to locate the suspect's vehicle, and it seemed to have simply disappeared into thin air. It couldn't have, I knew, and it couldn't have left town, so it had to be somewhere around here.

I walked to the street to meet the crime scene unit. They were led by Vanessa Comeaux, who had a degree in biochemistry and who'd been working in the crime lab for a little over a year now. She had handled quite a few high-profile cases for the sheriff's office in that short time, and she was quickly making a name for herself as a top-notch forensic scientist.

"Hey, Vanessa," I said when she climbed out of her Suburban with two other analysts, "I'm real glad to see you."

"I wish it were under better circumstances," she said, surveying the scene. "Can you show me what we're up against?"

I nodded and pointed out the locations of the decedents, as well as dozens of evidence cones that represented blood and other evidence from the additional victims. The blood and other bodily fluids that had been spilled would help to later recreate the scene and place each victim in the precise location where they had been struck by the vehicle. She already knew the sheriff's deputies who were guarding the scene, so there was no need to introduce them.

Once I was done, I expressed my intent to go inside the restaurant and view the video footage from the surveillance cameras.

"I spoke with the owners," I explained, "and they said the restaurant was locked up throughout the parade, so there should be no evidence inside the building other than the surveillance footage."

"If anything changes and you need me to go inside, just let me know," she said. She then turned to her team and began handing out assignments.

I waved Amy over. She had Rebecca with her, and the head waitress had agreed to give us access to the surveillance system. I had worked it several times in the past, so I was familiar with it. As I thought back to my times using the system, I remembered viewing footage from the two cameras in the front of the building, and a nagging doubt began to form in the pit of my stomach.

Once we were in the office and seated in front of the security system, I glanced up at Rebecca. "It might be best for you to wait in the other room," I said softly. "You won't want to see this."

She shook her head vigorously and hurried away, thanking me over her shoulder.

With a sigh, I accessed the northwestern-facing camera and selected a time much earlier in the day, hoping to capture the vehicles when they first arrived in the parking lot. Thanks to the rain from earlier, the parade had been delayed until seven, but the surveillance footage showed vehicles arriving as early as four—a full three hours before it was set to begin.

"Diehards," Amy muttered. "If I had my way and could get away with it, I'd arrive three hours after the parades ended."

I laughed. "I bet you would."

"You know how I hate those damned things."

"I hear ya." I began playing the footage from the time the first car arrived. It was the red car, the one that belonged to Miles Griffin. He pulled into the parking spot next to the vans. We were able to clearly see his face as he drove into the parking lot, but once he drove nearer to the building, the view of the windshield disappeared. After he had parked, we were only able to see the back end of the car. We couldn't even see Miles and his wife step out of the vehicle.

"Well, that ain't good," Amy said. "If the suspect's vehicle was pulled into the parking spot, we won't be able to see who comes and goes from the driver's door."

"Based on the burnout marks, I'm pretty sure Wesley backed his truck into the spot," I explained. "I'm just hoping it sticks out enough for us to see the suspect enter the vehicle."

"Do we really think someone stole Wesley's truck and killed them with it?" Amy scowled. "That would be one hell of a coincidence, and you don't believe in coincidences."

I only nodded, knowing she had a point. If someone did steal the truck and kill them with it, there was a chance they were targeted. If so, we would have to take a deep dive into their lives to find out who might want them dead.

I continued playing the video footage. One of the unknown vehicles showed up next and pulled into a spot, but we were unable to see the occupants because they exited and walked too close to the restaurant to be picked up by the security cameras. Jen and the other waitress arrived next with their kids. While they pulled in and were concealed upon their exit, we were able to clearly make them out when they left, because they headed straight for the exit to the parking lot.

"One thing's for certain," Amy said as she leaned over my shoulder, "we'll be able to clearly see the truck plow over them."

She was right. We had a crystal clear view of the area where Malory was now lying on the ground. I already knew it wouldn't be pretty.

CHAPTER 9

As Amy and I continued watching the footage, the sun began to go down and the shadows grew long. Finally, another vehicle turned into the parking lot. It was one of the cars that weren't supposed to park there. It was followed closely by the cook and, finally, Wesley's truck. It was nighttime now in the camera, but the angle and the infrared night vision afforded an excellent view into the windshield of the truck as it swooped by. I easily identified Malory in the passenger seat, and there was a clear view of the driver, who I thought looked like Wesley Chouest. I'd only met him a few times and his face looked different in the grayish hue of the infrared video, but I was pretty sure it was him. After whipping around, the truck backed into the spot that now stood vacant.

I leaned closer as the footage showed Malory and Wesley stepping from the vehicle. We couldn't quite see them, but we could see the doors swing open. After the doors closed, they came into view again. They approached Main Street and then headed north, disappearing in the upper, right-hand corner of the camera.

From that point on, I watched every inch of the screen intently. There was a lot of foot traffic, so it was hard to study every person that walked into view. Thus, I focused on the people who walked through the parking lot. If someone had stolen Wesley's truck, he or she might've driven another vehicle into the parking lot and left it there, or he or she might've been dropped off.

I glanced at the time on the computer. It was getting late and we needed some actionable information. With a sigh, I hit the fast-forward button to cover more real estate.

"Keep an eye on the truck," I told Amy. "I'll watch the crowd."

"Ten-four."

The parking lot filled up quickly after that, but no one approached the truck and no one appeared suspicious. Soon, the parade began to roll, and everyone left the parking lot to join the crowd that had already lined up on either side of Main Street. Despite the rain that had fallen earlier, the lines of bodies were three and four people deep in places. We watched as the first float rumbled by, and then the next, and the next. With each one that passed, the crowd broke into a frenzied scramble as revelers fought for the best throws to come off of each float.

"Why didn't the suspect strike while the parade was happening?" Amy wondered aloud. "He would've gotten more people."

"But he would've been captured," I said. "By waiting for the parade to end, he either knowingly or unknowingly waited for most of the police cars to drive on by and get boxed in with the floats. Had it not been for Baylor manning the barricades at the south end of town, he would've made a clean break."

"If he knowingly waited, then he's familiar with parades, which would mean he's from here," Amy mused. "If he wasn't waiting for the parade to end, then he must've been waiting for someone to show up, which would mean this was a targeted attack."

"I'm starting to think this is exactly what it is." I paused the footage and turned to look up at Amy. "We've got a lot of injuries, but only three dead. Cole died because he jumped in front of the truck to save a confused boy who found himself in the middle of the road facing an oncoming vehicle. As for Malory and Wesley, that was a direct hit. Had this been a terrorist attack, we'd have a lot more dead on our hands."

I pointed to the monitor, where hundreds of people were frozen in place. "That's a target-rich environment."

Amy nodded.

I resumed playing the video file, and Amy and I went back to carefully scrutinizing the footage.

"Come on," I mumbled after a while, "show yourself, you little piece of shit!"

As the parade lumbered on, a few people came in and out of the parking lot, but they were mostly revelers carrying bags of loot to their vehicles. They would empty the bags and then return to the street for more.

When the timestamp on the video reached eight o'clock, I detected a slight shift in the truck.

"What the hell was that?" I asked, wondering if maybe a gust of wind had blown through the parking lot.

"It looked like the truck shifted a little." Amy leaned so close to the monitor that I thought her nose would touch it. "Go back!"

I was about to hit the reverse icon when the screen went dark.

"What the hell?" I reversed the footage and played it again. Sure enough, the truck shifted just a little, as though someone had entered it, and then the screen went black. I quickly accessed the second camera at the front of the building and sped the footage forward to the same time period. A minute earlier, that one also went dark.

Amy and I stared at each other for a brief moment, and then we both leapt to our feet and bolted for the door to the office. When we burst out into the dining area, Rebecca jumped in her skin and let out a startled gasp.

"What's wrong?" she asked.

"Nothing," I called over my shoulder as we zigzagged between tables on our way to the front door.

Once outside, we hurried to the empty parking spot along the building where Wesley's truck had been parked earlier. I shook my head and grunted.

"Shit, this ain't good!" Amy muttered.

CHAPTER 10

Vanessa Comeaux saw Amy and me standing near the empty parking spot and walked over.

"What's going on?" she asked.

I pointed to the two security cameras that were fastened to the soffit along the front of the building. One was positioned slightly to the right of where Wesley's truck had been parked, and it was south-facing. The other was positioned farther to the left, and it was north-facing.

"Someone cut the wires on these cameras," I explained. "The footage went dark right around eight o'clock, which was about an hour and a half before the murders."

Vanessa nodded as she studied the camera above us thoughtfully. She then turned and looked at the other camera. The two delivery vans were parked directly under that camera.

"I'll process those vans for prints and DNA," Vanessa said. "The cameras are too high for even a tall person to reach and cut, so the suspect must've climbed on one of the vans to get the job done."

"Yes," I agreed, pointing above me. "We saw Wesley Chouest's truck shift a little bit right before the screen went dark, so it appears the suspect climbed onto the bumper to cut this camera."

"With the parade going in full swing, no one would've noticed a thing," Amy said. "Even after the parade, people would've been hurrying to their vehicles, most of them drunk, and hardly anyone would've been paying attention to their surroundings. By cutting the cameras, he eliminated what would've been the most reliable witnesses to the murder. This suspect ain't entirely stupid."

I cursed under my breath. We needed someone to tell us something. Surely, one or more of the witnesses had to have seen something useful. I turned back to Vanessa.

"Do you need me at the scene?"

"No, we've got it under control," she said. "I'll call you if I have any questions or if I find something immediately useful—like the killer's driver's license—but other than that, I'll submit all of the evidence to the lab first thing in the morning, and I'll have a report on your desk by tomorrow afternoon."

I thanked her and turned to Amy. "Can you pull the footage from the DVR?"

"Sure," she said. "I'll grab everything for the entire day, just in case the killer visited the place earlier."

I nodded and pulled out my phone to call Susan. When she answered, I asked for her location.

"I'm at the station," she said. "So far, four victims have been treated and released from the hospital, and two of them are en route to the station. The sheriff put a few detectives at the hospital and they're screening the victims and witnesses who show up. If they didn't see anything, the detectives are getting names and contact information and sending them on their way. If they saw something noteworthy, the detectives are directing them here."

"The two victims who are en route now," I began, "do we know what they saw?"

"I spoke with Lou Baker, but it was brief," she said. "He just told me they saw the whole thing and they wanted to help catch the monster who did it."

Lou Baker was a detective with the Chateau Parish Sheriff's Office, and he was a good one. We had worked a number of cases together, but we hadn't spoken since the incident between his brother, Jeremiah, and Takecia.

"Did Lou say anything about Jeremiah?" I asked.

"Not a word, but that doesn't mean much. There was a lot of noise in the background and he sounded busy as all hell."

I nodded, and then told Susan about the cut wire on the surveillance cameras.

"Well, that's not good," she said. "This isn't some out-of-control drunk who was running from demons."

"No, this was definitely intentional, and I'm leaning more and more toward Malory and Wesley being targeted."

"What an insult," Susan said with a grunt.

When she didn't expound, I asked her what she meant.

"To be run over by your own truck," she said. "That's just wrong on so many levels. It almost seems personal."

Personal, indeed.

"Do you know their parents?" I asked. "We'll need to notify them of the deaths and find out if they know anyone who might want to hurt them." Before Susan could respond, I added, "I hope they didn't find out through the grape vine."

"By now, I think everyone knows what happened and who were involved," Susan said. "But just in case, I'll grab Regan and we'll go make the death notifications."

I thanked her and then asked about the manhunt.

"I spoke with Melvin a few minutes ago," she said. "He told me they've got nothing. They've driven all the way down to the coast, cruised down every neighborhood, searched every park and cane field, and checked all the usual hiding spots out in the country. The truck is nowhere to be seen."

I had been afraid of that. "Does he have any ideas?"

"He thinks it's possible the killer lives here and parked the truck in his garage or barn. Since we can't go searching every property out there, all the killer has to do is keep the truck locked up, wait until the heat dies down, and then he'll be home free."

I started making my way toward the crime scene tape that was stretched across the front of the parking lot.

"What if the killer ditched the truck and hitched a ride out of here?" I offered. "He could've also swapped cars after he got south of town. Hell, he could be long gone by now."

"If that happened, how do we find him?"

I'd already been thinking about that, so I had an answer ready.

"It's been raining for days, so the ground's sopping wet," I said. "Have them check the bayou sides and every public lake or pond that can be approached by vehicle. If he ditched the truck in a bayou or lake, there should be tire tracks leading right up to the edge of the water. If we find the tracks, we'll find the truck."

"Good idea," Susan said hurriedly. "I'll pass it on to Melvin and all."

I ended the call just as Amy and Rebecca exited the restaurant and walked across the parking lot to meet me. I told Amy we needed to go to the police station to conduct some interviews, and I thanked Rebecca for her help.

"Um…" Rebecca hesitated, and shifted her feet. "I know y'all are busy and I hate to be a bother, but can y'all walk me to my car? I had to park far away and I'm kinda spooked by everything that's happened. I'm not usually like this. I guess I've never been this close to someone who's been killed. It's pretty scary."

"Absolutely." Amy put a hand on her shoulder. "I can even follow you home if you like."

CHAPTER 11

It was midnight when I finally made it to the police department and began interviewing the two victims. The first was a man who pushed a lady out of the path of the oncoming truck and got hit on the leg. Although he was struggling to walk, he didn't have any broken bones, and the ER doctor told him that he'd be fine. Upon questioning him, I learned that all he had seen were headlights and then the pavement—when he hit it.

The next victim was a young mother I'd met during a previous investigation I'd worked last winter. Her name was Joselyn Pitre. She was the mother of twins, which normally meant she would have two hands full, but considering her right arm was now wrapped in a cast and resting in a sling, she was about to fall on some challenging times. In addition to the cast, there were bandages on her bare shoulder, stitches above her left eye, and a nasty bruise on her forehead.

"Are you okay?" I asked Joselyn once Amy and I were seated across the desk from her in the interview room. "You look pretty banged up."

Despite the pain she must have been experiencing, she cracked a bit of a smile, but her bright blue eyes were sparkling with moisture.

"You know how they say your life flashes before your eyes when you're about to die?" she asked.

I nodded.

"Either I wasn't about to die, or it's not true, because the only thing I saw were headlights and the ground."

I cursed inwardly while smiling outwardly. If the only things she saw were the headlights and the ground, she would be as useless as the other victim. And I didn't blame her for being a bad witness—I blamed the asshole who plowed through the crowd in the middle of the night during the chaos that always follows a Mardi Gras parade.

I hesitated before asking the next question, because I hadn't gotten a detailed report on the identities of the injured yet. I did know that the death toll hadn't changed. There were a few victims who were critical, but as far as I knew, they were adults and they had all been flown to New Orleans.

"I'm guessing the twins weren't at the parade," I finally said, a bit cautiously.

"No, and thank God!" Joselyn's eyes swelled with tears. "Logan finally got a day off of work, so we got a babysitter and came to the parade. You know, sort of like a date night?"

I settled into my chair. I hadn't seen Logan in the waiting room when Amy and I had entered. There had only been an older man who appeared to be waiting for something or someone. Could it be that Logan was also among the injured?

"What about Logan?" I asked. "Did he get hit, too?"

"Oh, no!" Joselyn waved a dismissive hand. "He went home to relieve the babysitter. My dad met us at the hospital and he gave me a ride here."

"Well, I'm real sorry this happened to you," I began, hoping I might be able to extract something out of her. "Can you start from when you first got to the parade and give me a rundown of what happened leading up to when you were attacked?"

"Sure." She shifted the sling that held her cast. "Since we live so close to the parade route, we decided to just walk to where we wanted to be. At first, we weren't gonna go because we thought it would rain, but then the rain stopped and we decided to chance it. When we got on the route, we started off in front of that new pizza place. What's the name of it again?"

"The Pizza Bayou?" I offered.

"That's it," she said with a nod. "We stood there for a while, but when the parade made the first round, the crowd got kind of rowdy, so we decided to move. We weren't really trying to catch anything and we heard that they changed the route to make it faster because of the rain, so we started walking while the parade was still going down the bayou. We stopped a few times to talk to people we knew, and the parade had made the round and already started coming back up Main Street before I got to M & P Grill."

"What happened to Logan?" I asked when she stopped to catch a breath. She winced every time she moved, and I knew she had to be in extreme pain, so I wanted to get this over with as quickly as possible. "You said the parade turned around before you got to M & P, so where was Logan?"

"Oh, he stopped to talk to a friend in front of our street, but I kept going," she explained. "He talks to his friend all the time, so I don't know why he felt the need to stop and talk to him again tonight. But I was waiting for him. One of my friends was supposed to meet me in front of M & P Grill, and I haven't seen her in about a year. When I got to the restaurant I didn't see her, so I stood around waiting. I ended up not seeing her at all tonight."

"Is your friend okay?" I asked. "Have you heard from her?"

Joselyn nodded. "Oh, yeah, she called my phone a few times when everything was happening, but I wasn't able to talk to her until later. She said she was near Mechant Groceries when everything happened. They were buying more beer and she heard a truck going real fast and then she heard some gunshots."

"Did she see anything?"

"No, she was in the store when the truck passed."

I took a breath. "Okay, what happened after you got to the restaurant?"

"Well, I was there for a while looking for my friend," Joselyn said. "I wasn't really paying much attention to what was going on around me, but I remember seeing you stop and talk to this man in a rain suit. He was one of the ones who got hit, but he jumped in front of the truck to save a little boy. The truck didn't intentionally hit him."

I cocked my head slightly to the side when she mentioned that the driver hadn't intentionally hit Cole. How could she possibly know that? While I wanted to know the answer to that question, I didn't ask it just then. I let her continue with her statement.

"After you drove by, that Jamaican woman cop drove up and stopped to talk to the man in the rain suit." Joselyn grinned slyly. "I could tell they were flirting. I don't know what she told him, but he was real happy when she drove off. Anyway, that was the end of the parade and everybody started picking up their stuff to leave, but I was still standing there looking for my friend."

Joselyn took in a deep breath and let it out slowly. "Thank God she wasn't around, because she would've probably gotten run completely over. That girl's got worse luck than anybody I know."

I nodded to keep her talking, and she got the message.

"It was right around then that I heard a truck with a loud muffler start up," she continued. "I looked in the restaurant parking lot, but I didn't see any lights on. Just in case, I moved away from the entrance to the parking lot and kept looking for my friend."

"When you say you moved away from the entrance," I interjected, "in what direction did you go?"

"I went toward down the bayou."

"So, you ended up on the south side of the parking lot entrance?" When she stared blankly at me, I said, "The down-the-bayou side of the entrance, which would be the south side?"

"Yes!" She snapped her fingers. "The south side. And while I was standing there, I saw Malory and Wesley walking toward the restaurant. They were coming from up the bayou. I knew Malory, so I smiled and waved to her. She waved back and it looked like she was about to say something to me, but Wesley started talking to her. I didn't hear what he said at first, but then he raised his voice and said, "What in the hell are you doing in my truck?""

CHAPTER 12

I felt my ears instantly perk up like Achilles' did when he heard someone approaching the house at night.

"Wait a minute—Wesley actually *saw* the person in his truck?" I asked, leaning closer to Joselyn. "Are you sure that's what he said?"

"I'm positive." Her head bobbed up and down for confirmation. "He also demanded to know what the man was doing in his truck, but I didn't hear the man say anything back. He just revved up the engine and ran right at Malory and Wesley. He didn't even turn on his lights at first. He just ran right over them and then headed for the road. It wasn't until he reached the end of the parking lot that he flicked on the lights and started blowing the horn to make people get out of his way."

"I'm sorry I have to ask this next question," I began slowly, "but did you see what happened to Wesley and Malory after they were hit by the truck?"

"When the truck hit Wesley, he flew far back and I think he fell in the ditch," she said through pursed lips, "but it looked like Malory got caught under the tires. I was freaking out and I wasn't moving at first. It was just so crazy to see that happen right in front of me. When he turned on the headlights and blew the horn, I think that knocked me out of my trance, because I turned and started to run toward down the bayou. That's when I saw the man in the rain suit running toward me. I heard some noise behind me and a scream, and then the next thing I knew, something hit my arm hard and knocked me to the ground. My head bounced off the concrete and I think I blacked out for a second, because everything went quiet. And then all of a sudden, I could hear people screaming. I could still hear the loud muffler, but it was far away by now."

When Joselyn finished talking, I leaned slowly back in my chair, trying to picture the events as she had just described them. No one that I knew of had mentioned hearing a horn blowing. Was it really like Joselyn had said? Was he really trying to warn people that he was coming? Or had the bump on her head caused some confusion? I sure hoped the latter wasn't true, because the information she'd provided was crucial, and we needed her to be credible.

"Are you sure he was blowing the horn?" I asked.

"Absolutely," she said. "I don't know if it was because it was the loudest horn I ever heard or because it was right on top of me, but my ears are still ringing from it—that's how loud it was."

The fact that a concussion could also cause ringing in the ears didn't make me feel any better.

"What makes you think he was blowing it to make people get out of the way?" I asked, already knowing the answer to the second part of my question, but wanting to test her story. "Is it possible the horn was blowing because he had broken into the truck and it was the alarm sounding?"

"No, he was definitely the one blowing the horn, because it wasn't blowing before when he was just sitting in the truck."

"Okay, but what makes you think he was blowing it to warn people?"

Joselyn was thoughtful. "Well, what gave me that impression was because after he hit Wesley and Malory, he swerved a little to miss another lady that was about to step in front of the truck," she said. "The lady didn't realize what was happening and she would've probably also died if he hadn't of swerved to the left a little. It kind of made me think he ran over Malory and Wesley because Wesley was gonna try and stop him from stealing the truck."

I glanced over at Amy, and I could tell she was thinking the same thing I was thinking. This sounded more and more like a targeted killing, and Wesley and Malory had been the ones in this killer's crosshairs. It was possible only one of them had been the target and the other had been a casualty, so we would have to try and figure out which was which. Another thought came to me, and I addressed Joselyn again.

"When witnesses are describing a situation and they don't know the sex of the participants, they usually say *he* in general," I explained. "Were you doing that when you described the crime, or do you know for certain that it was a man stealing Wesley's truck?"

Joselyn's brow furrowed. "I couldn't really see the man in the truck, but I'm pretty sure Wesley called him an asshole at one point."

"At what point was that?"

"I think it was when he gunned the engine and peeled out of the parking spot," she said. "It all happened so fast at that point. I think they were just so shocked that it was happening at all, and they didn't even know what to do or say."

I looked to Amy and asked if she had any questions. She nodded and went through the story again, approaching it from different angles to try and stimulate Joselyn's memory, hoping to extract every bit of information she could.

After another ten minutes of questioning and not learning anything new, she nodded to turn it back over to me.

"Joselyn, did Logan see anything?" I asked. "I know he was farther away in front of Orange Way, but did he mention seeing anything at all?"

"Well, actually, he had already started heading toward M & P Grill to find me because the parade was over," she explained. "He said he was close enough to see the man in the rain suit getting hit."

"He did?"

"Yes, sir, he said there was a kid standing in the road and he saw the man jump right in front of the truck and push the kid out of the way." She shifted the strap on her sling to relieve the pressure on her neck before continuing. "He said it looked like the truck was trying to swerve to the left to avoid the little boy, but there were people on the shoulder and he thought some of them might've gotten—hey, wait a minute!"

She paused for a long moment, seemingly dumbfounded.

"What is it?" I asked when she didn't continue.

"I was one of those people on the shoulder!" she said. "I was running on the shoulder of the road and Logan said the kid was in the middle of the road. When the truck swerved toward the left to avoid the little boy, that must be when his side mirror hit me. He also hit this other little girl, because I saw her lying on the ground after I got up. She was almost in the ditch."

"Where'd you go when you got up?" I asked.

"Logan helped me to my feet and walked me back to the pizza place. An ambulance came by later and brought me to the hospital."

I asked a few more follow-up questions and then ended the interview. I told her I'd call if I needed anything more, and then grabbed my cell phone while Amy walked Joselyn to the lobby, where her dad was still waiting.

CHAPTER 13

When I was alone in the interview room, I called Sheriff Turner and asked him if he had any news for me. He told me his detectives were wrapping up the interviews at the hospital, but the information was scarce.

"Most people remember seeing a truck running through the crowd, but they can't even give an accurate description," he said with a grumble. "I swear, five people gave five different colors of the truck, and one even said it was a sedan. No one got a license plate, no one saw the driver, and no one had their phones out when it happened."

I cursed.

"What about you?" he asked.

I told him what we'd learned from Joselyn, and that seemed to immediately grab his attention.

"So, this might be a targeted case after all?"

"It's starting to look that way, but I'm not ruling anything out," I cautioned. "Have you heard anything from the victims who were flown to New Orleans?"

"The NOPD was kind enough to send a couple of their detectives to the hospital, and one of them called me a few minutes ago." Buck must've shoved the phone against his face, because I heard some muffled scratching noises that lasted for about twenty seconds. Finally, he was back on. "So, one of them is in serious but stable condition, and the other one's critical. I think the critical one was injured more so when his head hit the pavement. We got their names and my people have already started notifying family members. I spoke with Susan earlier, and she said she was handling the death notifications for the couple that was killed, and I made the notification to Cole Peterson's mom."

"You did?" I immediately stood straighter, my heart breaking for the woman. "How'd that happen?"

"She had heard from a neighbor that a firefighter had been injured, so she came to the hospital to check on him. It about killed her when I told her Cole didn't make it." Buck let out a long sigh. "This is the worst part of the job, Clint, and I'll never get used to it."

I nodded and lowered my head. I couldn't believe Cole was gone. The kid had been so full of life and possibilities just hours earlier, and now he was nothing but a memory.

"I'm gonna get this bastard, Buck," I said through gritted teeth, "and he'd better not resist arrest."

"If he does resist, I want to be there."

Buck promised he'd update me if there were any changes on the conditions of the victims, and I pulled the phone from my ear. When I looked up, Amy was standing there with a frown on her face.

"Susan and Regan just came in," she said, "and they've got Malory's and Wesley's parents with them. They're in the break room and it's not pretty. They're angry and they're heartbroken and they want answers."

"Do we need to go in there?"

"Actually, I think it's probably best if we don't. Susan met me in the hallway and said she's got them calm at the moment, and she thinks she can keep them that way, but it wouldn't take much to set them off." She sighed. "She said Wesley's dad wants to go on a murdering spree, and Malory's dad offered to supply all the weapons."

"Shit, I don't blame them one bit." I gathered up my notepad and tucked it under my arm. "Did you tell Susan what Joselyn gave us?"

"Yeah, and she said she'll try to find out if anyone had a vendetta against either of them."

I nodded. Susan was as capable as anyone I knew in getting information from people, and if Malory and Wesley had enemies and the parents knew about it, we'd have that information in no time. I waved for Amy to follow me, and then headed for my office.

"I'd like to hang around here just in case things go south, but I need to interview the Griffins," I explained, glancing at the time on my cell phone. It was creeping up on one o'clock, but I needed to speak with the owners of M & P Grill now. "I'll call and see if they'll agree to come in to the office now. If not, one of us will have to go interview them at their house while the other one stays here."

"You don't think Susan and Regan can handle them?" Amy asked, cocking her head sarcastically to the side. "It's only four against two."

"Of course they can handle them—but I don't want the parents getting hurt."

"Ah, you're right," Amy said flatly. "I'll do the interview. I don't want anything to do with beating up grieving parents. If they start trashing shit, I'll just walk away and let them at it. Hell, I might even help them, and then Susan would want to kick my ass."

I wasn't about to argue with her. Hell, I had no place to argue—not after what I'd done to the men who had killed my first wife and daughter.

"Why does it always have to be the good ones?" Amy mused aloud. "I knew Malory, and she was as good a person as they came. Maybe a little nosy, but I don't think I've ever met anyone as kind as she was. Why couldn't it be some cruel woman who deserved to die? Like that woman who hurt her kids east of here a few years back? Why couldn't it have happened to that bitch?"

"I don't know, Ames, I really don't." We had made it to my office, so I dropped into my chair and made the call.

As it turned out, neither Amy nor I had to leave the office to conduct the interviews. Victor Griffin picked up on the first ring and didn't even give me a chance to fully introduce myself before he was saying he needed to speak to me.

"I think I know who did this to Malory and her husband," he said. "There was trouble at the restaurant a few weeks ago, and I bet that little son of a gun is the one who caused trouble out there tonight. If it's okay with you, we can be there in five minutes. We're just down the road."

CHAPTER 14

Shade Rankin was heading north on Cypress Highway south of town when he noticed a desolate road that veered away from the highway and back south along a bayou that was smaller than Bayou Tail. He had never been down that road and didn't know what was back there, so he decided to go check it out. It appeared to be a desolate road, and since they were checking every possible hiding place for the suspect's truck, it seemed like a good place to search.

It had rained most of the day and the road was sloppy in places, so he stopped, slipped the gearshift in neutral, and activated the four-wheel-drive on the old Ford pickup truck. Since he was the newest officer here at the police department, he had gotten saddled with the oldest of the patrol cruisers, which didn't bother him at all—especially since it was a four-by-four. If he had been driving a new truck, he probably wouldn't have taken a chance on this road for fear of damaging it in some way, and if he had a Charger for a unit, he wouldn't be able to make it a mile on this road.

Since it looked like he was going off the grid, Shade called Melvin and shared his location.

"It's a good idea to check that road," Melvin said. "If you go down a ways, you'll see some rental camps hidden in the oaks off to the right side of the road along the bayou side. The woman who runs it is named Lucille Cheramie. She's probably sleeping, so you won't be able to talk to her, but you can check the camps to see if the suspect's truck is there. As far as I recall, there aren't any garages for the guests, so everyone's cars should be in plain view."

"Okay," Shade said, flicking his headlights to bright. "If I see anything even resembling the truck, I'll back off and give you a call."

"Ten-four."

Shade continued cruising down the bumpy, muddy road and, just like Melvin said, he soon came upon a stretch of land that boasted tall oak trees and a smattering of old camps. However, if Lucille Cheramie was sleeping, she must've been wearing earplugs, because there was a full-fledge party going on down by the bayou, complete with music, lights, and a large crowd of howling guests.

Shade surveyed the vehicles as he pulled into the driveway of the main house, which also appeared to serve as the office for the rental property. Nearly all of the vehicles were pickup trucks—with the exception of a tractor, a few motorcycles, a box truck, and a cargo van—and although there were two black Chevrolets, they didn't entirely match the description of the suspect's vehicle. While they both had lift kits, large tires, and prominent bumpers, they didn't have a primer black exterior. That kind of dull coat would be hard to miss in a crowd.

Not wanting to engage with a bunch of drunks but wanting to see if he could gather some information, Shade parked his truck and made his way down to the party. There was a boardwalk path leading to the bayou side and, despite the unevenness and a few broken boards, it made the going much easier than walking in sloppy mud.

Shade felt conscientious about his uniform. Although his green and tan BDUs were comfortable, he still wasn't used to displaying a badge and gun out in public, and he felt a little weird about it—as though all eyes turned to him when he entered a room. He didn't like attention, but attention was all he got once he'd donned a police uniform.

As he had feared, everyone turned to stare when the police officer approached the fun. The area where the party was taking place was along a long stretch of flat ground near the bayou. There were over a dozen picnic tables situated under a network of large tents. A wooden dance floor had been constructed to one side, and a cover band was entertaining the crowd from a raised wharf over the water. The bright lights on the wharf and those hanging from strings around the edges of the tent lit up the area like the daytime.

Shade stopped at the edge of the boardwalk and scanned the faces in the crowd. As luck would have it, the band was winding down its latest song—a cover of *Am I The Only One* by Aaron Lewis—so everyone heard and turned to stare when a man shouted, "Oh, shit, people! Who shot the sheriff?"

Another person hollered, "We promise we'll turn down the music, so you can leave now!"

Someone else screamed, "I didn't do it!"

If Shade had been given a dollar for every time he'd already heard someone say they "didn't do it" in his short career, he could retire early. In response, he only smiled and waved to the crowd as he tried to seek out the owner. He had no idea what Lucille Cheramie looked like, but he imagined she would be the one working the hardest while everyone drank beer and partied.

He was still surveying the crowd when he caught movement from his peripheral vision. He turned to see a bashful—but beautiful—looking girl approaching him with a shy smile on her face.

"Hello, officer," she said. "Can I help you?"

Shade scowled. Based on his conversation with Melvin, he had imagined Lucille Cheramie to be an older woman, not this young and beautiful girl standing before him.

The young woman giggled, seemingly recognizing Shade's confusion.

"I'm Daisy," she said, holding out a slender hand. "I'm Lucille Cheramie's assistant."

Shade took her hand, squeezed gently, and introduced himself.

"This is quite a party," he said. "It looks like fun."

"It's our first Cajun Mardi Gras Bash," said Daisy. "So far, it's been our most popular event in years. We've had people from all over the country come here during Mardi Gras and say they wish there was a place where they could celebrate with good food, music, and king cake, rather than having to stand out on the street waiting for plastic beads and cheap stuffed animals. So, Lucille decided to make their dreams come true."

"That's cool." The band had cranked up again, so Shade leaned closer to Daisy. "Have y'all heard about what happened in town?"

The young woman's brow furrowed and she shook her head. She leaned even closer to Shade and put her mouth close to his ear. "What happened?"

He shivered when the breath from her mouth tickled his ear. He leaned toward her ear and gave a brief accounting of what had happened, leaving out the gory details.

"We're looking for a black Chevrolet pickup truck," he said. "It's got a lift kit, large mud tires, and it's coated in a dull black primer paint. It should have damage to the front end."

When Shade pulled away from Daisy's ear, he saw that her face was twisted in horror. She clutched at her chest.

"Dear God!" she said loudly. "Do you know who was hurt? My mom lives in town and she goes to the parade."

"What's her name?" he asked, turning his ear to her.

The name wasn't one he recognized, but he hadn't been privy to a victims' list, if one even existed, so he told her he wasn't sure, but that someone would've contacted her by now if her mom had been a victim. He leaned close to her ear again and continued the conversation, turning his ear to her when she responded.

"How long has the party been going on?" he asked.

"All afternoon," she said. "We started at six and we're going until two."

"Did anyone show up late looking nervous?"

"Not that I noticed."

"If you hear or see anything suspicious, can you call the police department and share that information?"

"For sure," she said. "What's your name again?"

"Shade Rankin."

Daisy smiled warmly. "It's nice to meet you, Shade Rankin."

Shade smiled back and nodded his head. He then told her he would work the crowd, just in case someone saw anything, and they parted ways. He spent the next thirty minutes or so walking around and speaking with the guests of the Cajun Mardi Gras Bash. Most of them were drunk and many of the women tried to get him on the dance floor, but he politely waved them off and continued on.

After speaking to about a dozen people and getting nowhere, he decided it was a waste of time and he headed back toward his truck. He scanned the vehicles in the muddy parking lot once again on his way out, but none of them matched the description of the suspect vehicle.

"Well, that was a waste of time," he muttered to himself as he got back in his truck and radioed that he was clear of the party. As he was backing out, he remembered something Clint had told him. He'd said that no investigative step was a waste of time. Even if nothing was turned up, it was important that every effort was made. If nothing else, it would help to ensure that a thorough investigation had been conducted and that no stone had been left unturned.

Feeling a little better now about "wasting" the last half hour, Shade quickly sped out of the driveway and headed back toward the highway. That truck was out there somewhere, and he wanted to help find it before it injured or killed someone else.

CHAPTER 15

Mechant Loup Police Department

Amy and I decided to interview Victor and Faith Griffin separately. She took Faith to Interview Room One, and I took Victor to Interview Room Two.

"You said on the phone that there'd been trouble at the restaurant," I began. "Do you mind explaining what you meant?"

Victor, who had short gray hair and a sizeable belly, nodded. "Mind you, I didn't witness any of it, but Malory told me about it the day after it happened. I wanted to call the law, but she wasn't having it. She said that Wesley had taken care of the problem, and she preferred to leave it at that."

I nodded patiently, not saying anything. I was content to allow him to tell his story in his own way.

"It was the middle of January, a Saturday," he said, "maybe the fifteenth. Anyway, this young man comes into the restaurant and orders a burger. He was sitting alone in the corner. It's the winter time and it's the middle of the day, and we're slow in the winter, so it was only Malory and one of our cooks—a female—in the restaurant. Well, when this fellow was making his order, he starts saying inappropriate things to Malory about the size of her, um, her breasts, and he asks if he can see them."

Victor paused and licked his lips.

I scowled and leaned both arms on the desk, waiting for him to continue and feeling my blood starting to boil.

"Well, this guy didn't stop there," he explained. "When he was done giving his order, Malory asked if she could have the menu. The menu was on the table in front of him, but he just leans back and tells her she can take it if she wants it. When she reaches for it, he slides his hand up the back of her leg and squeezes her behind."

I was growing angrier by the second and Victor was growing more and more uncomfortable. I could tell he wasn't used to talking about things of this nature.

"It's okay, Mr. Griffin," I said, grateful that we'd separated the couple. "It's just you and me in here. Tell me what happened next. There's no judgment from me."

"Well, Malory went to the back and quickly called Wesley, as you would expect her to, you know?" He fidgeted in his chair. "Wesley, he was not a happy camper. He drove right to the restaurant, but he didn't do anything at first. He walked inside like a regular customer and took a table not far from the young man. Malory had stayed in the kitchen until he showed up, and she comes out once he's taken his seat. Well, right away, that young man with the attitude, he calls over to her and asks where she's been. He says he missed her and wants her to go sit in his lap. That was all it took."

Victor took a breath and glanced around the room.

"What is it?" I asked when he didn't continue.

"I mean, Wesley can't get in trouble for this, right?"

I cocked my head to the side. "Come again?"

"What I mean is, will this reflect poorly on his character?" Victor waved a hand. "I know he's gone, but I don't want to speak ill of the dead. If he were alive, could he be in trouble for what I'm about to tell you?"

"First off," I said, "I don't know what you're about to tell me, but if you're gonna tell me that he beat the shit out of that little punk, I'm here to say that I would've done the same damn thing."

Victor took a breath. "Okay, I understand. Yes, that's exactly what he did. He storms over to the young man, drags him out of his chair, and he pummels him right there on the floor of the restaurant. The whole event was captured on camera. I watched it a few times before it recorded over itself. I've never seen that side of Wesley. To me, when he'd come visit Malory at the restaurant, I always thought of him as a gentle giant. He wasn't a giant of a man, mind you, but he was above average in height and weight."

"Go back a step," I said. "Did you say the recording was deleted?"

"Yes, sir," Victor acknowledged. "After a certain time period—I think it's fifteen days—the DVR automatically deletes old footage to make room for new footage."

I sighed. "Okay, do you know the name of this little rodent that came in starting trouble?"

"No, sir, I don't, but my wife does." He snapped his fingers. "I think his first name is Dan, Danny or Daniel, but I don't remember his last name. Like I said, my wife will know."

"What happened after Wesley beat him down?" I asked.

"Oh, yeah, that's the most important part to this story." Victor straightened in his chair. "This young man, he tells Wesley that's he's going to pay dearly for what he did. He says it doesn't matter if it takes him his entire lifetime, he will surely pay him back. And then that's when the tires got slashed."

"Wait…what?" I asked. "When did this happen?"

"It was about two weeks ago, on a Saturday. Yep, that's when Wesley's tires got slashed."

I was thoughtful. I hadn't received any reports of tires being slashed within the last two weeks, and I couldn't remember ever seeing Wesley's name on a report.

"Where'd this happen?"

"Oh, at the restaurant," he said. "Malory was working the night shift that night and I couldn't be there, so Wesley drove her to work and hung around the place just in case something happened. Now, he didn't just hang around, mind you. He worked—and he worked a lot! I told Malory I wanted to put him on the payroll. Anyways, he parks his truck where Malory always parks her car, and when they go to leave, they find all four tires slashed. They said from the looks of it, someone stuck a large knife right through the sidewalls. It cost him a little more than two thousand dollars to replace the tires. I put up half the money. He didn't want me to, but I felt bad because it happened at my place of business and it was a result of him defending my waitress. I mean, I know it's his wife, but she was harassed by one of my customers, so I felt partially responsible."

It was at this point that Victor's head slowly began to droop and his chin began to tremble. Before long, his entire body was shaking and he was crying. As he sat there wringing his hands, he tried to talk, but his sentences were unintelligible. I waved him off and pulled a box of tissues from the desk drawer. I slid them across the table.

"Take your time, sir," I said softly. "This is difficult for all of us. It's okay to cry."

He nodded and dabbed at his eyes with the tissue. After a long minute of fighting hard to control his emotions, he decided to just talk right through them.

"I just feel like it was a bad move to come here and buy this business," he said through choking sobs. "Had I simply stayed in Texas where I belonged, none of this would've happened. I feel responsible for everything that's gone wrong. I…I'm responsible for this. It's my fault they're dead."

His words once again devolved into a string of unintelligible sentences. I sighed heavily. I knew that nothing I said would relieve his guilt, but I had to try.

"Sir, there's only one person responsible for what happened out there tonight—and it's the asshole who stole Wesley's truck and attacked them."

Victor continued babbling about something, but I still couldn't make out a word he was saying.

"Look," I finally said, feeling like I was running out of time, "you can either sit there feeling sorry for yourself, or you can man up and help me solve this case. The fact is; I need your help. You can't help me in this condition. It's okay to break down and cry, but I need you to do that later. Right now, I need to know everything you know, but I can't understand a damned thing you're saying."

As I had hoped, my rough tone and sharp words had jolted Victor out of his sorrow. He clamped his mouth shut and brushed the tears away from his eyes. Although his face was still twisted in sorrow, he seemed to be in better control of his faculties.

"Are you ready to continue?" I asked.

"Yes, sir."

"Okay, I don't remember seeing a report on a tire slashing at M & P Grill," I said. "Did they call it in?"

"No, Wesley refused to involve the police." Victor took a trembling breath. "I tried to convince him to call you guys, especially since we had the evidence to prove who it was, but he said he would leave it be for now. He didn't want to escalate anything. He said if the young man struck again, then he would involve the police."

"By evidence," I began, relieved that we were finally getting somewhere, "do you mean surveillance footage?"

"Yes, sir."

I quickly did the math in my head. "If this happened two weeks ago, on a Saturday, then you should still have the footage, right?"

Victor was thoughtful, but didn't respond right away.

"If your surveillance system records over old footage every fifteen days," I explained, "then we still have two days, because that Saturday would've been thirteen days ago. Right?"

I was hoping he was correct about the amount of days that the recordings were retained, but the look on his face made me worry.

"I mean, it should be." He glanced at his wristwatch. "It's Saturday now, so the footage will start to erase soon."

I jumped to my feet. "Then I need to go retrieve that video right now!"

Without hesitating, Victor reached into his pocket and produced a large key ring. He selected a silver key and, with trembling hands, removed it from the ring. He then slid it across the table. "Help yourself."

"Did you look at the footage?" I asked, already heading for the door.

"Malory did, but she said she couldn't be sure, but that it was probably the same guy from the restaurant—the one that Wesley beat up."

"What time did it happen?"

"Oh, I'm not sure." Victor shook his head. "I never saw it."

"Okay, just chill out here for a while," I said from the doorway. "As soon as Detective Cooke's done with your wife, y'all can leave and I'll call later to return the key."

"Just keep it."

I was about to disappear out the door when Victor stopped me.

"Um, Detective, can I go to the restroom?" he asked. "I need to break down."

CHAPTER 16

After showing Victor to the restroom, I hurried to Interview Room One and knocked on the door. Amy told me to enter. When I was inside with the door closed, I asked Amy if she was almost done.

"Yeah, she was just telling me about the fight between Wesley and Danny." Amy shook her head. "Can you believe that little shit? First Wanda and now Malory. That kid can't keep his hands off married women."

I scowled as I thought back to the case we'd worked that involved Wanda Pierce. "It was Danny *Kiger* who assaulted Malory?"

"Yep, one and the same."

"That little shit!" I sucked in a breath and quickly glanced over at Faith Griffin. I'd gotten the impression from her husband that cursing was frowned upon in their household. "I'm sorry ma'am, but I'm a flawed man. I've been known to do more than my share of cursing. I apologize."

"I'm not worried." She chuckled and waved a dismissive hand. "I do it, too, from time to time, but never in front of Victor. He doesn't like it when people curse. He says it goes against God's wishes. I challenged him once to show me in the Bible where any of the modern curse words are forbidden by the Lord, but he couldn't. Now, Miles? He curses all the time. Sometimes, I think he does it just to annoy his father."

When Faith noticed the quizzical expression on Amy's face, she explained that Miles was her son. I was tapping my foot now, wanting to interrupt them, but not wanting to be rude about it.

"That's how we found out about everything tonight," Faith continued. "Miles and Ivy came over and said their car was stuck in the parking lot, because there had been some kind of accident and it was being investigated. We heard later that it was, um…"

Faith allowed her voice to trail off and she lowered her head. A few tears fell from her eyes as she fought to keep her composure. She finally took a breath and wiped her face. Without looking up, she said, "We heard later that Malory and Wesley had been taken from us."

I only nodded, while Amy reached across the desk and took Faith's hands to comfort her.

"Um, Ames," I said softly, but quickly, "I've got to run to the restaurant to pull footage from the cameras."

Faith wiped her eyes and looked up. "Oh, the footage from that fight has been deleted," she explained. "The system records over itself every fourteen days."

"Wait—every *fourteen* days?" I blurted loudly, interrupting her.

Amy and Faith stared up at me in confusion.

"Yeah," Faith said, "it's got a two-week retention period, where it starts deleting everything on the back end within fourteen days."

"Shit!"

"What's going on?" Amy asked.

"I need to go," I said, and ran out of the room.

Susan and Regan were huddling in the hallway just outside of the break room when I sped past them. I didn't even slow down to say hello. I was running out of time. At this very second, the recording I needed could be falling into nothingness. I rushed into the dispatcher's station, snatched a flash drive from the supply cabinet, and then headed for the lobby.

"Clint!" Susan called after me. "What's wrong? Where in the hell are you going?"

"M & P Grill," I shot back. "I'm in a hurry."

CHAPTER 17

There was no traffic on Washington Avenue, so I was able to speed toward Main Street. There were still Troopers blocking off the crime scene at Market Street, so traffic was a little more congested than it would normally be at one forty-six in the morning, and I had to wait for several eighteen-wheelers and a few other vehicles to pass before I could get on the highway.

When I had finally reached the scene, I saw Vanessa kneeling on a makeshift bridge beside Wesley's body in the ditch. She was so intently involved in her examination that she didn't even look up when I approached the crime scene tape. The deputy who stood guard over the scene recognized me, and immediately lifted the tape so I could slip under it.

Not wanting to disturb Vanessa, I waved one of the other crime scene techs over.

"Am I clear to go back inside the restaurant?" I asked, trying to slow down enough for my words to make sense. I didn't want to sound like Victor had earlier.

"Yeah, we're done with the parking lot."

I nodded my thanks and hurried toward the entrance. Malory's body was gone, but there was still a dark blood stain on the concrete where she had spent her final seconds on earth. I gritted my teeth and tried to push the thought from my head as I hurried inside and to the office.

Once I was seated at the desk, my fingers flew across the keyboard. I quickly pulled up the south-facing camera that was positioned on the front of the building and checked the date range.

There were exactly fourteen days of recording stored, and I knew the footage from that Saturday was being dumped by the second.

Working as fast as I could, I shoved my flash drive into the USB port and accessed the retrieval system. I selected all the available footage from both of the front-facing cameras on that Saturday and told the machine to copy the footage to my flash drive.

Now, all I could do was wait. I drummed my fingers on the desk, hoping and praying I had made it in time. I found myself talking out loud to the DVR, and I didn't hear the front door open and close. The first indication that I wasn't alone was a tap on my shoulder.

I whirled around and saw Vanessa standing there.

"Hey," she said, smiling. "Is everything okay?"

"Yeah, I'm trying to download this footage before it disappears." I explained what we had learned from the Griffins, and I told her about the fourteen-day dump period.

"Oh, wow, you're cutting it close." Her blonde hair was plastered to her face, thanks to the protective gear she had been wearing earlier, and she reached up to peel away some strands. "I just wanted to let you know we're moving from the parking lot to the highway now. I'll be processing Cole Peterson's body next, while members of my team continue processing the locations where other victims were injured."

I nodded, glancing from her to the monitor to keep an eye on the progress of the download. A thought suddenly occurred to me.

"Hey, did you find any keys in Wesley's pockets?" I asked without looking at her. I'd already told her we believed he had been run over by his own truck, but I hadn't put a lot of thought into the manner in which the thief had stolen the truck. The truck was an old model, so it was possible to hotwire it without much trouble, but I wanted to know for sure.

"No, I didn't find any keys in his pockets." Vanessa consulted her notepad. She flipped a few pages and then scrunched up her mouth while she studied her notes. "He had eleven dollars and thirty-eight cents in loose bills and change in his front right pocket, a wallet in his rear right pocket, a bottle cap in his front left pocket, and his cell phone was in his rear left pocket. No keys."

I nodded. "Can you dump his cell phone as soon as possible? I need to know if he's had any threatening text messages or anything that might indicate problems with someone else. The same with Malory's phone. If there's a chance this has nothing to do with the fight at the restaurant, I want to know about it."

Vanessa nodded and jotted something in her notebook.

My download was nearly halfway completed. The moment of truth was fast approaching. While I waited, Vanessa went on to outline everything she had found and done so far, and the steps she planned for the remainder of the scene. She mentioned processing the van and surveillance cameras for DNA and prints, and she said they recovered a number of prints from the van, including a partial print from the top of the van.

That got my attention and pulled me away from the download progress.

"You found a partial on *top* of the van?" I asked, realizing this was significant.

"One of my techs did," she corrected. "You wouldn't expect a worker to be climbing around on top of the van, so I'm pretty sure that partial will belong to the person who cut the wires on the camera."

I spun around in my chair. "Holy shit! That's great! How soon can you run it?"

"Well, there's a bit of bad news."

I sank in my seat. "Hit me with it."

"The print isn't from an area that's typically rolled during bookings," she explained. "I'll have to examine it more closely in the lab, but it looks like it's from the outside portion of the right pinky. So, I won't be able to give you a suspect based on that, but I might be able to match it to someone if you develop a suspect and recover major case prints."

"I might have a suspect for you in a few minutes," I declared, turning back toward the monitor. "It turns out that Malory and Wesley were having problems with a local boy named Danny Kiger. He grabbed Malory's butt while she was working one day, and Wesley beat his face in."

"Good for him!"

"I know, right?" I said with a laugh. "Anyway, someone slashed all four of Wesley's truck tires two weeks ago, and they believe Danny did it in retaliation for the beating he got."

"Huh!" Vanessa was thoughtful. "And we're thinking this Danny fellow is also the one responsible for driving them down in Wesley's truck?"

"Well, I don't know what to think just yet, but he's our only hope right now." I shook my head. "We've got to go where the evidence is taking us and, unfortunately, we don't have much of it right now."

"Well, you bring me his prints," Vanessa began in a confident tone, "and I'll tell you for sure if it's him or not."

I thanked her and she turned to leave, while I turned back to the monitor. Ninety-five percent done.

My palms were sweating. My heart was racing. Finally, the progress report notified me that the download was 100% complete. Without wasting a second, I snatched the flash drive from the USB port. I flipped open a laptop on the desk and checked to see if it was pass-protected. To my relief, it wasn't. I shoved the flash drive into the USB port on the side, accessed the folder, and then began searching for the correct date and time.

The file names were fourteen digits long, representing the year, month, day, and time, so it was difficult to distinguish one from the other. I was still trying to find one from two Saturdays ago when I heard the front door to the restaurant burst open, followed quickly by the sound of boots pounding on the floor. I didn't have to look up to know that it was Amy.

"Did you find it?" she asked, her breath sounding heavy, as though she had been running.

"I don't know what time it happened, so I'm guessing here." I clicked on one of the files from the eight o'clock hour and played it. The truck had been backed into the lot like it had been yesterday during the parade, so we couldn't see the tires. "We won't be able to see anyone cutting the tires."

"Just go to the last one of the night," Amy said. "See if the height of the truck looks different in the camera."

I did as she instructed and, sure enough, there was an obvious difference in the height of the truck in the last file, versus the first file. I then started clicking on each previous file. As soon as the image came into view and I saw that the profile was lower, I exited and went to the next. Finally, I found a file that showed the truck in its original state.

"Here we go!" I sat back and allowed the footage to play. They were recorded in five-minute files and I didn't know at what point during those five minutes the tires had been cut, so I elected to be patient. We had saved the footage, and that's what was important.

About twenty seconds into the footage, a man was seen approaching the parking lot from the north. He was walking on the shoulder of the road, and he was checking his surroundings like a rabbit looking for a coyote. Due to the gray hue of the infrared night vision, it was hard to make out the color of his clothes, but he was definitely wearing a hoodie and he had the hood covering his head.

"This is gonna be our guy," I said, tapping the screen. "And he's built like Danny Kiger."

Amy only grunted. Her attention was so focused on the footage that she reminded me of when my grandma used to watch soap operas that she called the *stories*. If I opened my mouth to ask for anything, she would shush me immediately, and if I tried to interfere again, she would throw her shoe at me. Amy's boots were heavy, so I didn't interrupt her concentration again.

After loitering in front of the restaurant for about a minute, the man finally jumped the ditch that separated Main Street from the parking lot and made a mad dash toward the truck.

"Hmm," I mumbled, leaning closer to the monitor while trying not to get in Amy's way. "Is that a knife in his right hand?"

"It sure is," Amy said, "and it's a big one—at least an eight-inch blade, and he's carrying it like he's ready to use it."

As we continued to watch, the man disappeared from the camera's view, but it was very obvious what he did next, because the truck shivered four distinct times—presumably with each strike of the knife—and then slowly sank into a squatting position on its rims.

"Damn, he's caught red-handed," Amy said. "I don't understand why Wesley didn't report it. Danny doesn't have any money. With his record, he would've never been able to afford bail and he'd still be locked up. They would still be alive if they would've reported it."

"Yeah, but according to Victor Griffin, they didn't want to escalate things," I explained.

"And how'd that work out for them?" Amy's hands were on her hips and she was staring down at me. I was still watching the footage, but I could feel her eyes boring into the side of my face.

"I don't know, Ames," I finally said, as a crouching figure came into view near the front, passenger side of the truck. "Had they known what the future held, maybe they would've made a different decision, but they didn't have that benefit."

Amy sighed heavily and turned back to the monitor. She stabbed her index finger on the head of the crouching figure who seemed to be hiding because another car had turned into the parking lot.

"You lowlife piece of—"

"Shit!" I said, pounding the desk when the man turned toward the camera. "That's not Danny Kiger!"

CHAPTER 18

I stepped away from the computer screen and called Melvin. He answered right away.

"Hey, are y'all finding anything?" I asked, desperate for a break in the case.

"Not a thing," he said. "We've checked everything twice, and we're going back over our steps again. If he's still here, he's bedding down deep. I'm hoping he sticks his head up at some point, because if he doesn't, we might never find him."

"Did y'all check the bayou sides and lakes?" I asked, already knowing that they had. Once they were asked to do something, this group of officers jumped to it.

"Yeah, there's no sign anywhere of any vehicles going into the water," he said. "And with the rain we've had, it would easily show up."

I rubbed my face. Although my body was probably tired and hungry, I didn't feel it. I wanted to solve this case, and I wanted to solve it before sunrise. I wanted that asshole behind bars before he could hurt another person.

"Look, I'm about to text you a picture," I finally said."Let me know if you recognize this person."

I pulled the phone away from my ear and sent the screenshot I'd taken of the tire-slashing suspect. I then put the phone back to my ear and brought him up to speed.

"We originally thought Danny Kiger slashed Wesley's tires, but this guy shows up in the video," I explained. "We need to identify him as soon as we can. He might've also been involved in the murders tonight." I suddenly remembered what time it was and corrected myself. "I mean, last night."

Melvin was silent on the other end, but I could hear him shuffling the phone around. Finally, he said he didn't recognize the suspect.

"If he's from here, I've never seen him," he said. "What direction did he come from?"

"He walked up from the north. Amy and I backed up the video to see if we'd see him driving past the place, but we can't make out any faces in the vehicles because it's at night and the cameras are so far from the road."

"Just because it's not Danny, it doesn't mean he's not involved," Amy said over her shoulder. She was still going through the footage, trying to find anything useful. "He could've gotten one of his buddies to do the dirty deed."

She was right and, at the moment, he was our only suspect, so we had to pursue that lead. I thanked Melvin and ended the call.

"Let's head back to the office and run Danny's name," I said. "If he was late paying his water bill last month, I want to know about it."

"Danny doesn't have a water bill." Amy snatched up the flash drive and shut down the laptop. "He's probably still leaching off of Wanda or some other sugar momma who believes her glory years are behind her and he's the best she can get."

I shrugged and followed Amy outside. Once I'd locked up the restaurant, I sauntered over to where Vanessa was processing Cole's body. Just across the street from her, every man, woman and youngster who was a member of the fire department was huddled together in prayer. Some of them had candles and others held their cell phones up with the flashlight feature turned on.

I frowned. Cole was beloved by all, and he would be truly missed. I thought back to Amy's earlier reflection: *Why does it always have to be the good ones?*

Amy sped out of the parking lot first, so I followed her back to the police department. Once we were in my office, I accessed our warrant database and conducted a name search on Danny Kiger.

"We've got his ass!" I shouted. "He's got three warrants—one for burglary, one for domestic abuse battery, and another one for contempt of court—and there's a parole hold on him."

"Does it list the victim of the domestic violence?"

I scanned the documents. "No, it doesn't, but his latest address is listed as Wanda Pierce's house."

"Ugh, do you really think she's still with that loser?"

I shrugged. After printing the warrants and calling the sheriff's office to make sure the warrants were still valid, I called Sheriff Buck Turner to let him know I would be heading to Northern Chateau to interview Danny Kiger.

"He's got warrants," I added, "so is it okay if I turn him over to one of your guys if this ends up being a dead end? I don't have time to mess with peripheral charges right now."

"Oh, I understand perfectly," the sheriff said. "I'll have the shift lieutenant keep one of his north deputies free until you're ready for them. Do you need backup? I heard this kid's fast when he decides to run."

"Nah, I've got somebody even faster." I smiled as I said it, but didn't offer up the name. "Before I go, have there been any changes to the status of the victims?"

"Actually, yeah, there has."

My heart sank for a moment.

"All three patients in New Orleans are showing improvements," he said. "My detective tells me the doctors are optimistic that they'll all make full recoveries."

I exhaled the breath I didn't realize I'd been holding. "Thanks, sheriff."

My next call was to Shade Rankin.

"Hey, Clint, how are you?" the kid said when he answered the call. It had taken a lot of work to break him of the habit of addressing me formal, but it had finally paid off.

"I'm good. Melvin tells me y'all didn't turn up anything."

"Not yet, but we're still looking."

"Look, we're going after a rabbit," I explained. "I've dealt with him before and didn't have any problems with him, but he's got warrants now, so I think he'll try to run. Care to come along?"

"Absolutely!" he said. "I'd love to come along."

I didn't bother asking him about his injured leg. Brandon Berger, who was the head instructor for the Magnolia Parish Sheriff's Office Police Academy, had told me that Shade was the fastest and most physically fit recruit he'd ever seen. He said that on day one of the academy, Shade had shattered their record for most push-ups in two minutes, most sit-ups in two minutes, and most pull-ups.

Brandon said that Shade had started out in the middle of the pack in the running department, but, after a few weeks, he found his stride and broke the academy's long-standing record for the two-mile run. He said the only records that remained safe from Shade were the ones for heaviest bench press and heaviest leg press, but he assured me those records had been set by meatheads who could barely do a single pull-up, so it didn't really count.

Brandon had nearly choked on his tongue when I'd told him that Shade had been shot in the left leg three days before Hell Day, and that his doctor had recommended he sit out this academy and wait until the next one started.

"He never said a word about an injury," Brandon said. "And he certainly never mentioned being shot. Was this on duty?"

I explained what had happened and how he had saved my life. "He was supposed to show up to Hell Day with a doctor's note saying he was on limited duty," I said, "but I guess he didn't."

"We never had a clue," Brandon said. "It's winter, so we're wearing warm-ups and I never even saw a bandage."

Before ending that particular call, Brandon had also told me that Shade was one of the best fighters he'd ever seen, and he was competing with two other cadets for the top academic award. As for firearms proficiency, they weren't going to the range until the end of the academy, so that was yet to be determined, but he said Shade was one of the best overall cadets he'd ever had the privilege of teaching.

Although I'd known about Shade's record-setting performances at the police academy for about two weeks now, he had yet to mention them to any of us at the police department. I was starting to think he never would.

"Great," I said to Shade. "Let Melvin know you'll be with me, and then meet Amy and me at the police department."

"Did he ever tell you he set those records yet?" Amy asked when I'd pocketed my cell phone.

"Nope."

"Damn." She whistled. "I'd be bragging about that shit from sun up to sun down. I'd take out a billboard. Hell, an ad in the paper. Maybe even a television announcement."

I laughed. "I'm sure you would."

Shade still had a little more than a month left in the police academy, but he came out every weekend to volunteer. As soon as Shade graduated, Melvin would be placed permanently on the water, Shade would slip into one of the dayshift spots, and Baylor would move into a night slot. Even more than Shade, Baylor and Melvin couldn't wait for the kid to graduate.

I couldn't wait either, because I was hoping to someday steal him from Susan and create a new detective spot. More land had been opened up for development just to the north of town, and every available plot had been sold within days of becoming available, so the town would soon see another expansion.

In addition to that, we were becoming more and more of a tourist destination, so with more people visiting and more money rolling in, more criminals were also showing up to take advantage of unsuspecting folks and to try and take a giant bite of the pie. It was our job to make sure that if they did get a piece, it would be a slice of Miss Hilly's "special" pie from the movie *The Help*.

CHAPTER 19

Twenty minutes later, Shade was in the back seat of my Tahoe, Amy was in the front seat, and I was driving. I could tell Shade was trying to act nonchalant about the mission, but underneath that calm, cool, and collected veneer, he was excited.

"So, who is this guy we're going after?" he asked almost immediately.

As I drove us out of town, Amy explained how it was that we'd first come to meet Danny Kiger a little more than a year ago. In the rearview mirror, I could see Shade hanging on her every word.

"Oh, wow," he said when she was done. "That's the same case Melvin was telling me about earlier. We went to the Waxtuygi Wildlife Nature Park tonight to look for the suspect, and he actually showed me the outhouse where some of it happened. We didn't go down the trail to the campground, because it was obvious a truck hadn't gone back there, but we looked everywhere else the suspect might be."

Amy and Shade talked about the case at hand while I drove, myself lost in my own thoughts. We were driving through Central Chateau when Amy asked him how the police academy was going.

"Oh, I love it," he said. "Captain Brandon Berger is really cool. He talks a lot about you, Clint. He said you're one of the only detectives he knows who's solved every murder case you've worked. He says that's quite an accomplishment."

"I wish he'd stop saying that," I muttered. "It's a team effort. Even though my name's on the report, there are a lot of people that go into solving every case. From the dispatchers, to the patrol officers, to the forensic scientists, to the witnesses, and on and on—it truly takes a team to put a case together. And besides, he might jinx us."

Shade and Amy laughed, but I didn't. With each new case that came along, I was worried that it would finally be the one that would stump us. If that ever happened, I knew I would never be able to ride off into the sunset and enjoy time with my wife, kids, and grandkids, because I could never leave something like that undone. I just prayed it never happened.

Susan called me a few more minutes into the drive to say that Malory's and Wesley's parents had gone home.

"They're exhausted," she said. "I promised we'd wake them up if there were any new developments."

"Did they know of anyone who might want to hurt Malory or Wesley?" I asked.

"Well, other than the kid that Wesley beat up, they've got nothing," she said. "And Amy told me we think he's Danny Kiger?"

"Yeah, we're heading to his house now. We should be there in about ten minutes."

"Be safe."

"Always."

"I hate when you say that," she grumbled. "It sounds like you're taking things for granted."

"I love you, too," I said with a laugh and ended the call.

When I turned down Wanda Pierce's street, I decided to stop at Danny's previous address first, just in case he was staying there, but changed my mind the second his property came into view—the house was gone. I didn't know if there had been a fire or if it had gotten destroyed in the last hurricane that had blown through here, but whatever the case, the only thing left was a concrete slab and some miscellaneous trash around the edges.

"I guess he ain't home," Amy said with a smirk.

I nodded and headed for Wanda's house. We had been there before, but I almost didn't recognize the place this time. The bright lights that used to shine above the garage door were now dark. Grass grew tall in the yard. The trees hadn't been trimmed in some time. All-in-all, it looked like the place had been abandoned.

"Damn, she let her house go," Amy mumbled. "It's starting to look like Danny's used to."

I drove past the house so we could assess the area, and then turned around at the back of the street. As I cruised back toward the house, I asked Shade if he could make his way toward the garage door once we arrived, and asked Amy to head toward the right side of the house.

"I'll knock on the front door," I said. "If he makes a run for it, he'll probably come from the garage and head for the woods toward the back of the street." I gave Shade a nod in my rearview mirror. "Even if he slips past you, you'll be able to run him down before he hits the woods."

"I'll try my best," Shade said wryly, "but I don't know how fast he is. Plus, I'm wearing my gun belt, boots, and uniform. All this gear slows me down."

"I'm not worried," I said with a smile. "My money's on you."

I didn't reveal what I knew about his physical feats at the academy. Instead, I parked on the street and waved for them to spread out on the house. I gave them enough time to get into position, and then I approached the front door. Standing to the right side of the door and keeping my hand near my pistol, I banged on the wooden frame with my left hand and stood there waiting, ready for anything.

It was a quarter to three in the morning and I would've normally felt bad about waking someone up at this hour, but this was too important a lead to delay until daylight. As I stood there waiting, the doubt started to creep into my mind. If Danny hadn't possessed the stones to slash Wesley's tires himself, he wouldn't have possessed the stones to steal his truck and plow over him and his wife. There was no way the truck could've made it out of town, so it couldn't be on Wanda's property. Supposing Danny did have friends loyal enough to murder someone for him, how would I make him admit that? All he had to do was keep his mouth shut and we might never know who was responsible—that is, if he was even a part of this.

I sighed and banged on the door again, but this time even louder. I longed for an easy case for a change. I'd once worked a case where the perpetrator had dropped his driver's license at the crime scene. Easiest case ever. Why couldn't they all be like that?

Suddenly, I heard movement from inside the house. I stood alert and waited.

"Who is it?" a groggy voice asked without opening the door. "It's three o'clock in the damned morning!"

"Mrs. Pierce, it's Clint Wolf," I said loudly, "from the police department."

There was a moment of hesitation, and then I heard her throw the lock. When she opened the door, I saw a mess of red hair and a surly scowl staring back above a silk nightgown.

"What the hell do you want?"

"Well, ma'am," I said slowly, taking in the roughness of her appearance, "I'm looking for Danny Kiger."

"He doesn't live here anymore," she said, pulling her nightgown tighter around her and trying to fill the doorway.

I cocked my head to the side and glanced past her. From what I could see of the place, it was a wreck. Things had certainly gone downhill for her since she'd started messing around with Danny.

"Mind if I search your house?"

"Do you have a warrant?"

"No, but I do have enough probable cause to get one," I said. "Danny's a suspect in a sexual assault that occurred in Mechant Loup a couple of weeks ago, and he's listing your house as his address."

"Sexual assault?" her face twisted in confusion. "What on earth are you talking about? He hasn't been to Mechant Loup in forever."

"How would you know that if he doesn't live here?" I asked pointedly.

Wanda clamped her jaw shut. I could almost hear her curse under her breath.

"I've got a warrant for his arrest," I said. "If you won't let me in, then I'll surround the place to make sure he doesn't escape and apply for a search warrant. I'm only looking for Danny. I don't care what else you've got going on in your house. That's your business."

"What's that supposed to mean?" She folded her arms across her chest. "Are you calling me a criminal?"

"Not at all—"

Suddenly, there was a loud banging sound from the back of the house, followed by a lot of commotion. I whipped out my pistol and glared at Wanda.

"Is that Danny Kiger?"

She sighed heavily and nodded, moving out of the doorway. I rushed into the house, hollering over my shoulder that Danny was trying to make a getaway. I said it loud enough that I was sure Shade heard me, but I couldn't be sure if Amy did.

After rushing through the living room, I made my way down a spacious, but cluttered, hallway, and followed the noise to a bathroom to the left. As soon as I made the corner, I realized I was too late. The window above the bathtub was open and the thin fabric curtain was blowing in the breeze.

CHAPTER 20

Wanda Pierce's Residence—Near the Garage

Shade Rankin stood to the left side of the garage door, which was open, and waited in the dark shadows. He had seen firsthand what could happen if an officer stood in front of what Captain Brandon Berger referred to as the *fatal funnel*, and he wasn't about to let that happen to him.

When Shade heard Detective Wolf knock on the front door of the Pierce residence, he checked his weapon to make sure it was secured in his holster. It was only force of habit and not out of necessity, because he had a level three holster for his Beretta 92FS pistol, and it wasn't going anywhere unless he wanted it to.

After a moment of silence, when all that could be heard were the sound of the Cajun chorus frogs in a nearby ditch, Clint knocked a second time on the wooden door. This knock was a little louder than the last one, and Shade thought he heard movement from somewhere inside the house.

He crouched a little lower, preparing himself for a possible chase. More noise emitted from inside the house. Whatever was happening seemed to be happening directly on the opposite side of the interior garage door. He knew he couldn't enter the garage without permission or a warrant, so he was content to turn his ear toward the sound and wait. The next sounds he heard came from the front of the house, and then he heard a woman's voice. It was followed by Clint's voice. They seemed to be having a conversation, but he couldn't hear exactly what was being said.

A few seconds later, there was a loud banging sound from the other side of the garage door. It sounded as though something had fallen. There was more noise that sounded like a struggle—maybe someone trying to break open a door. And then Shade heard Clint say that Danny was escaping through a back window.

Shade quickly made his way toward the back of the house, but before he could reach it, a dark figure shot past his location and headed toward the back of the street. Without hesitating, Shade sprang forward and the chase was on.

From what Shade could gather in the darkness, the description of Danny had been accurate—he was a short fellow and he was fast. Thankfully, there was at least a waning crescent moon in the sky and it cast a faint glow over the soggy back yards through which they ran. While it wasn't bright, it did offer enough light for Shade to avoid the mud holes.

"Stop!" Shade hollered. "You're under arrest!"

He had learned enough at the academy to know that he needed to inform the suspect that he was under arrest so he could be charged with resisting if he ran. What they hadn't told him at the academy was that his announcement seemed to spur the suspect on, but it didn't matter. He was gaining on Danny Kiger.

The ground underfoot was as soggy as a wet sponge, and he loved the rhythmic sound of his feet pounding the sopping ground. He loved the thrill of the chase. He loved the feeling of closing in on the bad guy and taking him down.

Shade had closed the distance enough to take Danny down and he was about to tackle the shorter man when a flash of something appeared before them. Shade's reflexes had always been lightning fast and they'd never failed him, not even now. He immediately fell into a quarterback's slide, but Danny wasn't so lucky. The suspect hadn't noticed the clothesline strung up across their path and it caught him right across the chest. He let out a screech as he cut a back flip and landed hard on his neck.

Before Danny had a chance to realize what had happened, Shade was on him. He flipped the shorter man over, pinned both arms behind his back, and cuffed him.

"Danny Kiger, you have the right to remain silent," Shade said, not even out of breath. "Anything you say can and will be used against you in a court of law. You have the right—"

Approaching footsteps interrupted Shade. He looked up to see Clint running up through the darkness, followed closely by Amy.

"Watch out for the clothesline," he called quickly, standing next to it to make sure they saw it and stopped running. "Mr. Kiger got knocked on his ass by it."

Clint slowed to a stop and put his hand on the line. He took a few deep breaths and exhaled them slowly before speaking. "How far was that? A mile?"

"It felt more like two," Amy said, stopping beside Clint and resting an elbow on his shoulder. She then looked at Shade. "How old are you again?"

"Nineteen."

Amy blew out a lungful of air. "Damn, it must be nice to be that young. You're not even breathing hard."

Shade only smiled and helped Danny to his feet. He turned the suspect so Clint could speak to him, and the chief of detectives finished advising him of his rights.

"Why'd you run?" Clint asked when Danny acknowledged he understood his rights.

Danny was a straggly looking man. He was breathing gingerly as he stared around at the trio of officers who surrounded him. His eyes finally settled on Shade.

"God damn it, you're pretty fast," he finally said. "I turned around when I felt you breathing down my neck and that's why I didn't see the clothesline. Otherwise, you would've never caught me."

Shade smiled again and nodded. "Okay, buddy."

Clint grabbed one of Danny's arms and Shade grabbed the other one, and they all walked back to Wanda Pierce's house. When they reached the house, Shade saw a vehicle in the driveway that hadn't been there earlier.

"Who's showing up at three in the morning?" Amy asked, peeling away from the group and heading for the front door. It was closed, but the lights were on inside the house.

"Hold him here," Clint said. "I'll bring my Tahoe closer."

Shade nodded and told Danny to get to his knees. He complied, and just as soon as Clint walked off, Shade heard voices sounding from the front door. Keeping a hand on Danny's shoulder, he turned and looked toward the house, and that's when his heart stopped dead in his chest.

CHAPTER 21

In front of Wanda Pierce's residence

I pulled my Tahoe into the driveway and stopped in front of where Shade had Danny kneeling on the concrete. Danny looked even worse than the last time I'd seen him. The kid was a loser through and through, and he was rapidly dragging Wanda down with him. Maybe now that he was going away for a long time, she might have a chance at getting her life back together.

I shut off my Tahoe and approached Shade, but he didn't seem to notice me. I looked in the direction he was staring and saw Amy, Wanda, and Alice Pierce standing there. A smile immediately came to my face when I saw Wanda's daughter. The last time I'd seen the young Pierce, she had been a mess. Now, she seemed to be in total control and she was speaking to her mother like one would speak to a child.

"It's time for you to snap out of it," I heard Alice say. "You've felt sorry for yourself long enough. It's time for you to get your life back on track."

Wanda was crying, pointing toward Danny, and saying something I couldn't understand.

Alice turned icy blue eyes toward Danny, and that stare gave a new meaning to *looks can kill.* I noticed her face softened a bit when she looked up and saw Shade. I wasn't positive, but I could've sworn their eyes locked for a second, and then Alice was reproaching her mother again.

"The best thing that can happen to you is for that lowlife asshole to go away for a long time," she said in a stern, but loving voice. "He's been dragging you down, Mom. I've tried to warn you that he was bad news, but you wouldn't listen. And now look what's happened. It's because of him that the cops are at your house at three in the morning. He led them on a foot chase, for Pete's sake! Someone could've gotten hurt."

Wanda continued to sob and Alice wrapped her arms around her mother. Amy put a hand on Alice's shoulder, said something I couldn't hear, and then walked over to me and Shade as we were strapping Danny into the back seat of my Tahoe.

"Keep an eye on our guest," I said to Amy. "I want to say hi to Alice."

I waved for Shade to follow me, but he hesitated and licked his dried lips.

"I'm good here," he said. "I don't want to impose."

"No, it's okay," I said quietly. "She was a victim of a shooting we worked a while back. I want you to meet her."

Shade nodded and followed me to the front of the house. Alice's eyes lit up when she saw me. She let go of her mom and hugged my neck.

"Detective Wolf, it's so good to see you again."

"Likewise," I said, indicating Shade with a nod of my head. "This is Shade Rankin. He's one of our police officers."

Shade smiled and gave a nod as he shook Alice's hand. She smiled back at him. It was a much different smile than she'd directed at me. I then turned to Wanda.

"Look, Mrs. Pierce, I could arrest you for harboring a fugitive," I said, "but you've already been through enough. I overheard what Alice said to you, and she's right. It's time for you to move on from Danny. He's going away for a long time, and even if he wasn't, he's not good for you. He's a bad man."

Wanda took a shivering breath and nodded. She must've gone to bed with mascara on, because it was now smeared down her cheeks like black tears.

"Thank you," she said in a hoarse voice. "I know you could arrest me, and I thought you were going to."

"She did think she was going to jail," Alice said, smiling in relief. "She called me and said I'd have to bail her out, but she wouldn't tell me what she did wrong."

"I'm sorry for lying," Wanda continued. "I…it's…it's just that Danny's all I've got now that Alice moved out."

"Mom," Alice said, the motherly tone returning to her voice, "you know the only reason I moved out was because you let Danny move in. Dad never wanted me around Danny, and it was for good reason. If Danny's gone, I'll come back and stay with you until I finish college, but you've got to clean this place up."

I told Alice that it was good to see her again, I apologized to Wanda for having to do what we did, and then I turned to leave. Shade followed me, but I could almost hear his boots dragging the ground as he tore himself away.

When we reached the Tahoe, I tossed him my keys. Although I hadn't warned him of my intentions, he snatched them deftly out of the air.

"What're these for?" he asked.

"You drive," I said. "I want to interview this clown on the way to the police station. We're running out of time, and we need answers like yesterday."

CHAPTER 22

"Man, this is some bullshit," Danny said when I climbed in the back seat with him, and Shade began to back out of the driveway. "Y'all are always coming after me and accusing me of shit I didn't do."

"Is that so?" I calmly asked.

"Yeah, it is! Remember the last time y'all barged into my house and conducted an illegal search and seizure? It was all for nothing."

I didn't bother reminding him that he had given us permission to search and we hadn't seized anything. Instead, I brought his attention to the day he'd grabbed Malory on the ass in M & P Grill.

"Man, she's lying!" he said. "I did no such thing!"

"Look, Danny Boy, I'm gonna ask you some questions about a crime that could land you in prison for the rest of your life," I explained slowly. "If you lie about the sexual assault, I'll have to assume you're lying about this other crime, and I'll have to just lock you away forever."

"Life?" His eyes grew wide and he leaned his back against the door. "What in the hell are you talking about? Are you saying I murdered somebody?"

I only smiled and stared knowingly at him, waiting for him to speak again. I wanted to see what he would say.

"Is this about that stuff that happened in Mechant Loup?" He smirked. "Yeah, it's got to be, because that's where you're from. Man, I was with Wanda all night. We were making love. You can ask her."

"Oh, you mean like last time?" I grunted, remembering the

previous case I'd worked with him. "Well, you know what's different now?"

"What's that?"

"Wanda's word is mud now," I explained. "She's a proven liar. She said you weren't there, but we found you there, so she's no longer a credible witness. Since she lied about you not being there when you were, I've got to believe she'd lie about you being there when you weren't."

That seemed to twist Danny's brain into knots, and he scowled as though trying to decipher what I'd said.

"I've got some simple questions for you," I continued. "The way you answer these questions will greatly determine how much of your life will be spent behind bars. Are you ready?"

Danny hesitated, and then nodded slowly.

"Did you eat at M & P Grill last month?"

"Yeah, I think so."

"Did you flirt with Malory Chouest?"

"I mean, I don't know her last name, but there was a waitress coming on to me while I was there. She wanted some of this, but I didn't let her have it. I'm a kept man. Wanda's the only woman for me."

I tried not to vomit.

"Did you touch this woman on the ass without her permission?"

"I never—"

"Before you answer that question," I interrupted, "I want you to remember that your answers will determine how much time you spend in prison. You should also consider the fact that we've pulled all the footage from the surveillance cameras—both inside and out—and we already know the answers to every question we're asking you."

Danny gulped. "What do you mean by how many years I'll be in prison? According to my parole officer, I'm only backing up six years. I'll be back out in four, maybe sooner if the jails get overcrowded again."

"We're talking about life in prison—without the benefit of parole or suspension of sentence," I said.

"I already told you I wasn't in Mechant Loup tonight."

"And I already told you that you don't have a credible alibi witness," I countered. "In order for us to believe you about tonight, you've got to tell the truth about everything."

Danny shifted nervously in his seat. "Man, I don't like this."

"You'll like it even less being locked up for life." I turned in my seat so I was facing him directly. "Now, why did you grab Malory on the ass?"

"Look, about that," he began, "I was just messing around. I didn't mean anything by it. I'll even apologize to her if it helps."

The fact that he thought he could apologize to Malory either meant he genuinely thought she was still alive, or he was acting. Based on my many years of interviewing liars, if I had to guess, I'd say he really thought she was still alive—and that didn't bode well for him being involved. Surely, if he had gotten an accomplice to steal Wesley's truck and run them down, he would've known by now that the mission had been successful.

"Okay, what happened after you grabbed her ass?" I asked.

"Well, that's when that big corn-fed asshole came in there and jumped me when I wasn't ready." He puffed out his chest like a peacock, only he looked more like a Japanese bantam rooster. "He's lucky he sucker punched me, because I would've brought it in a fair fight."

"Remember, Danny, we pulled security footage from the restaurant."

That seemed to deflate him.

"Okay, now tell me about the slashed tires," I said, wondering how far to push it. I couldn't tell him I saw him on the tape, because then he would know I was bluffing. "The ones on Wesley's truck."

"I didn't do that shit!" He shook his head emphatically. "That wasn't me!"

Although I was convinced it wasn't him, the way he denied it made me think he knew something about it. But what did he know? And how would I extract that information from him?

"Now's the moment of truth, son," I said in a somber tone. "Here's your one and only chance to convince me you had nothing to do with the murders that happened in Mechant Loup. Tell me everything you know about the slashed tires."

"Look, I admit I was mad about the ass-whipping." He stopped to lick his lips again. "I know I told him that I'd pay him back, and…and I mean, I was thinking about it, but I wasn't really gonna do it. I was just, you know, thinking about it."

"Go on, son," I said, "tell me what you were thinking of doing."

"Okay, well, last night, I got one of my friends to bring me to town for the parade." He shifted in his seat. "I saw Malory and her boyfriend—what's his name again?"

"Wesley," I said, realizing that he wasn't talking about the night the tires were slashed. Since he was talking freely, I didn't want to stop him, but I was growing more curious by the second about where this was heading.

"Yeah, that's it," he said. "I saw Malory and Wesley standing not far from the bridge waiting for the parade to start, and I figured the truck would be parked where it always is by the restaurant. I thought this might be a good chance to get my revenge, so I made my way down there and hung around near the shoulder of the road waiting for my chance."

"What do you mean by waiting for your chance?"

"I was waiting for people to clear out of the parking lot," he said. "When the parade finally made its way to the restaurant, people went to the road and the parking lot was emptied. I waited a bit longer, because I wanted to be sure I wasn't seen. I knew y'all had warrants for me and I didn't want to get busted, so I kinda hid by some cars for a while."

Danny shifted again in his seat before continuing.

"Anyway, I was about to make my move when this man walked into the parking lot," he said. "He was kinda tall and he looked pretty tough. Anyway, he climbed on the bumper of this van next to the building and I saw him messing with the cameras."

My heart just about shot to my throat, and it was all I could do to keep my poker face on.

"What did he do to the cameras?" I asked in a nonchalant voice.

"I don't know, but I figured he was spray-painting it." He shrugged. "Me, I never realized they had cameras, so I would've gotten busted if I would've messed with his truck."

"What were you planning on doing to his truck?" I asked.

"I had bought a bag of sugar at the convenience store on the corner, and I was gonna pour it in his gas tank."

You little asshole.

"Go on," I said, concealing the contempt I felt. "What happened next?"

"Well, at first I thought the guy was gonna break into the restaurant, and I knew I was gonna get blamed for it if I was seen in the parking lot. So, I got down between two cars and was crawling out of the parking lot when I saw him climb onto the back of the truck. I think there must've been another camera on the building, because he was messing with something on the edge of the roof." Danny shook his head. "If you have the footage, you know I didn't do nothing to the truck."

"Just keep talking," I said. "I'll let you know how you did when you're done."

"Oh, I'm telling the God's-honest truth," he said, lifting a shoulder because his hands were cuffed behind his back. "You can check the cameras and see that before he messed with them, I was in between the cars."

"What happened next?"

"Well, when he got off the back bumper of the truck, he got inside the truck somehow." Danny shook his head. "I don't know if he already had a key or if it was unlocked, but I just know he got inside the truck and he just sat there."

"Did he start it?"

"Not while I was there. He just sat in the driver's seat like he was waiting for something."

"Did you get a look at his face?" I asked, wanting to show him the picture of the man from the tire-slashing video.

"I mean, I saw him a little bit, but I probably couldn't pick him out of a lineup, if that's what you're asking."

"Would you recognize him if you saw him again?"

He shrugged. "Maybe so, but I'm not positive."

"What'd you do next?"

"Oh, I got the hell out of there." He shivered. "I was scared to death of being seen around that restaurant. I knew that whatever that guy did, I would be blamed for it—and I was right. When y'all came knocking on the door, I knew y'all saw me in the camera and I knew y'all were gonna accuse me of whatever happened out there. I also knew y'all wouldn't believe a word I would say, so that's why I ran. And I would've gotten away, too, if that Speedy Gonzales hadn't caught me."

"When you say you got the hell out of there, what do you mean?" I asked.

"I headed back to the convenience store where I left my friend," he said. "We crossed the bridge, got in his car, and hauled ass back to Northern Chateau. He called me later and told me he heard some people got killed. He wasn't sure how it happened, but he said he would find out and call me back. He never did."

"Who's your friend and what's his number?"

He hesitated. "Will he be in trouble?"

I studied Danny Kiger for a long moment before I said anything else. He had just put himself at the murder scene and he'd provided information that was corroborated by surveillance footage. Only the killer or someone at the scene would know everything that he knew. I remembered looking at the footage and I hadn't seen anyone hiding between the cars. Did it mean he was lying, or did it mean he was too far away for the camera to pick him up?

If the former was true, he might very well be our killer. If he was the killer, what had he done with the truck? I knew he didn't leave town with it, that much was for certain.

"If you're responsible for what happened in town tonight and your friend helped you escape, he'll be going to jail right beside you," I said. "But if you didn't kill those people and he merely gave you a ride home from the parade, then I won't bother him. Now, what's his name and number?"

Danny took a deep breath and let it out slowly. Finally, after a long moment of silence, he nodded and gave up the information.

CHAPTER 23

After arriving at the police department, Shade and Amy escorted Danny Kiger to the holding cell while I contacted his friend by phone. If a face-to-face interview was necessary at some point, I could conduct it later, but I needed him on the record as soon as possible before word got to him that Danny was in custody.

I had to call twice before he answered, but once I got him on the phone the conversation was brief, and he corroborated everything Danny had told us. He said he hadn't made it as far as the restaurant at any point during the night, so other than exonerating Danny, he was of no use to us.

"Well, what's the word?" Amy asked when she and Shade sauntered into my office. "Was Danny lying?"

"Nope." I shook my head. "He was telling the truth."

"No shit?" Amy scowled. "My money was on him lying."

I drummed my fingers on the desk, lost in thought. I hated having to rely on Danny's word, given his past, but, unfortunately, we couldn't pick our witnesses. We had to play the cards we were dealt.

"Hey, Clint," Shade said, "is it okay if I get back on the road? I'd like to keep helping Melvin search for the suspect's truck—unless you need me here, of course."

"No, we're good for now." I thanked him for his help. "As always, you did a good job out there."

He nodded and quickly made his exit. The kid didn't like compliments and he didn't like standing still when there was work to be done. I liked those things about him.

"Why don't we show Danny the picture of the tire-slasher?" Amy suggested when we were alone. "See if he's the same fellow who stole Wesley's truck."

"Good idea. Do you think you can get a good image from that video? It looked decent when we were playing it, but it got real grainy when I froze the frame."

"I'll see what I can do." Amy went to her office and began working on the video while I puzzled over what to do next. I needed the truck. It would provide a ton of information and possible evidence. Once we found it, we would know if it had been hotwired or if Wesley had left the keys in it. We might also find the suspect's DNA or fingerprints in the truck. We should definitely be able to recover blood evidence from the portions of the truck that had collided with our victims. If we could link a suspect and the victims to the same truck, we would be in business.

I glanced at the clock. It was already past four in the morning and I felt bad about what I was about to do, but I needed to know if Wesley had a habit of keeping his keys in his truck. I picked up my desk phone and dialed Rebecca Theriot's number. When the head waitress answered, she sounded wide awake. *Of course she is*, I thought. *How is she supposed to sleep after a night like this?*

"Rebecca, this is Clint Wolf from the police department," I said, and then apologized for bothering her at this hour. When she told me it was no bother, I got right to the point. "Do you know if Wesley had a habit of keeping his keys in his truck?"

"Um…" She was thoughtful. "I don't think so, because I've gone places with them before and I remember getting to the truck first and him having to hit the unlock button on the keyless remote. In fact, we went to New Orleans a couple of months ago and I distinctively remember him pointing the keyless remote at the truck and hitting the button to lock it."

"I understand locking it in New Orleans," I said. "They get more car thefts than we get mosquitoes, but what about at the restaurant? Is it possible he felt comfortable enough to just leave the keys inside the truck while he was inside or walking around town?"

"I'm not sure about that."

"Okay, thanks."

"Detective…"

"Yeah?"

"Am I in danger?" I detected a tremor in Rebecca's voice. "Is it possible that the killer's targeting people from the restaurant?"

I hadn't thought about that and I didn't know for sure why the killer had struck, so I didn't want to immediately dismiss the idea.

"There's no indication that anyone was specifically targeted," I said, picking my words carefully, "but it wouldn't hurt to take extra precautions."

"Like what?"

"Well, where are you staying right now?"

"I came to my mom and dad's house for the night."

"That's good," I said. "Maybe plan to stay there until we resolve this case. With luck, that won't take too long."

"And what if you never solve it?"

"Goodnight, Rebecca, and thank you for everything." I hung up the phone without addressing her last comment. I didn't want to entertain that thought at the moment, so I got busy. I headed for Amy's office, which was down the hall from mine, and asked if she had produced a still picture from the video.

"It's coming out now," she announced, her hand waiting on her printer. It was spitting out a grayish image of the man who had turned to face the camera.

"Did you check the footage again to see if Danny appears in the shadows of the parking lot?"

"I tried," she said, "but I couldn't make anything out. He would've been so far away that he would've been reduced to a blurry blob that blended into the background."

I sighed and nodded. When the photo was done printing, she glanced at it, grimaced, and then handed it to me.

"Is that the best you can do?" I asked.

She nodded. "That's it."

"Shit." I turned and headed for the jail cell. Amy was hot on my heels. We didn't stop until we were on the opposite side of the bars from Danny, who had stretched out on one of the cots. He scrambled to his feet when he saw us.

"Am I getting out?" he asked excitedly. "Did you verify my story? Can I leave now?"

I ignored his questions, shoved the photo through the bars. "Do you recognize this guy?"

Danny took the photo and held it to the light. He squinted as he studied it. "Huh, I don't know him. Who is he?"

"Is this the guy you saw cut the cameras and break into Wesley's truck?"

"Man, that guy was so far away that it was hard to make out what he looked like." Danny started shaking his head. "I can't be sure, but it doesn't look like the same man."

"If you didn't see him, how can you be sure this isn't him?" I challenged.

"I don't know. He just doesn't look like him. The shape of him is all wrong. The guy that cut the cameras looked a little thicker, you know? Like he had more muscles or he was just heavier."

I reclaimed the photo and turned to leave.

"What about me?"

I stopped and turned to look at him. "You've got warrants—you're going to jail."

"But I helped you!" Danny slammed his right fist against one of the bars, but then cried out in pain and dropped to his knees, cradling his hand.

"Smart move," I said with a smirk and a shake of my head. As I headed for the door, I called over my shoulder, "the medics will have a look at you when you get to the jail."

I walked straight to the dispatcher's station, where I heard Susan speaking to someone on the phone. When she hung up, she told me that more of our victims had been released from the hospital, but the initial interviews conducted by the sheriff's detectives had turned up nothing.

"Buck said things are looking good for all of our victims," she said. "It looks like we won't lose anymore."

I frowned. While that was good news, we had already lost too many. Hell, one was too many, but to lose three citizens of such a small town? That would have a personal impact on nearly all of our citizens.

"Can you call Wesley's parents?" I asked. "I want to search his house. We need to find his spare key, and we need to look through whatever electronics he has at home."

"What if he wasn't targeted?" Susan offered. "What if someone wanted to steal the truck and was just sitting there waiting for the crowd to thin out, when Wesley shows up and blocks his path? Caught in the act, the suspect rushes out of there in a panic and runs everyone down."

It was as likely a scenario as any at this point, so I didn't dismiss the idea. "Everything's on the table," I said with a sigh. "Until we catch the suspect and know for sure, we have no clue what we're dealing with."

CHAPTER 24

Two hours later...

When Amy and I stepped out of Wesley and Malory's house, the sun was shining. I glanced at the time on my cell phone. It was almost six thirty, and I was starting to feel the pressure of the case crashing down on me. Despite our officers combing the area all night and into the morning and putting the word out to the majority of the town's population, there hadn't been a hint of the suspect's whereabouts.

I'd even sent the description out to the state police and surrounding agencies just in case the suspect had managed to slip past the checkpoint we'd set up on the north end of town, but we hadn't received any tips from those agencies. I began to worry about the possibility that the suspect had somehow slipped through town and over the bridge during the chaos that followed the deadly attack, and before we'd had time to set up the checkpoint. While it didn't seem possible, I couldn't rule anything out.

"Where to next?" asked Amy.

Like me, she was still running on pure adrenalin and wasn't a bit tired. We were focused on finding the killer, nothing more. In fact, none of our officers or the sheriff's deputies who had come out to help had slept a wink, and even though I'd suggested they turn in for a few hours, no one had taken me up on the offer.

I hated to admit it, but I was almost out of ideas. Vanessa was putting a rush on the DNA analysis from the swabs she had collected off of the security cameras, but we couldn't expect anything back until the end of the day, at the very earliest. Even if they were able to extract a profile from the swabs, it still wouldn't tell us much unless the suspect had been arrested before and his DNA was in the system.

"Earth to Clint," Amy said. "If you don't come back to me soon, I'll have to put you in a home."

I shook my head and turned toward Amy. Strands of her blonde hair had pulled free from her ponytail and dangled around her ears, while other pieces hung in front of her face.

"I don't know, Ames." I pulled out my keys and used the key fob to unlock the door to my Tahoe as I started heading in that direction. "Until forensics come back, we're stuck trying to find the—"

I stopped so suddenly in my tracks that Amy ran into the back of me. She muttered a curse word or three and doubled down on sending me to a nursing home.

"What the hell's wrong with you?" she asked, squeezing around me on the sidewalk and heading to my Tahoe. "Did you fall asleep while walking?"

"The keys to Wesley's truck," I said, holding up my own set. "They weren't in his pocket. They were in his hands."

Amy stopped, turned around, and cocked her head to the side. "What?"

"Vanessa checked Wesley's pockets, but his keys weren't there," I reminded her. "That made us think he might've left them in his truck, but I bet they were in his hands. Think about it—what's the first thing you do as you approach your vehicle?"

"You pull out your keys and hit the unlock button, but what does that matter?" Amy shrugged. "Whether he had his keys or not, what difference does it make?"

"We didn't find his spare key in the house," I reminded her. "If we can find his main set at the scene, then that means someone either hotwired the truck or used the spare. If they used the spare, then that means it's someone close to him—someone who had access to his house."

Amy nodded, and I could tell the gears were spinning. "I see where you're going with this, but the scene has already been searched. If his keys were there, wouldn't Vanessa and her team have found them?"

"I asked her to check his pockets, and she did," I said, moving quickly toward my SUV now, "but they weren't in his pockets when he went airborne—they were in his hands. That means they ended up in the ditch with him. The ditch is full of water and, while I'm sure Vanessa passed her hands in the water to search for whatever might be there, it would've been impossible for her to find the keys."

"How's that?" Amy asked as she climbed into the passenger side of the Tahoe while I jumped into the driver's seat.

"Someone had checked on the body before I did," I explained, "and their footprints left giant holes in the ditch. They probably stepped on the keys and buried them in the mud. We'll need a metal detector to find them now."

Amy whistled. "Okay, now *that* makes sense."

Although we could go a couple of days without sleep, we needed food for energy, so I dropped Amy off at Granny's Bakery with my credit card and a request for five dozen donuts. I then hurried to the police department, retrieved the metal detector from the supply room, and returned to pick up Amy.

I called for the nearest Mechant Loup officer to meet us at M & P Grill to grab the donuts and deliver them to our officers and the deputies still working the area, and that turned out to be Melvin.

"Anything new?" I asked while Amy handed him the boxes of goodies.

"Nope, not a thing." Melvin set the boxes on the seat beside him and turned back toward me. "I was thinking about going door to door and asking for permission to search everyone's garages. If they tell me to go to hell, well, then I'd just have to go to hell, but if they let me have a peek inside, we can at least begin to eliminate a lot of hiding places."

I shot an inquiring glance at Amy, and she only shrugged.

"Did you talk to Susan?" I asked.

"She said to run it by you."

I was a firm believer in the Fourth Amendment and how we, as police officers, had a duty to protect our citizens from any unreasonable searches and seizures. To knock on someone's door and ask for permission was not unreasonable, but it was an inconvenience, and I felt uncomfortable going to random homes and bothering random people who were minding their own business and going about their lives. As I mulled it over, I remembered Amy sending the photo of the suspect from the tire slashing to all of our officers, and an idea came to me.

"Look, we know the suspect made it south of town, so hit the first few neighborhoods in that area and conduct a canvass," I suggested. "During the canvass, ask them if they've seen such a truck in their neighborhood, inform them that we think the suspect might have stashed the truck in a garage or barn, and see if they'll invite you inside for a look. If someone comes to the door that matches the description of the man who slashed Wesley's tires, thank them, back away and call me, but don't take your eyes off the house."

"Got it!" Melvin said with a nod, and then headed north to deliver the donuts to the deputies at the checkpoint.

The scene was clear and the road was open again, so traffic was flowing this morning, albeit not as heavy as one would expect. It seemed the news of last night's tragedy had spread across town and had a sobering effect on its residents, and most of them seemed content to hide out at home if they didn't have to be out and about.

I started to unload my gear and barely a minute had gone by when Melvin sped past our location, heading south. I heard his voice come over the radio as he called for our other officers to meet him at Mechant Groceries.

"Do you think they'll do any good?" Amy asked.

I paused with my hand on the metal detector, thoughtful.

"Who knows?" I finally said. "I don't know what to think at this point. I know if I was the suspect and I had the truck hidden in my garage, I wouldn't let the cops search it. On the other hand, just because someone doesn't let the cops search their garage, it doesn't mean they're guilty. They might not want to be bothered. I understand and I wouldn't blame them."

"I guess you wouldn't," Amy said with a smirk. "I don't know even one old man who likes to be disturbed from his cat nap."

CHAPTER 25

After donning a pair of hip boots and firing up the metal detector, I made my way toward the ditch where Wesley had come to rest after being hit by the truck. I glanced at the street as I walked. The sheriff hadn't sent his vans filled with trustees to clean up yet, so Main Street bore the evidence of last night's parade all up and down its sideburns.

Plastic beads of all lengths and colors littered both shoulders of the street. In addition, assorted candies, miniature plastic footballs, and even a few stuffed animals were included in the mix. And the litter wasn't confined to the street. It extended across the ditches and into front yards and parking lots of the businesses that lined Main Street. If a man didn't know better, he'd think a giant piñata exploded over Mechant Loup.

I made it to the ditch and carefully followed the deep footprints from the night before. I made damned sure not to slip on my descent into the ditch, because I was positive Amy had her cell phone ready to film. Not only would she never let me live it down, but she would probably find some way to blast it all over social media or send it to some modern-day version of America's Funniest Videos.

Once I was on a steady footing, I began working the metal detector all around me, paying particular attention to the deep footsteps in the mud. When I didn't hit on anything above the water, I glanced up at Amy.

"Do you think this thing is waterproof?" I asked.

"There's only one way to find out."

I shrugged and dunked the coil under the brackish water, working it back and forth along the bottom of the ditch. After a few strokes, it let out a loud and sharp beep. I'd used metal detectors at crime scenes before, and the alert was similar to the sound the detector made when I'd find a brass shell casing. It gave me hope.

"This might be it." I handed the metal detector to Amy and squatted close to the water to feel for the keys. Once my arm was submerged to the elbow and I was feeling around with my fingers, I felt a shoe impression in the mud. I ran my fingers along the bottom of the indentation, but didn't find anything. I was sure that's where the metal detector had alerted, so I gently stabbed my fingers deeper into the mud. It was soft and gooey. I made a face.

"What is it?" Amy asked.

"It feels like sewage, and it smells like it, too."

"Do you want gloves?"

"It's too late now."

I was about to try a different spot when my fingers brushed against something narrow, circular, and smooth. I shoved my hand deeper in the mud and hit pay dirt. I could feel the keyless remote and the keys on the ring before I pulled it into view.

"I've got it," I said. "Tell Melvin to get back here."

Amy's brow furrowed. "Why?"

"I've got an idea."

After Amy made the call to Melvin, I handed the muddy keys to her and then pulled out my own keys. To her dismay, I dropped them into the water and shoved them deep into the mud.

"What in the hell are you doing?" she asked.

I waited a few seconds, retrieved my keys, and then pressed the red button on the key fob. The lights on my Tahoe began to flash and the horn blasted.

"It still works," I said with a grin. "We'll give Melvin those keys and have him drive around the neighborhoods pressing the alarm button. If the truck is parked in one of those garages or barns, he'll know it when the alarm goes off."

"Damn, I'm glad I waited to put you in a home," she said. "I see I can still learn a few tricks from the old man."

I laughed. "If you put me in a home, they'd give me right back, this I promise you."

I walked over to the restaurant and rinsed off my hip boots with a garden hose that was located on the south side of the building. I changed into my combat boots while Amy rinsed off the keys. I was just drying off the metal detector when Melvin joined us in the parking lot. Before he could say a word, Amy tossed him the keys.

He snatched the key ring deftly from the air with one hand and studied it. Realization immediately spread across his face.

"I'm on it!" he said, and sped out the parking lot, heading back to where he'd come.

As for me, I called Susan and told her we needed the names of Wesley's closest friends, and we needed to know if Malory had any male friends who would've had access to their home.

"We found Wesley's main set of keys in the ditch," I explained, "but we couldn't find the spare at his house. This means the suspect either hotwired his truck or stole it using the spare. Since there was no evidence of a busted window at the scene, I'm thinking he had the spare."

"What if Malory had it on her key ring?" Susan suggested.

I scowled. I hadn't thought of that. While we'd found a spare key for her car hanging on a hook at their house, we hadn't located the main key for her vehicle. I was sure it was probably in her purse inside the truck, and if she had the spare key to Wesley's truck on her ring, then it was once again possible that the suspect had broken into the truck and stumbled upon the spare key. We needed to know more about that spare key.

"Can you check with the Chouests about Wesley's friends?" I asked again. She had already established a rapport with the parents, and I was certain they would feel more comfortable dealing with a familiar face. "We need to know which friends frequented their residence and who might be the type to swipe a spare key and do something like this. As ugly as it might sound to them, we need to know if it was possible that either of them was having an affair. You've got to be real pissed off to run two people down in cold blood."

"Sure, just stay with me," she said. "I'll call from my desk phone."

I climbed into the Tahoe with Amy and waited while Susan made the call. Although it was February here in Louisiana, the temperature was very comfortable and the sun was shining, making for a beautiful day—to those who didn't know better, of course. To the rest of us, the feeling of death hung heavy in the air, and I felt my gaze being drawn to the spot where Cole Peterson had lost his life.

While his fellow members of the fire department had vacated the area sometime during the early morning hours, they had left behind a shrine of sorts to honor the young man. A wooden cross had been hammered into the ground, and a fire department helmet had been mounted on top of it. A pair of boots had also been laid at the foot of the cross.

As I listened to my wife's soft voice in the background, I replayed my last conversation with Cole, and I made a silent vow to find the man responsible for his untimely death.

I glanced over at Amy and saw that she was also studying the spot where Cole had been killed. It was hard to miss, because it was stained in blood.

All of a sudden, there was excited chatter on the other end of the phone, and I heard Susan apologize to someone, whom I presumed was probably Wesley's dad. She then got back on the phone with me.

"Clint, we just got a call about the stolen truck," she said hurriedly. "The caller stated it's parked down a cane road north of the Bayou View Apartments, and it looks like it was meant to be hidden, because it was far down the road and tucked away in some trees."

Before Susan could finish talking, I had fired up the engine and was racing toward Market Street, which led to the bridge that separated the east side of town from the west side.

"I'm on my way," I told Susan. "Let Melvin know what's going on!"

I tossed my phone down and told Amy exactly what Susan had just said. Although I was driving, I could see a scowl of skepticism spread across her face.

"If it looked like it was meant to be hidden in the trees," she said, "then how'd the caller find it?"

I didn't have an answer for her, so I just drove to the scene as fast as I safely could.

CHAPTER 26

When I reached the end of Market Street and raced across the bridge, I caught sight of Susan's Tahoe turning off of Washington Avenue and onto Back Street. I was glad that she was coming. I asked Amy if she could contact Vanessa and tell her what was going on.

"If it's the right truck, we'll let her process it," I said.

The most important evidence that we could possibly recover from the suspect's vehicle would be DNA and prints, and Vanessa was an expert at recovering both of those things.

Once I turned onto Cypress Highway, I raced to the north until I reached the Bayou View Apartments, and then I slowed down. I cruised along the highway, stopping often to look down cane field roads that intersected with the highway. Thanks to all the rain we'd had yesterday, it was easy to tell if anyone had traversed those roads and, lucky for us, there hadn't been much traffic in this area. We reached Waxtuygi Road without seeing any signs of the vehicle, so we continued on. When we had gone about another mile, Amy grabbed my arm and pointed to a cane field road on the right side of the highway, where a gate was open.

"Tire tracks," she said. "Someone's definitely been back here."

I hesitated, not wanting to destroy any tread evidence that might be visible in the mud. From our vantage point the tracks looked smeared, but I didn't want to take any chances. I picked up my cell phone and called Melvin before exiting my Tahoe.

"Hey, this is Clint," I said when he answered. "Did you search the area north of the Waxtuygi Nature Park last night or this morning?"

"Yeah," he said. "It was all clear."

"How far down Cypress Highway did you go?"

"All the way until it dead-ends," he said. "Why? Did you find the truck? Is it the one?"

"We haven't found it yet, but there are tracks leading down a cane field road just north of Waxtuygi Road," I explained. "It's the first long road you come to after the nature park."

"Then that's it!" he said. "None of those roads had tire tracks on them last night, so we didn't go down them. We left them clean. If there're tracks there now, then someone's been down there after we checked the area…"

His voice trailed off and he stopped talking.

"Wait, isn't that the road with the gate across it?"

"Yeah," I said, "but it's open."

"That gate was locked last night," he said, his voice growing in intensity. "Check it to see if they used a key or if it's busted."

My heart was thumping in my chest. I glanced at Amy. She could hear Melvin and she asked if I wanted her to check it out. I gave a nod.

"Amy's checking it out now," I said. Susan's Tahoe appeared in my rearview mirror and she pulled it to the shoulder of the road.

"It's busted open," Amy hollered. "It looks like they drove right through the gate."

"This could be it," I told Melvin. "Get here as soon as you can."

I stepped from the driver's seat and headed for the rear gate of my Tahoe, where Susan met me.

"Do we have any information on the caller?" I asked as I opened the rear gate.

"No," she said. "It was a male subject. He didn't leave a name and he called from a blocked number."

I cursed, grabbed my AR-10, and slung it around my neck. Neither Susan nor Amy asked why I'd grabbed my rifle. They didn't need to because they both knew that a handgun was no match for a vehicle.

I approached the muddy tracks and the busted gate and surveyed the area. The middle of the bar tube gate was dented and twisted, and a length of chain dangled from the side opposite the hinges. The narrow post to which the chain had been attached was now resting on the ground.

I squatted in front of the tracks. They were fresh, but it was hard to tell how fresh, thanks to the complete inundation that had taken place during yesterday's rain. However, one thing was certain: these tracks had not been made before the rain or they would've been washed away, so they had definitely been made when the gate had been crashed in.

Within a few minutes, Melvin, Shade, and Takecia pulled up, all of them ready for business. I heard Regan and Baylor call out over the radio to say that they were also en route. Susan radioed for them to set up a perimeter when they arrived, and she let them know that we would be searching the road for the suspects. She then turned to give me a nod.

I indicated Shade's truck with a nod of my head. "Shade, since your truck's the oldest, why don't you use it to block the road in case they get past us?"

"Yeah, let's see them bust through his truck like they busted through that gate," Amy said. "If they make it through to the other side, I'll personally help them escape."

Shade grinned and did as I'd asked. I then waited while they all armed themselves with long guns. When they were all ready, we separated and began making our way on foot along the muddy road. Susan, Takecia, and I took the right side of the road, while Melvin, Regan, and Shade took the left side. We remained about ten feet apart to avoid cluttering, and I assigned everyone a different area of responsibility to avoid any potential crossfire situations should the need for gunfire arise.

The sugarcane in this area had been harvested at the end of last month, but the canal on the right side of the muddy road was lined with tall trees and thick underbrush, so it was hard to see very far into the wide-open field to that side.

The mud was soft and we sank to our ankles with almost every step we took, so the going was slow. We must've traveled a little over four hundred yards before I saw a break in the trees up ahead to the right. It appeared that the tire tracks disappeared in that direction. Since it was on the same side of the road as Melvin and his crew, I motioned for him to hold his position.

With a wave to Susan and Takecia to sit tight, I continued along our side of the road, moving closer to the opening and keeping my rifle trained in that direction. When I was almost directly across from it, I could see that it was a cross-section of road that led to a thick wooded area. Parked in front of that wooded area was a black truck with a lift kit and large tires. It looked like someone had just driven it right into the trees and left it. This could be it!

CHAPTER 27

I immediately took a knee in the mud and carefully studied the scene over the front sight of my rifle. Everything was quiet. So quiet, in fact, that I could hear my heart beating in my ears. I waved Melvin and his crew closer to the opening, and then I signaled that I was going to approach the truck from the left side of the tree line. I motioned for Melvin to follow on the right side and for everyone else to hold their positions.

Melvin kept pace with me as I crept toward the truck. I could see right away that it wasn't the dull, black primer color that Baylor had identified as being the suspect's vehicle, but the other descriptions matched. What if Baylor had been mistaken?

I immediately dismissed the notion. While mistakes in identifications had been known to happen during high-stress situations, Baylor was no tenderfoot. He was a seasoned police officer and had been in his share of gunfights. I squinted and studied what I could see of the truck some more as Melvin and I got closer. Perhaps, if it was speeding toward me in the middle of the night, I might think it had a dull tint to it.

The deep tracks in the sloppy mud led right up to the tires of the pickup. I paused frequently to study my surroundings. What if this was a trap? I glanced at Melvin, who was also searching the trees with his eyes.

After waiting a few seconds more, I eased up beside the truck and tried to peer in through the passenger's side rear window, but it was tinted. I couldn't make it to the front passenger's door because a large tree branch was pressed up against it, and it seemed impossible for anyone to have escaped through that point of egress. I moved stealthily to the driver's side and glanced down at the ground. There were boot tracks in the mud. They began at the driver's door and led directly away from the truck and into the woods to my left. I was nowhere as good as Melvin when it came to tracking, but even I could tell these impressions had been made after the rain, just like the tire tracks.

I glanced at Melvin to see what he thought, and he pointed to where the tracks disappeared in the woods, and I knew he wanted to follow them. I gave a nod and backed off so he could go to work.

When he disappeared into the trees to the east, I turned my rifle toward the west and sat back on my haunches to wait. I glanced over my shoulder to where Susan and everyone else were waiting. What if we had been led into a trap? What if someone was sitting in the truck right now, waiting to open up on us with gunfire? I got Susan's attention and pointed my ring and index fingers to my eyes and motioned around me, letting everyone know to stay alert.

I listened intently for the slightest of sounds or shifting of weight inside the truck, but all was quiet. Not just from the truck, but there were no sounds from the woods that surrounded us either. No rustling of leaves. No snapping of twigs. No singing of birds. Hell, I didn't even hear Melvin moving, and he was just inside the trees and within spitting distance of me. I felt naked where I was. Even though I had the truck for cover, I felt like danger might be lurking inside of it, so I crouched a little lower.

I glanced in Susan's direction and was relieved to see that they had all moved to positions of cover. They were all on high alert. I was tempted to open the driver's side door and check inside the truck, but I didn't want to disturb the shoe impressions in the mud.

After several long minutes, Melvin reemerged from the trees to my right. He stopped beside me, squatted, and indicated the truck.

"That truck could've been here as much as four hours ago, maybe more." He didn't whisper, so I took it as an indication that we were alone in the woods. "There's only one set of tire tracks leading into this place, and it belongs to the truck. That means no one drove back here to see it."

"The caller's our suspect, then?"

He nodded. "He's either the one who left it here or he's working with the one who did, but no random person drove back here and saw the truck to report it."

I breathed a little easier. If the caller was the suspect, then the truck was definitely empty, because the suspect wasn't about to turn himself in.

Melvin leaned back and pointed toward the woods to our left. "It appears one man—the driver—exited the truck and headed off into the woods, going directly east, and then circling around to head west, traveling parallel to that mud road we came in on. He left a trail plain enough for a blind man to follow, heading straight for the highway, and he was in a hurry. It would be faster for me to head back to the highway from the road we came in on and pick up his track there, because the fields are as sloppy as all hell, but I'm gonna follow his tracks just in case he threw something along the way."

I was thoughtful, going over this information in my head. Melvin's strong suit was man tracking and the behavior of people in the woods, so I always deferred to his wisdom in that regard. And while I never felt comfortable watching Melvin head out into the wilderness alone, I knew he worked better that way. He was like a ghost in the swamps and woodlands around here, and if someone joined him, they would be more of a liability than an asset.

"While I'm back-tracking the suspect, I'll have Shade and Regan head back to the highway to search the shoulder of the road," he continued. "They should be able to find the spot where he came out of the fields. If they can't find the spot, then that means he's doubling back."

My head snapped around. "Is that a possibility?"

"It's always a possibility, although I don't think it's likely." Melvin shook his head. "This guy's not woods savvy. He might be able to run people down in the streets with a truck, but he wouldn't be catching anyone in the woods."

"So, you think this is the suspect's truck?"

"Shit, Clint, I don't know," he said with a shake of his head. "That's your department."

I nodded and straightened up as Melvin approached Shade and Regan. I waved for Susan and Amy to join me and told them what Melvin had found.

"Can y'all guard the area while I search the truck?" I asked. "Melvin doesn't think he doubled-back, but he said anything's possible, so…"

Susan nodded and entered the woods to my right, holding her AR-15 at the ready. Amy took up a position on the opposite side.

After I watched Melvin disappear into the trees, and Shade and Regan had headed back up the road, I turned my attention to the truck.

I began my inspection by making a wide arc from the passenger's side around back to the driver's side, studying every inch of the outer panels. When I reached the front door of the truck, I stopped and studied the tree branches that cloaked the entire front of the vehicle. Even the windshield was covered. I had a chainsaw in my Tahoe, but it did me no good now.

I made my way back to the passenger's side and dropped to my knees to get beneath the level of the branches. I crawled forward and stopped when I reached the front of the truck. It had a heavy-duty iron bumper with a winch attached to it and, although it appeared rugged, there was obviously some recent damage from when it had crashed through the gate. There was a large dent in the cover plate of the winch, and the passenger-side headlight was busted.

I backed out from under the branches and moved to the driver's side, where I again dropped to my knees. I could feel the cold wetness from the muddy ground that had seeped through my pants, and I didn't like it. I had just reached the front corner of the bumper and had pushed a large tree limb away from the truck when something caught my eye on my side of the winch.

Thanks to the truck having been driven into the trees, it was too dark to make out anything definitively, so I pulled out my cell phone and flipped to the flashlight feature. When the light illuminated the bumper and the corner of the winch, I sucked in my breath. There was blood on the winch, on the bumper, and smeared onto the headlight. There was also what appeared to be a piece of fabric dangling from a groove in the bumper.

I slowly backed out of the overhanging branches and—careful not to disturb the shoe impressions—made my way to the rear driver's side door. Using the tail of my shirt, I tried the doorknob. It was unlocked. Just in case, I stood to the side and drew my pistol with my right hand, and jerked the door open with my left hand.

I immediately confirmed that the truck was empty. I was able to confirm something else, too—there were three bullet holes in the front windshield.

CHAPTER 28

After calling Vanessa to give her the details of what I'd found and calling dispatch to run a license plate check on the truck, I called for Baylor to drive my Tahoe to our location. We would need it once Vanessa arrived to take over the scene, and his Dodge Charger would never make it back here.

Susan, Amy, and I were standing behind the truck discussing the possibilities when I heard the engine on my Tahoe roaring toward us. The road was a sloppy mess and even with four-wheel-drive it would be a challenge to get in and out of here.

Finally, Baylor pulled my Tahoe onto more stable ground across from the cut where the truck was located, and he jumped out of the driver's seat. He immediately shook his head when he took in the truck.

"That's not it," he said. "That's not the truck I shot."

There was a gnawing in the pit of my stomach. I wanted desperately to believe that this was the truck, but—in spite of all of the evidence—I took one look into Baylor's eyes and knew that he was positive.

"There's blood on the front grill and three bullet holes in the windshield." I opened the back door and waved for him to have a look.

He backed out still shaking his head.

"Those aren't my bullet holes. I shot low because the driver had ducked down, and I also didn't want my bullets to bust through the back windshield. I wanted my bullets to rip through the dash and get him, but I guess there was too much glass and metal between me and him." He shot a thumb toward the windshield. "Those bullets are a little higher, like someone was trying to make head shots, and the grouping is wider. I shot a fist-sized group, while that one's about ten inches."

I nodded as I listened to him. I was starting to get the picture of what was happening, but I needed more confirmation. I always believed in following the evidence—no matter where it led—and the evidence was telling me this was the truck that had killed Cole, Malory, and Wesley, and that it was the same truck at which Baylor had shot.

However, I'd also been doing this long enough to know that evidence could be manipulated, and I was afraid that's what was happening now. Why or how, I didn't know, but I had a hunch that things were not as they seemed. But how would I prove it? And if this truck had been planted as a decoy, where was the actual truck? And what about the blood evidence? Was it human blood or animal blood? If human, whose blood was it? If the DNA from the front of this truck matched the reference samples from our victims, how would we disprove this as being the truck involved in the attack?

As these questions swirled through my mind, I picked up my cell phone. It had been ringing and was about to go to voicemail, but I caught it in time.

"This is Clint," I said absently, still trying to rectify my dilemma.

"Hey, this is Lindsey."

Lindsey Savoie was our daytime dispatcher. She had been with the police department longer than most of our officers, myself included, and she was the best we had.

"Give me the good news," I said, knowing the license plate would come back stolen. I had seen the truck keys dangling from the ignition, but I was sure that only meant the owner had left his truck running or left the keys in the truck. It had probably been stolen from a gas station or convenience store.

"I don't know if it's good news, but I've got the registration back on that truck," she said. "It's a black Chevy pickup registered to Max Broussard. His address is off of Back Street."

"Where was it stolen from?"

"Oh, it wasn't reported stolen," she said. "There's no two-nine on it."

I scowled and turned to look at the truck. It hadn't been stolen? It was almost ten o'clock on Saturday morning. The murders had happened twelve hours ago, and if we were to believe this truck was involved, it must have been stolen before the murders. Hell, it would've been stolen before the parade began at seven.

"Did you check our database to see if he's ever been involved in anything?"

"Yeah and no," she said. "He also doesn't have a criminal history. Not even a speeding ticket."

"What's his house number?"

She told me and I wrote it on my hand. I thanked her and walked to where Susan, Baylor, and Amy were now standing. I told them what was going on.

"Amy, as soon as Vanessa and her crew get here, we're gonna pull this Max Broussard fellow in and interrogate the piss out of him." I turned to Susan. "Can you call Wesley's dad and find out if he knows anything about this man?"

She nodded and pulled out her phone.

I was about to pull out my own phone to call Shade when Baylor stepped up.

"Hey, do you believe me about that truck?"

"Absolutely," I said without hesitation.

"Even though there's blood and bullet holes in it?"

I nodded and told him my theory.

He cocked his head to the side. "Why would someone go through all of that trouble to try and throw us off?"

I stood frozen, thinking over his question. It was a good one, and one to which I didn't have an immediate answer. I began to imagine I was a criminal. If I had just stolen a truck and run down a bunch of people, why would I steal a second one and make it look like that one had been involved in the murders?

Try as I might, I couldn't think of a reason why I would've done something like that. I would've ditched the first truck and gotten the hell out of Dodge. To steal a second truck would've exposed me to more risk—*unnecessary* risk.

Finally, I just shook my head. "I have no clue, Baylor."

CHAPTER 29

Amy and I didn't have to wait long for Vanessa and her crime scene techs to show up. Luckily for Vanessa, Sheriff Turner had seen fit to purchase four-by-four UTVs—complete with transport trailers—for the crime scene unit, and they were able to reach our location with no problem.

I gave Susan and Baylor a ride to their vehicles, and then I checked on Shade and Regan. They were trudging along the shoulder of the highway when I spotted them, and they walked over to the Tahoe.

"Anything?" I asked.

"Not so far," Regan said. "We just got word from Melvin, and he said he's about halfway to the highway. He says he hasn't found anything yet except for the man's tracks."

I nodded and whipped my Tahoe around in the roadway, rocking in my seat as we hit a large pothole. Since this portion of Cypress Highway dead-ended to the north, the town had quit resurfacing the road years ago, and it was getting a bit bumpy.

Amy and I headed back to town, going straight to Max Broussard's address. We found his place on the bayou side almost directly across from Bayou View Pub. As I glanced at the old barroom, I nodded appreciatively when I noticed something I'd never seen there before.

Max Broussard's house was a square cinderblock job, painted an ugly yellow, and there was a tiny metal shed to the left of the house. The shed was almost the size of his house. Aside from the front door, the only other opening we could see in the house was to the right of the doorway, and it was a window covered with latticework. A portable generator was on the ground next to the front door, and there was a satellite dish attached to the top, right corner of the house.

I moved to the left of the doorway and Amy sidled to the right. She gave me a nod to let me know she was ready, and I rapped loudly on the storm door. We didn't know what to expect, but we were dealing with a potential killer, so we expected the worst. That's not what we got. Instead, an aged man opened the main door to the house and peered out through the glass of the storm door.

"Hey, there, officers," he said, almost as though forcing himself to sound cheerful. "What's going on?"

I didn't waste any time.

"Max Broussard?" I guessed.

"That's me." He nodded. "Yes, sir, I'm Max."

"Where's your truck, Max?"

"Why, I don't know," he said. "I was about to call the police department and report it stolen."

"Is that so?"

"Yes, sir, it is." He pushed through the storm door and indicated his empty driveway. "When I got up this morning to come out here and have my morning coffee, I noticed it was gone."

I studied the man. He was a bad liar, but that didn't mean he would be easy to break.

"Any idea when your truck was stolen?" I asked, knowing that most theft victims could only give a range—the last time they saw it to the first time they noticed it missing—but I wanted to see what he would say.

"Well, it must've been around ten o'clock last night." He glanced down at a faded wristwatch. "Yeah, it was around ten o'clock last night, because that's when I thought I heard it start up. I didn't go look at it, because I have a neighbor whose truck sounds just like mine and I thought it was his truck, but when I had my coffee this morning, that's when I noticed it was gone."

I was thoughtful. If his truck was stolen at ten last night, then it would've been stolen after the murders and after the parade had ended. However, because of the murder, the roads had been shut down and everything had come to a standstill, so it would've been difficult for someone to steal his truck and drive it out of here.

"What time did you have your coffee this morning?" I asked.

"Oh, it was around six in the morning."

"And why haven't you called it in yet?"

"I was waiting to see if it would come back," he explained. "I have a bad habit of leaving my keys in the truck, so I thought maybe someone had borrowed it and would bring it back. I was trying to give them a chance to do the right thing."

I took a patient breath. "Mr. Broussard, what would you say if I told you that we have reason to believe your truck was stolen earlier than ten o'clock last night?"

"Oh, I'd say that was impossible."

"Oh, yeah, and how's that?"

"Because I heard it start up at ten," he explained. "So, I know that's when it was taken."

I sighed. "Did you hear about the murders last night in town?"

He hesitated, and I knew he was trying to decide how to answer me. Finally, when he thought he was taking too long, he nodded. "I did."

"And do you know what happened?"

"Yes, they said someone in a stolen black truck killed some people, but it couldn't have been my truck."

"Why not?" I asked.

"Because my truck was parked in my yard at that time."

"What if I told you we found your truck and it's got blood all over the grill?" I offered, trying to get a reaction from him. "And three bullet holes in the windshield from one of our officers firing some shots as it tried to run him down?"

"It was stolen, so I can't speak to what happened after it was taken from my possession," he said calmly, although his face had blanched a little. "So, y'all were able to recover my truck?"

I nodded. "But it'll be a while before we can give it back. It's being processed for more evidence as we speak, and that could take days. If the DA wants to hold it for trial, then it could be months to years before you get it back."

"But…but I need my truck! I can't go everywhere on foot." He looked desperately from me to Amy. "Please, I've got to get my truck back! I can't survive without it."

"You didn't seem too worried about it," I said. "I mean, it's been over four hours since you noticed it missing and you still haven't filed a report."

"But you already found it, so there's no need to file a report anymore, right?"

I knew he was lying, but I didn't know why, and until I knew why he was lying, I couldn't alleviate his concerns and get him to tell us the truth.

"What are you worried about?" I asked.

"I'm worried about not being able to get my truck back." He shook his head. "That would ruin us."

I glanced toward the house. "Are you married or have a girlfriend?"

"I…I'm married."

"What's your wife's name?"

"Mable."

I nodded, indicated the house. "Is she inside?"

He shook his head.

"Where is she?" I asked.

"She's working at the pharmacy. She stocks the shelves there. It doesn't pay a lot, but it helps us get by."

"Look, Mr. Broussard," I began in a soft tone, "some things aren't adding up with your story. I know it's just because we knocked on your door unexpectedly and confused you. However, I need to know what really happened with the truck so I can get on with this investigation. Three people died and many others are hurt, so I need to find whoever did this, and I need to find them fast. So, can you help me?"

"I…I don't know how I can help you."

"You can help by telling me the real story about when your truck was stolen." I fixed him with a long stare. "You could help save more lives by cooperating with us. You would be a hero."

He stared back at me for a long moment, but then his eyes shifted downward. "I don't know anything."

I sighed again, not wanting to do this, but having no choice. I gave Amy a nod and she walked over to keep him company while I retreated to my Tahoe. Once inside, I grabbed my cell phone and called the pharmacy.

CHAPTER 30

When Mable Broussard came to the phone, I introduced myself and said I was calling about the theft report her husband wanted to file on his missing truck. She seemed cautious.

"Okay, and who is this again?"

I again explained who I was, and I said I was at her house speaking with Max.

"We were talking to him about his stolen truck," I explained, hating to deceive this woman, but not having time to play around with her lying husband, "but he got upset when I told him we found it damaged."

"You found it?"

"Yes, ma'am, but it's been in a wreck and it's damaged," I said. "Not so bad that it can't be fixed, but it's definitely damaged."

"Oh, no, he loved that truck!"

"Yeah, he's pretty upset." I glanced toward Max, who was staring intently at me. "So upset, in fact, that he's having trouble remembering his own birthday. My partner's with him right now trying to calm him down."

"Oh, no! Maybe I should come home!"

"No, that's not necessary," I said quickly. "I can see him and it looks like he's smiling now. Anyway, I was wondering if you could tell me what you know about the theft. It might help us figure out who did it."

"I...I don't know anything about it." She sounded confused. "I wasn't there when it was stolen."

"Where were you?" I asked, wondering if she had maybe gone to the parade alone last night.

"I was home."

I resisted the urge to react to her statement. I needed to act like I already knew that information, and I needed to shift gears subtly.

"Can you remember everything Max told you about the theft?"

"Is…is he in some sort of trouble?" she asked. "I know he was real upset when he heard about the black Chevy truck that hit those people in town. Some of our friends were saying it was Max's truck, and he was worried he would be responsible because he always leaves the keys inside."

"Oh, no, Max is in no trouble at all," I said in as reassuring a tone as I could. "It doesn't matter if he left the truck running. That doesn't give someone else the right to steal it and do whatever they want with it. But anyway, getting back to what Max told you about his truck being stolen…"

"Oh, all he said was that he parked it where he normally does and then he went to his deer stand to hunt," she explained. "He said he was in his stand for about two hours when he heard a truck that sounded like his start up. He said he hunts behind a neighborhood, so he thought it was someone else's truck at first. He said he shot his deer and it started raining while he was cleaning it, so he hurried back to the truck to get his raincoat. That's when he noticed the truck was gone."

"What day was this again?"

"Well, he went out night before last, but he didn't get back until yesterday afternoon," she said. "He called his brother to go get him, because his brother has a four-by-four dually, and it was real muddy out there. His brother helped him clean the deer and then gave him a ride home. It was less meat for us, and we certainly need the food right now, thanks to all the prices going up, but if his brother wouldn't have helped him, the meat would've spoiled."

I shook my head as I stared at Max. "So, he went hunting Thursday night, and that's when his truck was stolen?"

"Yes, sir."

"What time did he leave Thursday night?"

"Oh, it was right around ten o'clock," she said. "I was just starting to watch the late news when he left."

"Do you know why he waited until today to report it stolen?" I asked. She didn't need to know that we were the ones who initiated contact with him.

"Um, well, he told me the other day that he had already reported it stolen, and he was waiting to hear back from the police."

"I see." I thanked her for her time and ended the call. I had more questions than ever now, but not all of them were for Max Broussard.

I stepped out of my Tahoe and ambled toward Amy and Max. I shook my head when I was standing in front of the older man.

"What is it?" he asked when I just stood there looking at him.

"We can do this one of two ways," I said. "I can get a search warrant for your freezer to go recover the meat from the illegal deer you killed while night spotting, or you can tell me the truth about your truck and show me the spot where it was stolen from."

His mouth opened and closed several times before he spoke again. When he did, it was to deny night hunting.

"I don't care if you were hunting in broad daylight or at night," I said with a grunt. "Deer season's over, so it's all illegal. Now, do you want to go to jail for illegal hunting, or do you want to show me where your truck was stolen?"

He swallowed hard. "How do I know you won't just arrest me anyway?"

"Do I look like a game warden to you?"

He shook his head slowly.

"On a normal day, I would call in the wardens and have them tear your house apart recovering that illegal meat," I said, and then softened my tone, "but I know you've fallen on hard times and you're just trying to feed your family."

Max pursed his lips and nodded, his mouth quivering just a little.

"All I care about is the theft of your truck," I reiterated. "If you cooperate with me, I'll forget I know anything about an illegal deer, but only if you promise not to do it again."

"I swear, I'll never do that again as long as I live!" He shook his head in confirmation. "It was the first time I've ever done an illegal hunt, and my truck goes and gets stolen. I took that as a sign that I was doing something wrong. That's why I didn't report it stolen. Mable's sick and she's working as hard as she can to help out. I get social security, but it's not much, and she'll lose it if I go to jail. I need to be here to take care of her and we need that income."

I fished out one of my business cards and handed it to him. "If you get hungry again, call me."

He started to object, but I put out a hand.

"This ain't a charity offer," I said. "I'll put you to work and you'll earn that money the honest way."

He smiled and took the card. "Thank you, detective. I really appreciate that."

I nodded and waved him toward my Tahoe. "Now, show us

where the theft happened before I change my mind and call the game warden."

Max didn't waste time scrambling into my SUV. Amy allowed him to sit in the front so he could point the way, and he led us south along Back Street and onto Old Blackbird Highway. He told me to keep driving until we were approaching Rooster Drive, and then he told me to turn down a road that led to some cow pastures west of the highway.

It was muddy, so I stopped to put it in four-wheel-drive, and then continued down the road until we reached a locked gate. He pointed toward the gate.

"I parked my truck right there and then walked to the woods," he said. "Um, I…I was doing some night spotting, but I didn't see anything at night. I was about to leave in the morning when I saw a few does move into the area. They were too far away, so I just waited in the tree stand."

"Is it your tree stand?" I asked.

He shook his head. "My buddy owns the land and it's his tree stand. He let me hunt here once, but he doesn't know what I did. Do you have to tell him? It would be really embarrassing, and he wouldn't let me come hunt during the season. It's how we get most of our meat for the year."

"I don't even know his name," I muttered, stepping out of the Tahoe to have a look around. Amy joined me and we found some tire tracks that might have been made by his truck leaving, but they were faint and had definitely happened before yesterday's rain. We found another set of tire tracks that we assumed were from his brother's truck, because they were dually tracks and they were deep in the mud, indicating the dually had been here after the rains came.

And then there was a single track that followed the edge of the road. It was faint and had nearly been washed out from the rain, but it was visible enough for us to determine that it had definitely been made by a dirt bike. I took pictures of all of the tread evidence with my cell phone, and then grabbed my camera for better photos.

"Do you really think that these tracks are involved with the theft?" Amy asked when I was done, arching an eyebrow.

I didn't know, but I definitely didn't believe that the suspects had randomly happened upon this field and found a truck matching the rough description of Wesley's truck.

"For some reason, our suspect selected Wesley's truck for the crime and this truck for the cover-up," I said. "Once they found Max's truck, they followed him around until they had a chance to steal it. I'm betting if they hadn't stolen Max's truck yesterday, they would've waited to steal Wesley's truck."

"You think so?"

I nodded my head. "I believe Max's truck was stolen for the sole purpose of throwing us off the scent. For some reason, they abandoned his truck in hopes that we would find it and think we'd found the real truck, and then we would think it was over. When we didn't find it fast enough, they planted a call to lead us to it."

"And the blood?" she asked. "Do you think it's real?"

"I think it's from Wesley's truck," I said. "I think they scraped the blood evidence from his truck after the murders were committed and then smeared it onto Max's truck. They know that once forensics comes back on Max's truck and the blood matches the victims, it's over. Max's Chevrolet officially becomes the suspect vehicle and we stop looking for Wesley's truck."

"I don't know, Clint, it doesn't make any sense to me."

"Unless they wanted to make a clean getaway with Wesley's truck," I surmised. "If we look at it that way, then this makes perfect sense."

"So…" Her voice trailed off and then her eyes widened. "Shit! They're trying to get Wesley's truck out of town!"

CHAPTER 31

As soon as I turned off of the pasture road and headed north on Old Blackbird Highway, I was dialing Susan's phone. She had been coordinating the efforts with the sheriff's office to seal off the town. When she answered, I told her what we thought about the suspects trying to get Wesley's truck out of town.

"They planted Max's truck to make us stop looking," I explained. "This was planned from the beginning. It was how they were gonna get out of here with Wesley's truck."

"If what you're saying is true," she said deliberatively, "then they didn't just steal the truck to use as a weapon—they planned on keeping it."

"Yeah, I guess so."

"But what's so special about this truck, Clint? Out of all the trucks in the world, why this one?"

"I don't have an answer for you yet," I admitted, suddenly remembering the spare key. "Did you ever get to talk to Mr. Chouest about Wesley's spare key?"

"No, we got called to come out here to mess with this truck," she said, "but I'll head there as soon as I'm done here."

"Oh, and put the deputies at the checkpoint on high alert," I said hurriedly. "They need to be ready for anything, including a ramming attack. They've already run down twenty-one people, so what's a few more?"

"So, we think he's got an accomplice now?"

I told her about the possible involvement of a dirt bike, and how we needed to keep our eyes out for one.

"Amy and I are heading to Bayou View Pub to look at their cameras," I explained. "We think the suspects were casing Max's house and they followed him yesterday when he left to go hunting. And it didn't really matter where he was going—he was losing his truck yesterday, or they weren't stealing Wesley's truck, because they needed a patsy vehicle. If we can get a good description of the dirt bike, I'll pass it on."

"Wait a minute," Susan said, her voice laced with disappointment. "Bayou View Pub doesn't have any video cameras."

"They do now," I said with a smile. "I saw them when I was across the street at Max's house."

"What if they're dummy cameras?"

I groaned. That would be my luck.

As soon as I ended the call with Susan, I called Melvin. He answered on the second ring, and he did so just as I was pulling up to Max's house. I quickly thanked Max for his help and asked Melvin if he'd found anything.

I saw Max take a deep breath and let it all out in a long sigh of relief when Amy and I drove off. He had probably thought that we would change our minds—or that we were lying to him—when we said we wouldn't arrest him or call the game warden for him having killed the deer out of season.

"I didn't find anything along the trail," Melvin said in response to my question, "but Regan located a few drops of blood along the shoulder of the road. Vanessa did a presumptive test on it and it's human. The blood from the stolen truck back here is also human, and Vanessa said she'll know by the end of the day if it belongs to our victims."

I parked in the Bayou View Pub lot and shut off the engine, thinking about the blood that had been found on the side of the road. I glanced up at the cameras, but couldn't tell if they were dummies or not.

"Did y'all check the gate for blood?" I asked.

"Yeah, Vanessa took some swabs," Melvin said. "She said it looks like there's some blood transfer from the truck to the gate. She didn't do a presumptive blood test on that yet, but she's pretty sure it's human. What do you think it means, Clint?"

I told him my theory, and added a wrinkle that I'd just considered with the new information he'd provided.

"You can't go driving around in a truck that has human blood on the front grill," I explained, "so they waited until they reached that cane field road to plant the blood. They might've watched a few episodes of Dateline, but they're not as smart as they think they are. While they did the right thing in planting the blood before they drove through the gate to make us think it had been there all along, they should've checked for blood on the road where they worked to plant the evidence."

"Since we're spit-balling," Melvin said, "I have my own idea about how the suspect might've gotten out of here."

"How's that?"

"I think he left on a dirt bike."

I had shut off my engine and was stepping out of the Tahoe when he mentioned the dirt bike. I froze in place, with one leg dangling out of my vehicle.

"What makes you say that?" I asked.

"I found a single track in the gravel on the shoulder of the road about a hundred yards north of where the suspect came out of the fields," he said. "On its own, that doesn't seem like much, but I found a similar track near where Regan located the blood. It's not a smooth pattern. It's got large grips like a dirt bike tire."

Amy was already heading for the door to the barroom, so I quickly told Melvin about the single track we'd found on the pasture road. I dug out my phone and accessed one of the images as I talked about it.

"The track was fainter than the truck tracks, because it looked like it had been made before the rain." I hit the *send* button on my cell phone. "I'm sending you a picture now."

I tapped my foot impatiently while watching the progress on my phone. Finally, it made that familiar sound to indicate it had been sent and my phone showed that it had been delivered.

"Got it," Melvin finally said. "Oh, shit, Clint, this has to be it! This is the same type of tire track I found over here. I can't be positive it's the exact same one, but the tread patterns are similar. We'll take some good photos and see if we can make a cast of it."

"Good deal," I said, and ended the call. I hurried up the concrete steps and made my way across the wooden porch, my boots echoing against the hollow boards, and then pushed through the wooden door.

The bar was dark inside and I had to blink a few times before my eyes adjusted to the dimness of the place. I had heard Amy's voice immediately upon entering, and I headed in that direction. When I reached the bar, I found her talking to Ed Brody, the owner of the place.

"They're real," Amy said, beaming. "He's pulling up the footage."

"Hey, Ed, I thought y'all didn't believe in spy cameras," I said jokingly, feeling relieved. "I mean, considering certain members of your clientele like to show up with women who aren't their wives."

"They've had to get over it," Ed said from around a cigarette. "I'm not taking any chances nowadays. I want to know who comes and goes around here. I even have it wired to my cell phone. I can check in on the place twenty-four, seven."

I watched as the white-haired man squinted through the smoke at his laptop. He glanced up once at Amy.

"Thursday night, right?"

Amy nodded.

"What time?"

Amy glanced at me. "What time did Mable say he left?"

"It was ten o'clock," I said, leaning forward so I could watch the footage as Ed played it. He waved me off and turned the laptop to face us.

"It's set to Thursday at ten." Smoke puffed from his mouth as he spoke. "Just hit the little buttons at the bottom. You can go forward, backward, and speed it up."

I thanked him and watched as Amy took over the controls. She backed up the footage to a little before ten, when the truck was still in the driveway, and then let it play.

As we watched, the front door to the house opened and Max Broussard stepped out carrying two bags. He opened the rear, passenger door and placed both bags on the back seat, and then returned inside the house. When he reappeared, he was carrying an AR-15 that had a scope mounted to the carry handle. Even though he was across the street and the footage was a little grainy, I could plainly see that there was a thirty-round magazine extending from the well.

"Thank God the rifle wasn't stolen with the truck," I muttered. "That'd be one more thing we'd have to worry about."

Amy pushed a lock of blonde hair behind her ear and nodded. She was reaching for the keyboard to the laptop when she suddenly froze in place. "What in the hell is that?"

CHAPTER 32

North of Waxtuygi Road

After ending the call with Clint, Susan turned to watch the red rollback tow truck fight its way along the muddy road toward Cypress Highway. The stolen truck had been secured to the flatbed and the added weight was pushing the back tires deeper into the mud. While that might prove beneficial, it could also be a hindrance, as the truck was almost buried to the axle.

"Do you think he'll make it?" Vanessa asked.

"I sure hope so," Susan said, watching the tires spin frantically. "I won't be able to drag him out with my Tahoe."

"He said he could do it." Vanessa shook her head and walked off to help her team load their gear in the back of her Suburban.

Susan also shook her head and turned away. Takecia and Regan had gone back to searching for Wesley's truck, while Melvin and Shade had hung around to collect photographs and take a cast of the dirt bike tire track. Shade had never taken a cast, so Melvin was showing him how to do it.

The two officers were still huddled over the tire track next to where Regan had found the blood when Susan ambled over to stand over them.

Melvin looked up. "It should be hard in another ten to twelve minutes."

She nodded and they talked briefly about the possibilities of the dirt bike being involved, and how best to search for it. They were still strategizing when the roaring of the tow truck engine was upon them. They all turned in time to see the truck finally break free from the soft mud and lurch onto the harder surface along the shoulder of the road.

Susan shook her head in awe as she stared at the deep ruts that led back to the place where they'd located the stolen pickup. "I can't believe he made it out of there!"

She glanced at Melvin and Shade, then cocked her head to the side. Shade's eyes were wide and he was staring at the truck with his mouth agape. She turned to see what had gotten his attention. Earlier, when the truck had been smashed into the trees, there wasn't much to see. Now, the whole truck was exposed atop the flatbed, and the bullet holes in the windshield were clearly visible. Was that what Shade was gawking at?

Susan turned back to Shade. "What is it?"

"I know that truck."

Melvin snapped his head around to look at Shade. "Wait…what? You know this truck?"

Shade nodded and used his arm to wipe beads of sweat from his face. Although it had been cool during the night and earlier in the morning, the sun had been shining throughout the day and things were warming up considerably.

"Last night, when I was driving around looking for the other stolen truck," Shade explained, "I made my way to Lucille Cheramie's place. They were having some kind of party. They called it a Cajun Mardi Gras Bash, or something. It was the first of its kind. Anyway, there were a lot of vehicles parked amongst the oak trees, and there was a truck that looked just like that one parked there."

"Are you sure?" Susan asked, stepping closer to Shade. "This truck was at Lucille Cheramie's place?"

"I'm pretty damned sure. Out of all the trucks there, there were only two black Chevrolet trucks, and one of them had a bumper exactly like that one." He pointed toward the front of the truck. "I've never seen a bumper like it before, and it's weird that I would suddenly see two of them on two black Chevrolet pickups within a few hours of each other."

"That is weird," Susan said. "I have to go talk to Wesley's dad, but you need to give Clint a call right away and tell him what you saw." She turned to Melvin. "Clint's at the Bayou View Pub with Amy. He'll probably want y'all to go with him to Lucille's place, so you need to get out of here and head in that direction. I'll recover the cast."

Melvin hesitated, glanced down at the plaster and then over at

Shade, who was speaking quickly into his cell phone. Susan could tell that Melvin eagerly wanted to rush out of there and go to where the potential action might be, but he also didn't want to shirk his responsibilities.

"It's almost dry," he finally said. "I can do it."

"I have to wait for Vanessa and her team to clear out of here anyway," Susan said. "Get out of here. Go find these bastards."

She didn't have to tell Melvin again. He leapt to his feet and ran to his truck, waving for Shade to do the same. She smiled as she watched them hurry off like two eager boys heading to play ball with their neighborhood friends, and she said a silent prayer that they would be safe.

She then turned toward the tow truck, where Vanessa and her team were climbing all over the bed, wrapping the stolen Chevrolet in brand new tarps to preserve any evidence that might still exist. It took them about fifteen minutes, and Susan recovered the cast of the dirt bike track while they worked.

Once Vanessa had climbed down, she strolled toward Susan and peeled off her latex gloves.

"Tell Clint if he keeps calling me out like this," Vanessa said with a smile, "there's no way I'll have those reports done by this afternoon."

Susan laughed and watched them leave. She then closed the gate and secured it as best she could. She didn't know who owned the property, but she'd have to do some research at some point and make the proper notifications. But right now, she had to speak to Wesley's dad and find out who could've possibly gotten their hands on his son's spare key.

As she drove to town, she called her own house. Her mom must've seen the caller ID and let Grace answer the phone, because she was greeted by her daughter's sweet voice.

"Mommy!" Grace screeched. "Are you coming home?"

Susan's heart swelled with emotion at the sheer excitement in her daughter's voice just from getting to speak with her mom.

"Oh, Gracie, I sure wish I could come home to you," she said wistfully. "Daddy and I are trying to catch some bad guys."

"Aw, that's okay, Mommy," Grace said soothingly. "You can come home after you work."

Susan laughed. She continued talking to Grace on her drive across town, and she didn't hang up until she arrived at the Chouest residence. There was a fleeting moment, as she reached for her notepad on the dash, that she remembered tossing an item on that same dashboard a little more than a year ago. She had been too scared to look back then and things had gotten in the way, delaying her answer. She wouldn't be scared this time. She would find out, and she would do it right away.

CHAPTER 33

Bayou View Pub

Amy backed up the footage and played it a second time. We watched again as Max loaded up his truck and drove away. About thirty seconds after he had left, a man suddenly materialized from the ground near the shed, not twenty feet from where the truck had been parked. In a low crouch, he headed back toward the bayou and disappeared in the darkness off screen to the left, which would've been north of the house.

"Where'd he come from?" I asked. "Was that our suspect trying to steal the truck?"

"I think so." Amy allowed the footage to continue to play, and sure enough, about two minutes later, a large-framed dirt bike with large tires appeared in the camera's view from the north, racing southward along the shoulder of the road. The headlights—if it had any—were off, and there were two dark figures crouched low on the bike.

"Holy shit!" I said. "Those are our suspects and they're tailing Max!"

Without saying a word, Amy quickly reversed the footage until it reached ten o'clock. She then slowed down the reverse speed and watched. It was dark near the shed and his movements were subtle, but we were able to spot the man come into the camera view at around nine-thirty and slowly inch his way toward Max's truck. When Max stepped out at ten, he foiled the man's theft attempt.

"Damn it," I said. "Had Max just waited a few more minutes, we would've had the theft on camera."

Amy remained quiet as her fingers danced across the keyboard. My phone rang and I glanced at it. Shade Rankin.

I stepped away and answered. "Hey, what's up?"

"Clint, this truck that was pulled out of the woods, I recognize it."

I stopped dead in my tracks. "From where?"

He told me about some Mardi Gras Bash that had been taking place at Lucille Cheramie's campground last night, and how he had seen a black Chevy truck outfitted with the exact same bumper as was on Max's truck.

"Where are you right now?" I asked, feeling my heart racing with excitement. This was the best lead we'd had since the murders happened, and I wasn't about to let it slip away.

"Melvin and I are about to leave the Waxtuygi area," he said. "We can go wherever you need us."

"Get back to the campground ASAP," I said, "and don't let anyone leave. Block the damned road if you have to. Amy and I will be there in a minute."

I hurried back to Amy and told her what Shade had said. I wasn't sure if she heard me or not, because she just kept working on the laptop, never looking up or nodding.

"Are we done here?" I asked, wanting to leave right away. Just because the truck was no longer at Lucille Cheramie's campground, it didn't mean the suspects were no longer there. Even if they had left, Lucille might be able to tell us which one of her guests had been driving the black Chevy pickup with the unique bumper.

Max had heard the truck start up two hours after he was in his deer stand, and he'd left for his hunt at ten o'clock on Thursday night. Shade had possibly seen the same truck late last night or early this morning, so it would've been parked at Lucille's campground for at least twenty-four hours, and most likely much longer.

We also knew we were now looking for at least one dirt bike, so that would help to narrow down our search. If we could associate one or two men from the campground with a black Chevy truck and a dirt bike, we should be golden.

Amy hadn't answered, so I asked again if she was done.

"Not quite," she mumbled. "You need to see something."

I waited impatiently but eagerly, knowing it was probably good. Finally, she hit a button and waved me over. I leaned over her shoulder and watched as footage from two days earlier played. The timestamp said it was noon, and I could see that the sun was shining bright. So far, it appeared to be just another lazy day in Mechant

Loup.

As I continued to watch, a large-framed dirt bike with two riders came into view—it was the same bike with the same two suspects from Thursday night's footage! But this time, thanks to the daylight, I could see clearly that the bike was red and white.

"Play it again," I said.

Amy reversed it, played it until the suspects were directly in front of Max's house, and then paused the footage. While I could see the suspects clearly, I could tell very little about them other than they appeared a little bulky thanks to their outfits. The one on the back of the bike seemed a little shorter, but they could've been anyone in town. They both wore riding clothes and gloves, so I couldn't even tell the color of their skin, and their helmets had tinted face shields.

"Damn it!" I said. "Why couldn't they be a couple of real outlaws who refuse to wear helmets?"

"As you saw, they were cruising town looking for something." Amy reversed the footage and let it play through again. "Look how the one on the back of the bike taps the driver on the shoulder and points to Max's truck. They found what they were looking for—they found the truck they wanted to steal."

She was right. As we had figured, our suspects had driven around town looking for a truck to use as a patsy. Once they had located Max's pickup, they then cased the place and waited for the right opportunity to steal it. Had they done the same for Wesley's truck? I still couldn't understand why they felt the need to frame Max's pickup to give cover to Wesley's truck. I'd never heard of such a thing. Not only did it baffle me, but it also intrigued me. I accepted the challenge, and hoped we were up to solving it.

Amy had paused the frame again and I stared at the image of the suspects. There they were, in broad daylight for all the world to see, and we still didn't have a clue who we were chasing.

"Send that picture to Lindsey, and tell her to broadcast it to every law enforcement agency in the state," I said. "And text it to all of our people and to the sheriff, so he can get it out to his people. These bastards might've been driving around right under our noses all day, and we would've never known it."

As Amy captured the files and sent them to herself for dissemination, I thanked Ed Brody.

"You've been a big help," I said. "I'm glad you decided to install those cameras."

"Just catch those sumbitches," he said. "I'm friends with Logan Pitre, and I heard his wife got hurt last night."

I nodded and thanked him again. Once Amy had what she needed, we hurried outside and jumped in my Tahoe. As we headed north along Back Street and drove past Max Broussard's house, Amy pointed to his shed.

"The ground right there is flat and wide open," she said. "It's crazy how Max never saw the suspect. You know, if they had wanted him dead, we'd have an unsolved murder on our hands."

I stole a sideways glance at her. "Amy, we have *three* unsolved murders on our hands."

"Well, we'd have another one," she said with a toss of her hair, "and Max would've never known what hit him. It's crazy how unaware of his surroundings he was, but if you think about it, aren't we all? At least, in our own front yards?"

She had a point. I couldn't remember the last time I'd bothered to look at my short-cropped grass as I was heading to or from my truck at home in the dark. I thought for a brief moment that I might approach things a little differently now that I'd seen the video, but then I quickly dismissed the idea, knowing I wouldn't give a shit. I'd keep walking right on by that short grass without a second glance.

Amy pointed when we turned off of Cypress Highway and headed down the road that led to the campground.

I smiled when I saw that Melvin and Shade had positioned their trucks to block off the road, and both men had armed themselves with their AR-15s.

"Ain't nobody coming in or out of that campground unless they want them to," Amy said. "Even if the suspects left the campground, they'll be captured trying to get back in."

I nodded. They had set up the roadblock far enough down the road that no one could see them from Cypress Highway, which meant a driver would have already committed to traveling down the muddy and bumpy road by the time they saw the roadblock, and by then, it would be too late. Of course, there was the chance that the suspects had already returned to the campground on the dirt bike, and I was hoping we would find it.

CHAPTER 34

I stopped briefly at the roadblock and showed Melvin and Shade the picture of the dirt bike.

"That's a Honda 650," Shade said. "Those things are fast."

"How fast?" I asked.

"A hundred plus."

I whistled. "That's fast for a dirt bike."

"Some can get up over 120," he said. "It's crazy scary at that speed, so you'd have to be pretty crazy or desperate to try it."

I nodded thoughtfully and then asked Amy if she wouldn't mind staying with Melvin while Shade came with me.

"Shade saw Max's truck at the party," I explained, "so I'll need him to point out the exact location. And, if anyone decides to run, I'll just sic him on them."

"Shade, get ready," Amy said with a smirk, "because that old man ain't never gonna run again. You'll be catching all of his rabbits."

"I don't blame him," Melvin said. "The kid's got a bullet in his leg and he can still outrun all of us by a mile."

"By the way, how is your leg?" I asked when Shade had gotten into my Tahoe and we were heading toward the campground. "Still no pain?"

Shade slapped his left leg. "It's as good as new. Thankfully, the bullet didn't hit a bone or tendon."

"Yeah, we were lucky that day." I scowled at the memory, and thought of how different this very day would've been for Susan and Grace had things not gone our way in Mississippi. In this line of work, things could go from sunshine and unicorns to hellfire and bullets in an instant. While it was a hazard of the job, it was also what kept most of us sharp—and Lord knows, we needed to be as sharp as we could be right now, because we were dealing with two ruthless *sumbitches*, as Ed Brody had called them.

The Tahoe rocked gently as the four-by-four pushed us down the sloppy roadway and into view of the campground. I hadn't been to Lucille Cheramie's spread in quite some time, but everything still had a familiar look to it. Well, except for the network of tents that had been set up over the picnic tables. Normally, visitors ate under the umbrella of oak trees that lined the bayou side, but with the rain storm that had blown through yesterday, they'd been forced to improvise. They were lucky the wind hadn't been fierce, otherwise those tents would've turned to kites and everything would've ended up in the swamps.

I pulled up near the main house and parked. From the moment the campground came into view, I was scanning the parking areas in search of Wesley's truck.

"Most of the vehicles are gone." Shade pointed to a vacant area in the middle of a muddy opening. "That truck with the unique bumper was parked there, and there was another black Chevy truck farther down. There were a few motorcycles scattered around, but none of them looked like the picture of the dirt bike that Amy sent out."

I cursed. "So, there's a good chance they weren't staying in a camp, otherwise their truck would've been parked under one of the carports."

"I guess so," Shade said. "I've never been back here before last night, so I don't know much about the place."

"Well, here goes nothing." We stepped out and made our way along an uneven sidewalk and up a ramp that led to a screened-in porch.

"I didn't talk to anyone here at the main house," Shade explained, pointing toward a large tent near the water's edge. "The party was going on out there and I found Mrs. Cheramie's assistant. I spoke with her and some of the people at the party, but none of them knew anything and no one looked like the wanted poster of the man who slashed the tires."

I nodded and knocked on the screen door. Within seconds, it opened and a young girl was standing there. Her eyes immediately turned to Shade and she smiled, her face burning red. Recognizing her interest in Shade, I eased back and gave him a nod. If she liked him, she would tell him everything he wanted to know—even if she wasn't supposed to tell it.

"Hey, how's it going?" Shade asked smoothly. "Your name's Daisy, right?"

She smiled. "You remembered."

"Yeah, I did. Look, this is my boss, Detective Clint Wolf." Shade indicated me with a nod of his head. "He's working that case I told you about last night. As it turns out, the suspect's truck was parked out in the front last night."

Daisy's eyes grew wide. "What?"

"Yeah, and I was hoping you might be able to help us identify the men who were in that truck." Shade waved a hand. "Maybe tell us who was staying in each camp, what they were driving, and how many people were in their parties…stuff like that."

Daisy stammered for a moment, but finally found her voice. "Um, Lucille's not here at the moment, and she has all the records. I don't have access to that kind of information."

"You have eyes don't you?" Shade asked with a smile. "Can you maybe point me to the camp that had a black Chevy truck parked in front of it?"

"None of them did."

"No?"

Daisy shook her head. "I don't know the difference between a Chevy and a Ford, other than a Ford is supposed to be tougher, but I didn't see any kind of black truck parked by the camps."

Shade's shoulders seemed to sag a little, and I felt mine do the same. He pointed to the front yard.

"The truck was parked right over there when I came by last night," he insisted. "They had to have been at the party."

"There were so many people at the party." Daisy shook her head slowly. "I just don't know who was driving any of the trucks out there."

"Is it possible they stayed at one of the camps but didn't park in front of it?" he asked, trying to attack the problem from a different angle. As long as he was working through it, I wasn't going to interrupt him. It was a great way to gain some experience.

"Oh, that's definitely possible." Daisy nodded her head. "And you know what else? We have some tent pads set up all through the woods, and we had a lot of people rent those spots for the party. In fact, we sold out. We were completely full. I know a few people called in and asked for refunds when they saw the weather, but we had a waiting list and the spots filled up again as soon as someone cancelled."

"Can we have a look at the tent pads?"

"Sure." She pointed toward the picnic tables. "There's a path by the water that heads down the bayou. Just start following it past the camps and you'll run into where the tents go. Some of those people already left, but most of them are still hanging around. Those who are left are staying until tomorrow."

Shade nodded thoughtfully. "Oh," he finally said. "Did you see anyone riding around here on a dirt bike?"

"You know what, I heard one, but I didn't see it." She folded her arms across her chest. "My brother used to have one and it makes a loud whining sound. That's what I heard. It's not like those big motorcycles we get here—those Harleys. Those sound like a roar, but the bike I heard sounded like a whine. I also know that the Harleys that come through here won't crank up their engines late at night, because they know it disturbs the other guests. This dirt bike didn't care. I heard it coming and going late into the night, and it left early this morning."

Shade and I exchanged quick glances.

"Did it come back at some point?" Shade asked.

Daisy was thoughtful. "I don't really remember, because I was real busy picking up the mess all morning, and we had a lot of motorcycles come and go through here already today. I remember them leaving this morning, because they were the first ones to make noise. Everyone else was still hung over and sleeping." She smirked. "We cooked breakfast for over a hundred people, but barely fifty showed up. Anyway, the dirt bike might've come back later, but I didn't notice it. I was too busy working."

I glanced toward the picnic tables. There were a few dozen people sitting out there, some of them with coffee cups, and others with plates of beignets. Even from that distance, I could still see the mountain of powdered sugar on top of the beignets. They looked like snow-covered peaks.

Shade glanced at me and shrugged, as though wondering what else he should ask.

"Ma'am," I began, "could you tell what direction the dirt bike noise came from?"

"No, sir. I never did see them. I just know they were away from the water. Like, they didn't ride it down by the picnic tables or anything. They kept it toward the woods."

"How about this man," I said, pulling out my cell phone and bringing up the image of the man who slashed Wesley's truck tires. "Have you seen him around here?"

She leaned close and studied the image. "Oh, wow, it looks so gray. It's hard to make out his features."

I sighed. "Yeah, it was captured at night from an infrared surveillance camera. We did the best we could to clean it up."

"I don't recognize him."

I nodded and stepped away from the screened porch, surveyed the front of the property. There were a couple of street motorcycles scattered around the shaded area under the oak trees. Most of them were covered in mud, as were nearly all the vehicles that were still parked in the area. I didn't see any dirt bikes. Although the ground was marked up from vehicles driving all through it, I hadn't noticed any dirt bike tracks when we'd first walked up. Of course, that didn't mean there weren't any. They could've easily been driven over by other vehicles.

Shade indicated the soffit on the main house. "I don't suppose y'all have surveillance cameras out here, do y'all?"

"No," Daisy said. "Lucille doesn't like to be spied upon, so she said she would never spy on her guests. She likes to keep things simple out here. She wants to stay as close to nature as possible."

"Where is Mrs. Cheramie right now?" Shade asked.

"Oh, she went to town to get more supplies. We're out of flour and milk, and we're running low on coffee." Daisy shot a slender thumb toward the campground. "We need to feed the people who are staying through tomorrow, and they expect to have Lucille's world-famous beignets for breakfast."

"Does she have a cell phone?" Shade asked.

Daisy nodded.

"Can you call her and ask if she can give you access to the visitor logs?" Shade had an easy-going way about him, and it drew Daisy in. She seemed willing to do whatever he asked of her. "Let her know we think the killers are hiding out here."

Daisy waved for us to follow her inside, and we found ourselves in a crowded kitchen that smelled of fried seafood. I could hear the sizzling of grease from somewhere deep inside the house, and I knew they were cooking lunch for their guests. My stomach growled like an angry tiger, and I wondered what I wouldn't give for a handful of fried shrimp.

Daisy was very convincing as she spoke with Lucille. She nodded and moved about the room, apparently following Lucille's instructions. I saw her remove a small key from under a jar that rode high atop a cupboard, and then she disappeared into the house. When she returned, she was holding a worn notebook.

"This is it," she said, beaming as she handed the book to Shade. "This is where she keeps the names, locations, and phone numbers of everyone who rents a place over here."

Shade handed the book to me and I opened to the last pages with entries. Everything was handwritten, and the writing looked like chicken scratch. The entries from Friday took up two pages. I flipped back to Thursday, and that filled a single page. I shook my head. I didn't know what I expected to see, but there were names and locations that meant absolutely nothing to me. We knew our suspects drove a dirt bike and they thought they were slick, but that was about it.

Finally, I just pulled out my cell phone and took pictures of every page, beginning with the most recent one and working my way back to the day before Wesley's tires had been slashed. Although the names didn't mean anything today, they might mean something later.

When I was finished, I handed the book back to Daisy and thanked her for her time.

Shade thanked her, too, and we told her that we would be hanging around for a while to check out the campground.

CHAPTER 35

Once Shade and I had walked away from the house and were making our way down to the path by the water, I called Amy and let her know what was happening.

"Any movement on your end?" I asked.

"No," she said. "No traffic at all."

"Well, keep an eye out for the dirt bike," I said. "It seems they left early in the morning and they might not have come back yet."

After ending the call, I shoved my phone in my pocket and glanced toward the bayou. There, not a dozen feet away, was a large alligator resting on the bank sunning itself. I pointed it out to Shade.

"Man, I never get tired of seeing those giant lizards," he said. "I wish I could take one as a pet."

I laughed, and then scowled. "Have you ever heard the story of Godzator?"

He shook his head, so I told the story of my first encounter with the giant prehistoric beast. Meanwhile, we walked down the path that extended past the camps and led through the trees to where the tent pads were located. On our way to the tents, we walked around each of the camps just in case the dirt bike had been stashed there, but we had no luck.

Once we got past the camps and entered the thicker forest, we began to encounter a smattering of tents along the pathway. Each time we'd come upon a tent with people milling about, I'd stop talking about Godzator long enough to ask a few questions, and then I'd continue the story until we reached the next tent. All the while, I was searching for a man who looked like the picture I carried on my cell phone.

We walked by a number of tents that were zipped up tight with no movement inside, so it was possible the suspects were still in there sleeping. We could hear snoring coming from some of the tents, and it was only during those times that I remembered we hadn't slept for over twenty-four hours. As we were approaching the next tent along the pathway, it became painfully obvious that a couple was having sex inside. We tiptoed past that one, not wanting to ruin their mood, but then Shade asked if I thought it might be our suspects.

"What if they heard or saw us approaching and knew we were cops, so they pretended to have sex to throw us off?" he asked.

"You've been watching too many movies," I said with a laugh, but then stopped in my tracks. I remembered the figure on the back of the dirt bike being smaller than the driver. "But what if you're right? What if our suspects are boyfriend and girlfriend?"

"Should we interrupt them, then?" he asked, glancing cautiously back toward the tent. "Or would that just be cruel if it wasn't them?"

I thought about it, but then shook my head. "I think the suspects are too busy trying to figure a way out of here. I'm sure they feel the walls closing in on them, so—even if they are boyfriend and girlfriend—they're too busy for sex right now."

We rounded a curve in the path and came upon a bright yellow tent with a woman standing near a picnic table brushing her teeth. Her hair was a mess and she wore nothing but a long undershirt and a scowl. By the look on her face, she could use a hangover omelet.

I waited until she had rinsed out her mouth before introducing ourselves.

"We're investigating a murder that happened in town," I explained. "Someone attacked the parade—"

"Did you say a murder?" Her eyes widened and she dropped her toothbrush, suddenly very curious. "What happened?"

"Someone stole a truck and ran down a bunch of people," I said. "We've got a lot of injured and three dead, and we're thinking the suspects might've been staying here at the campground."

She walked over and stuck out a hand. "I'm NOPD," she said, shaking my hand first and then Shade's. "I work the burglary and robbery division. My husband and I ride our bikes out here every Friday before Mardi Gras. It's our only day off during Carnival season, so God knows, we need the break."

I nodded and glanced beyond her tent, where a couple of old Indian motorcycles were resting on kickstands. Although yesterday had been muddy, there wasn't a speck of dust or mud on these two. I imagined they had wiped them down after the rain. That kind of loving care said a lot about them and their bikes.

"Did you happen to hear a dirt bike running around the area?" I asked, pulling out my cell phone to show her the daytime picture Amy had captured of the dirt bike. I also showed her the picture of the man who had slashed Wesley's tires. "The assistant who works these grounds says she heard a dirt bike leave the area early this morning, but she doesn't know if they came back."

"Oh, he sure did leave first thing this morning, before daylight, and he woke my ass up," the female NOPD officer said with a grunt. She shot a thumb toward the east. "There must be a bike path through the trees in that direction, because that's where I heard him. I never saw him or his damned dirt bike, or I probably would've shot the little prick."

She looked at the images on my phone again and said she would keep an eye out for them. "So, there are two of them on one bike?"

I nodded. "We think so."

"Okay. Do you have a card?"

I fished one out and handed it to her, and then Shade and I headed for the trees. I glanced over my shoulder in the woman's direction once, wondering if she was really a cop. It had been an informal questioning and she wasn't required by law to provide any answers, so there had been no need to ask for identification. But what if she was working with the suspects and she was steering us away from them?

Shade must've been thinking the same thing I was thinking, because he asked if I thought it was a trick.

"I don't think so, but I'm not willing to bet on anything at this point." I turned my attention back to the woods in front of us. As we stealthily made our way through a stand of young oak trees—keeping about ten feet apart—I dropped my hand to my pistol. All was quiet in front of us, and I didn't know if that was a good thing or not. Behind us, I could hear stirring sounds as campers went about their day. At one point, a vehicle fired up from the direction of the main house, and I wondered if that was our suspects leaving. If it was, Melvin and Amy would stop them.

Shade and I had traveled several hundred yards into the woods when we finally came upon a narrow walking trail, but more than walking had taken place here. Deep tire tracks had been cut into the soft mud, and they were consistent with the tracks from the pasture road where Max Broussard's truck had been stolen. Not only that, but they were fresh.

I looked to the left, which would've led to the main building, and then to the right, which would take us deeper into the woods. What if we were running down an empty rabbit hole? What if these happened to be the tracks of some random teenager out for a weekend ride on his dirt bike?

I glanced at Shade, who had walked closer to the tracks and was squatting beside them.

"Found something?" I asked.

"Boot impressions," he said. "It looks like somebody walked through here heading back to the campground, and their boot prints are on top of the tire tracks."

I whipped out my cell phone and called Melvin. "Shade and I are following a dirt bike trail into the woods, but it looks like someone headed back toward the campground on foot. The boot tracks are similar to the ones you found near the abandoned truck. This might be our suspect."

"Do you have one set of boot tracks or two?" he asked.

"Only one at this point." I looked toward the right, where the trail disappeared deeper into the woods to the south. "The other suspect might've stayed with the bike, but it seems like they've definitely split up."

"What if they know we're on to them?" Melvin asked. "What if they know we know about the dirt bike?"

"I don't know how they could know that." I frowned. None of us had stopped long enough to watch the news, so I had no idea what was being said in the media. "We didn't put anything out about the dirt bike, so it shouldn't be in the news."

"Maybe they're watching us."

Just as the words left Melvin's mouth, a chill reverberated up and down my neck, and I took a quick glance around me. I didn't see or hear anything, but the woods were so dense in this area that an army could've been hiding within throwing distance.

CHAPTER 36

The Chouest Residence

Susan parked her Tahoe in the driveway of Mr. and Mrs. Chouest's residence, and let Lindsey know where she was. She then stepped out and walked to the front door. She took a breath before knocking. She needed to gather herself. It was hard to watch these poor people fall apart. She wanted to break down crying with them, but she knew she couldn't. She had to be strong for them.

Before she knocked, the door swished open and Mr. Chouest was standing there.

"Chief, did you find out anything?" Mr. Chouest was speaking in a low voice, and Susan figured that probably meant Mrs. Chouest had finally drifted off to sleep.

"We don't have anything concrete," Susan said softly, glancing around for a place to sit and talk.

"Why don't you come to the patio?" Mr. Chouest gently pulled the front door closed and led Susan around to the patio, where there was a wrought iron table and four chairs centered beneath a ceiling fan that was gently spinning.

Once they were seated, Susan showed Mr. Chouest the photo she'd recently received from Amy that depicted the two possible suspects on the red and white dirt bike.

"Do you recognize this bike or these suspects?" Susan asked gently. "I know they have helmets on, but does anything about them seem familiar?"

Mr. Chouest's eyes were bloodshot and swollen, so he had to rub and squint and turn the cell phone at different angles to make it out. He finally shook his head. "No, they don't look familiar. Are these the ones responsible for murdering my boy?"

"We don't know for sure, but we believe so," Susan said. "What we're having a problem figuring out is how they managed to steal the truck. It's possible the truck was hotwired, but there was no evidence of a broken window at the scene. He could've jimmied it open, but that would've taken time and there would've been a risk of him being seen."

Mr. Chouest just nodded and stared at Susan.

"So, we were thinking that it's possible someone got their hands on Wesley's spare key, and gained access to his truck—"

"Wesley didn't have a spare key," he interrupted.

Susan's brow furrowed. "What?"

"Yeah, when he bought the truck, it didn't have a spare key," he explained. "That's why he was very careful to never lose his key, because it was the only one he had. If he lost it, he knew he'd be screwed."

Susan leaned back in her chair, her mind working. The iron back felt good as her tired muscles relaxed into it. Lately, she had been more tired than normal, and the last twenty-four hours were kicking her ass.

"Where'd he buy the truck?" she finally asked.

"Rupe's Dealership," he said, "across the bridge."

"And when did he buy it?"

"Oh, he hasn't had it long," Mr. Chouest said. "It's only been about six or eight months. He saw it parked in their front lot and he fell in love with that ugly primer black color. I prefer my paint job to be shiny, but Wesley always did like that dull look. Hell, he wouldn't read a book if the cover was shiny. He said fishing bait was shiny, so he didn't trust shiny things."

Susan smiled warmly as she listened to Mr. Chouest speak so fondly of his son. That they were a loving and close-knit family was obvious.

When he stopped talking, the elder man scowled. "Is there something to this key thing?"

"I don't know," Susan admitted, "but I'm definitely gonna look into it."

Before she could leave, she had to answer a dozen, or so, questions about the investigation, and she did so without hesitation or hurry. She would spend all day there if it would help to make the man feel better. When he was done, he stood and let out a long sigh.

"I appreciate all you're doing," he said, "but please find these people soon. I don't know how much longer I can just sit around here waiting for something to happen before I start hunting them down myself."

"I understand, sir." Susan shook his hand. "You have my number. You can call anytime, day or night."

"I know." He nodded. "You've been great."

CHAPTER 37

Susan's mind was still racing as she returned to her Tahoe and drove toward Rupe's dealership. Traffic was jammed up at the bridge because of the checkpoint, and she waited patiently until it was her turn to approach the band of deputies stationed there.

"Hey, Chief," said Gretchen Verdin, who stood beside the center line with her German shepherd, Geronimo. "How are you?"

"Good." Susan indicated the line of cars leaving town. "Anything suspicious coming through here?"

"Not so far." Gretchen frowned. "Since we're limited on what we can do, I don't know how effective we're being."

"Your mere presence here is keeping that truck in town," Susan said. "They won't dare drive it out of here knowing we've got a checkpoint in place. The longer we can keep it in town, the better our chances of capturing them."

Gretchen nodded. "I guess you're right."

Susan gave her a nod and drove on to the dealership, which was located on the west side of the highway and just past the bridge. Once inside, she asked to speak with the owner, Julie Rupe. The woman behind the counter didn't waste time, and within a minute Susan was sitting with Julie in her office.

"Are you here about what happened last night?" Julie asked, her voice barely over a whisper.

"Yeah, I need some information from you."

"Sure, whatever I can do." Julie shook her head. "I can't believe that. People are saying it's a terrorist attack. I mean, I thought terrorists only attacked large cities. I didn't think they would start showing up in small towns—"

Susan raised a hand to interrupt her. "We don't believe this is a terrorist attack," she said. "We think it was a targeted attack, and I need everything you have on the sale of a dull black Chevy pickup to Wesley Chouest. According to his dad, he bought the truck here between six and eight months ago."

"Is that the truck that was used in the attack?"

Susan nodded. "We were operating off of the possibility that someone used a spare key, but it turns out Wesley never got a spare key during the sales transaction."

Julie had already turned to her computer and was tapping away at the keyboard. She stopped typing when Susan said the last part.

"Wait, do you think someone here had something to do with the murders?"

"I'm not thinking anything at the moment," Susan said. "I just want to get my hands on that spare key."

Julie nodded, and then continued her search. "Okay, give me a second. I'll have to pull the file."

Once Julie had stepped out of her office, Susan called Clint.

"What are you doing?" she asked when he answered.

"Shade and I are tracking down the dirt bike." He spoke in a hushed tone, and she got the feeling he thought he might be closing in on the suspects. "What's up?"

"Never mind," she said. "Call me when it's safe."

Before Clint could object, she ended the call. She didn't want to be the cause of him being discovered and attacked while stalking a suspect. Besides, Julie had just returned with the file and dropped it on her desk. She rifled through it and then handed Susan a yellow document.

Susan took it and saw that it was the vehicle invoice. It showed that the Chevrolet Silverado was sold to Wesley in June of the previous year. He had traded in an older truck—a Ford F-150 Supercrew—and gotten $1,000 in value for the trade-in.

Next, Julie handed Susan the title, but that didn't offer up any new information, and neither did the sales contract.

"Who sold him the truck?" Susan asked, scanning the invoice, and then answering her own question. "It was Tiffany. I want to talk to Tiffany."

Julie picked up her phone and told someone on the other end to send Tiffany into her office.

After about a minute of waiting, there was a soft knock on the door.

"Come in," Julie said.

A young woman with short hair and an easy smile entered. "They said you wanted to talk to me, Mrs. Rupe."

Julie introduced Tiffany to Susan and the two shook hands. Susan handed Tiffany the sales invoice.

"Do you remember making this sale?" she asked. "It was seven months ago, it was a primer black Chevy pickup that was sold to Wesley Chouest."

Tiffany swallowed hard. "I heard he was the one who died last night. I became friends with him on social media after I sold him the truck, and I saw a bunch of people tagging his page with memories they had of him."

Susan nodded. "What can you tell me about the spare key to his truck?"

"Um, let's see," Tiffany said, scrunching up her face. "I'm pretty sure we couldn't find the spare key to that truck. Wesley had asked about it when he was here signing the papers, and I checked the box, but I couldn't find it. Don was the one who got it as a trade-in, and I asked him about the spare key, but he said he didn't know. He was supposed to check with the original owner and get back with me so I could get the key to Wesley, but you know how Don is. I asked him three or four times and he kept saying he was on it, but he never got back with me."

Julie was already on her phone calling for Don to get in her office right away. The door opened and a man with slicked-back hair entered. He glanced down at Susan and smiled, but she didn't return the favor. Julie jumped in right away.

"Where in the hell is the spare key to Wesley Chouest's truck?" she asked heatedly. "Tiffany has asked you three or four times over the last six months to get that key, but you keep blowing her off."

Don lost his bluster and began to stammer.

"I want answers," Julie said, "not excuses. Did you or did you not talk to the original owners?"

"I…um, you know, I've been so busy that I forgot to call her." He swallowed hard. "I'm sorry, it just slipped my mind."

"Go get the file," Julie said. When he was gone, she shook her head. "That's the laziest son-of-a-bitch I've ever had working for me. Randall would've thrown him out on his ass a long time ago."

Susan only nodded. She wasn't interested in their office politics, she only wanted to get her hands on the spare key—and she wanted to interrogate the person who had it.

When Don returned, he handed the file to Julie with a hand that shook. Julie snatched it away and gave it to Susan, and then asked, "Do you have any questions for Don?"

Susan glanced at the vehicle invoice. It detailed the sale of a Jeep Grand Cherokee to Abby Bruce, of Mechant Loup, and it showed that she had traded in the Chevy Silverado. She hadn't done much better than Wesley had on his trade-in, having hauled in $2,500, put she had also put down almost $12,000 in cash.

"Tell me about the spare key to the primer black Chevy Silverado," Susan said, standing to look Don directly in the eyes.

He stood there fidgeting. "Um, well, I don't think I ever got the spare key from the original owner. I think I tried calling to ask her about it, but I don't think she answered."

"Did you leave a message?"

"Yeah…I mean, I'm sure I did." He swallowed. "Yeah, probably."

"What do you know about this Abby Bruce?"

"Nothing, really." He was thoughtful. "I think she said something about being from out of town and meeting somebody from here at a football game. I think they got married and she moved here. That's about all I know. I did see her with her husband or boyfriend at the store, but I only waved and kept going."

"Did you take that opportunity to ask her about the spare key?" Susan asked pointedly.

Don only shook his head.

Susan turned to Julie. "I don't have anything more for him."

Julie fixed Don with a cold stare and then, in a silently deadly voice, said, "Go home. You're done for the day."

When Don had left, Susan took her time studying the sales contract and other documents from the dealership. There wasn't much to gather from it all. After having listened to Don, she wasn't sure if Abby ever had the key, or if Don had misplaced it.

Julie must've been thinking the same thing, because she turned to Tiffany and told her to turn the place upside down looking for the key. "I want everyone working on this," she said. "Search every inch of this place, including Don's office."

Tiffany balked. "You…you want me to search his office?"

"I want you to search every drawer in his desk, every file in his cabinets, and every shelf on his bookcase." She stabbed the desk with her finger. "Randall built this place from the ground up, and I'll be damned if I'll let a weasel like Don bring disrepute on my husband's name."

"Yes, ma'am." Tiffany hurried off to conduct her search.

"If the key is in this building, we'll find it," Julie said. "You can believe that."

Susan thanked her, but told her she would pay a visit to Abby anyway. "There's a chance she traded the truck in without the spare, and if she did, only she can tell me that for sure."

Julie apologized for the trouble. "I'll deal with Don, don't you worry about that. You shouldn't have your time wasted by the incompetence of others."

Susan waved her off and tapped the name and address on the invoice. "It's okay, please go easy on him. I have what I need."

CHAPTER 38

Somewhere in the woods near Cheramie's Campground

"She hung up on me," I told Shade in a low voice when Susan abruptly ended the phone call.

"Why?" he whispered.

"I guess she could tell we were stalking someone." I shrugged. "She loves me and doesn't want me to get dead out here."

"You know, I never thought about getting married before," he said, a wistful expression falling across his face. "I've always just thought that I would date forever and stay single, but seeing you and the chief and little Gracie…it's really cool. I just hope I find a wife as cool as Chief Wolf someday, and not end up with someone like my mom."

I frowned and nodded. I didn't know what to say to that, so I said nothing, and shoved my cell phone back in my pocket.

We then continued along the muddy trail, following our elusive suspects and hoping to get lucky. We had earlier decided to parallel the suspect's route from the edge of the trees that skirted the trail, just in case we would suddenly turn a corner and encounter the suspects. If at all possible, we wanted to see them before they saw us, because that would give us a decided advantage. However, that meant we had to watch where we stepped so we didn't snap branches or rustle any leaves and give away our presence. Thus, the going was much slower than simply trudging through the slop.

As we got farther and farther away from the campground, I began to have doubts that we were doing the right thing. If these dirt bike tracks had been made by some local kid out for a joy ride, we would have wasted a tremendous amount of time and energy, while the real suspects were out there plotting their escape from town.

I was about to voice my concerns when a noise suddenly sounded in the distance. It didn't register at first and I kept walking until Shade grabbed my arm.

"That's a dirt bike firing up!" he hissed, pointing in the direction we were heading. "The suspect's either coming this way or getting out of here."

I drew my pistol and crept to the edge of the trees to peer down the trail. The path was straight for about 200 yards before it veered to the left and out of sight in the trees. The sound that we had heard was coming from that direction, and it was absolutely a dirt bike. The operator revved the engine a few times, and then we heard it kick into gear.

Shade and I waited for a moment, listening intently, and then we got our answer—it was heading right for us!

Holding my pistol in my left hand, I pulled out my cell phone and called Melvin to tell him the suspects were on the move and heading our way.

"We're gonna try to stop the bike," I said. "If he gets through us, be ready to confront him on the road."

I tossed my phone back in my pocket, and headed for the opposite side of the trail. Gripping my pistol firmly in both hands, I stood beside a tree and waited. I glanced once at Shade. He had dropped to a knee and had taken up a left-handed position beside a thick cypress tree, holding his pistol at the ready.

The sound of the dirt bike was growing louder and it was rapidly getting closer. Suddenly, it appeared around the bend in the distance and I immediately saw a flash of red as it bounced roughly across the uneven road. It was the same dirt bike we had seen in the surveillance footage!

Without hesitating, I stepped out from behind the tree and moved to the center of the road, leveling my pistol at the rider.

"Stop now, you son of a bitch," I bellowed, knowing he couldn't possibly hear me, "or I'll shoot you right off the back of that bike!"

I could tell the rider saw me immediately, because he instantly skidded to a stop. I felt something beside me and knew Shade had also stepped out from behind his tree. We both stood there aiming our pistols at the suspect, who sat there frozen, his bike running beneath him.

"Get off the bike and remove your helmet!" I hollered, taking a step closer to the suspect. He was about thirty yards away, so I wasn't sure if he could hear me, but I did know one thing—if he revved up that engine and started coming toward us, I was going to make good on my promise. I'd already seen the damage he could do with a truck, and I wasn't about to find out how artful he was with a dirt bike.

"What's he doing?" Shade asked.

"I don't know." I took another step closer and repeated my demands. The suspect had both hands on the handlebars, but the helmet was swiveling from side to side. Wait a minute—he was looking for a way out!

I began walking quickly forward now, yelling at him to step off of the bike. Shade was matching my stride and we had closed to within twenty yards when the suspect seemed to make up his mind. He jerked the handlebars toward his right and revved the engine. With a roar, the rear tire spit mud into the air and the bike shot into the trees, where it disappeared from our view.

"Shit!" I sprinted forward. I wasn't going to shoot a fleeing suspect, especially when I couldn't articulate that he was a threat to the public at large, so all I could do was run toward where I'd last seen him and hope I'd find him crashed into a tree.

Shade had sprung into action a full second faster than me. I cursed the aging process and ran as fast as I could, but I couldn't come close to catching the kid. He hit the spot where the dirt bike disappeared in a flash, and then he, himself, faded into the trees. I could still hear the engine screaming, so I knew the suspect hadn't crashed yet and he was escaping.

I stopped running for a second and pulled out my cell phone. I called Melvin and tried to control my breathing while I waited for him to answer.

"He's heading east through the woods," I hollered when he finally came on. "We've got a single suspect on the red Honda and I think he's trying to circle back to this trail or he's looking for a way to reach Cypress Highway."

"I'll get Regan to start heading this way from the south area, and Baylor's coming from across town," Melvin said. "Amy's on the radio alerting the checkpoint. Takecia just got here, so I'll send her to the campground in case he stops there."

"Okay," I said, still huffing. "I'm going look for Shade."

The suspect had traveled deep into the woods by now, and it sounded like he was circling toward the north. I started running in the direction of the fading sound of the dirt bike, dodging trees as I did so. I was hoping Shade hadn't gotten hurt dashing into the woods like he had. In the swamps, it was easy to step in a hole and break a leg or trip on a cypress knee and end up face-planted into a tree. The faster one ran, the greater the danger, and Shade was about as fast as they came.

"Shade!" I called as I raced through the forest. "Where are you?"

There was no answer. I tried to scan the ground as I ran, but it was hard to find any tracks in the blanket of leaves that covered the forest floor. We were on more solid ground now, and I was about to enter a thick stand of pine trees when I stopped and looked to the left and right, where the trees were thinner. I decided to circle the pine grove to the left, and that's when I came across a slough that had fresh tire tracks and boot impressions going right down the center of it.

"Shade!" The dirt bike was a distant hum now, and everything on our end of the forest had grown quiet once again, except for the chatter on my police radio. Now that we weren't trying to be stealthy any more, I had it turned up loud so I could hear the progress of the chase. It seemed as though they were still trying to locate the suspect, and I was worried that he would once again get away.

After a few more seconds of moving forward, I heard Shade's voice come over the radio to give the suspect's last known location. He sounded disappointed that he hadn't run down a dirt bike that could reach speeds in excess of 100 miles per hour.

I stopped walking and listened, and finally heard him moving through the woods.

"Hey, Shade, I'm over here," I called out, wanting to give him an orientation point.

"I'm coming," he finally said, his voice a lot nearer than I had expected it to be. "He came out on a cane field road and headed back toward the highway. I called it in."

His voice was strong now, and I soon saw him picking his way through the woods toward me.

CHAPTER 39

As I waited for Shade to reach me, I pulled out my cell phone and called Susan. She answered immediately.

"Hey, I heard the chatter on the radio," she said before I had a chance to say a word. "Is everyone okay?"

"Yeah, he got away through the woods," I explained. "We encountered him on a path behind Lucille's campground. I'm not sure where he was coming from, but it wasn't much farther down the path, because we heard him crank up the engine. Shade and I are gonna check it out and see what he was doing down there. With luck, it'll lead us to Wesley's truck."

"You think it could be down there?"

I nodded. "The road's wide enough for a truck, and it seems they've been riding that dirt bike back and forth through here, so they would've wiped out any tracks the truck would've made."

"Well, be careful," she said.

"Sure." I glanced up as Shade reached me. He looked mad. I grinned and shook my head. I wanted to tell him that no man could outrun a dirt bike, but I didn't think it would help. So, instead, I asked Susan why she had called earlier.

"I've got a lead on the spare key," she said. "Mr. Chouest said Wesley only got one key when he bought the truck."

"No kidding?"

"Yeah. He bought it from Rupe's Dealership. They acquired it by trade-in from a woman named Abby Bruce. She lives here in town with her husband, Chuck Bruce. I'm heading there now to talk to her."

"Be careful."

"I will. I got Lindsey to run a criminal history on Abby and her husband. They're both clean. Neither of them even have a speeding ticket."

"Okay," I said, knowing Susan could take care of herself. "Let me know what happens."

I waved for Shade to follow me and we headed back to the muddy road. I turned up my radio so we could hear any progress that might be made on the chase, and we then began back-tracking the dirt bike. I glanced over at Shade after we had gone a few dozen yards. He didn't seem to be breathing hard at all. Had I not known better, I would've thought he'd just stepped out of his truck.

"You mad you didn't catch him?" I asked.

"I almost got him," he said, shaking his head. "He took a turn to miss a big tree and his bike slipped a little, throwing him off balance. He fell into another tree and had to struggle to get the bike back up. I got to within a few yards before he was gone again. I could almost feel him in my hands."

I slapped his back. "We might not be able to catch our suspects at first, but we always catch them eventually. We have two distinct advantages over the bad guys—the size of our gang and the speed of our radios. They can't outrun a BOLO and they can't escape the long arm of the law. They might be able to evade us for a while, but we'll eventually get every last one of them."

I didn't know if I was saying that for his sake or mine, but I definitely needed to hear it, too.

We continued trudging along the trail, keeping our pistols ready and our heads on a swivel. We each cast a frequent glance over our shoulders to check our six o'clock position, and even looked up into the trees. While I didn't expect an attack from above, one could never be too careful.

After we had traveled another two or three hundred yards, we reached a spot where the dirt bike tracks veered sharply to the left into a narrow opening through a thick patch of underbrush. We both stopped and glanced at each other. I indicated I would go first. Shade nodded, and I proceeded to make my way as quietly as I could through the opening.

My heart pounded with anticipation. There was no way that Wesley's truck could've passed through this wall of tangled branches and leaves, so my hopes of finding the stolen vehicle had greatly diminished. However, there was a distinct possibility that we might find some other sort of evidence that could help us identify the killers. If this was their outlaw camp and they thought it was secure, they might've left behind maps or documents or something else that might give away who they were. If nothing else, I could get Vanessa and her team to come out here and scrub everything for DNA and prints, and we might soon be able to bring this case to a close.

I was crouched low as I walked. We were in a stretch of shadows, but I soon saw light at the end of nature's wooden tunnel. Keeping my pistol out in front of me, I picked my way as quietly as I could, moving one foot first and then the other, until I had reached the very edge of the tiny clearing.

The first thing I saw was a three- or four-man dome tent, and it was zipped up. Some dry leaves, twigs, and a few logs had been thrown together to make a fire, but it appeared their attempt had been futile, given everything from here to the coast was saturated from the downpour we'd had yesterday.

When I was sure there were no hostiles around the tent, I squeezed into the opening to make room for Shade to join me. I immediately saw a spot to the right where the dirt bike had been stashed, and there was a tarp on the ground that had apparently been used to keep it dry.

Shade moved like a whisper beside me and headed straight for the tent. He lifted his pistol and aimed it through the mosquito netting of the ventilation port. I had stopped what I was doing and aimed my own pistol at the tent. If anyone opened up on Shade, I would fill that tent full of holes. I scowled as I thought back to the case I'd worked with Alice Pierce, and then blinked away the image.

Shade had relaxed and was now leaning forward and peering through the netting. He suddenly whistled. "Clint, you need to see this."

CHAPTER 40

Northbound on Cypress Highway

The light bar on Regan Steed's Dodge Charger whistled as she sped down the highway. Shade had radioed several seconds earlier to say the suspect had cut through the woods on a dirt bike and then accessed a cane field road that led back to Cypress Highway. Regan was approaching Mechant Loup from the south on Cypress Highway and Baylor had just radioed to say he was crossing over into Mechant Loup East, so they would have him boxed in if he decided to stay on the highway.

Regan frowned. If the suspect decided to hit the cane fields again, she would never be able to catch him in her Charger, and he could easily lose himself in the network of muddy roads that crisscrossed the land. She was new to the area—being originally from Tellico Plains, Tennessee—and had made a concerted effort to spend some downtime speaking to the old folks around town and trying to learn the ways of the swamp people. During one such conversation, an old man had told her that he and his buddies used to ride their horses across the vast expanse of cane fields and through the swamps beyond it to make their way to New Orleans. He said it was only about thirty miles to the east, but it would take them about a day and a half to get there because of the rough terrain and the numerous bayous they had to swim across.

Based on what the old man had said, Regan didn't believe a dirt bike could make it to New Orleans, but it definitely seemed possible to hide out for a long time in those vast swamplands.

Regan was just thinking a helicopter would come in handy, when

Melvin called over the radio and asked dispatch to request one from the sheriff's office. She smiled like she'd just guessed an answer to a puzzle on Wheel of Fortune, but that smile faded as she neared town and saw a flash of movement from the fields to the right. There—riding like he was breaking out of hell—was the red dirt bike everyone had been talking about. He was going so fast that the back tire would occasionally slide to the left or right and he would nearly lose control in the soft mud.

Regan was farther from the point where the cane road met up with Cypress Highway than the dirt bike was, but she was traveling faster. She looked from the bike to the intersecting point and back to the bike again. If she continued at this speed, she would reach the intersecting point at the same time. If she were justified in using deadly force, that might be a winning strategy, but she wasn't. If she didn't want to crash into the bike, she either needed to slow down or speed up. If she sped up, she would reach the intersecting point first and would be able to set up a road block, but if he sped past her, he would be gone.

Making her decision quickly, Regan hit the brakes and pulled to the shoulder. Trusting that Baylor would make it across town in time to seal off the northern portion of Cypress Highway, she whipped her vehicle around in the road and waited on the southbound shoulder, her foot hovered over the accelerator and her eyes remained glued to the rearview mirror.

As she watched, the front of the dirt bike dipped sharply as the suspect neared the intersection, and Regan gripped the steering wheel in anticipation. Baylor had just called out on the police radio that he was crossing the Market Street Bridge, and Takecia radioed that she was out with a couple of subjects at the campground where the suspect on the dirt bike had last been seen.

"Come on," Regan said, "turn this way."

And it did. The dirt bike slowed to a manageable speed when it reached Cypress Highway, and then it headed south. In an attempt not to alert the rider on the dirt bike, Regan's light bar was off and her siren wasn't blaring, but she was sure he would recognize her vehicle as a police cruiser as soon as he saw it—and that would be any second now, because he was rapidly gaining speed and closing in on her location.

As soon as it appeared he was committed to heading south, Regan stomped the accelerator to the floor. She left a layer of rubber on the asphalt as her vehicle shot off to the south. Within seconds, she was approaching sixty miles per hour, but it wasn't fast enough.

The dirt bike was already traveling at speeds much greater than that, because it blew past her like she was parked.

Cursing loudly, Regan punched the steering wheel and demanded more of her Charger. She kept her foot to the floor and a white-knuckled grip on the steering wheel as the vehicle picked up speed. The dirt bike had been reduced to a small blob in the distance and had been shrinking at an alarming rate, but the shrinkage began to slow as the horses in her engine started doing their jobs. The needle slid past eighty and was heading to ninety. She snatched up her radio and informed dispatch that she was in pursuit. She reported her location, direction of travel, and speed. She also gave a description of the suspect and bike, and reported that it didn't have a license plate.

As she thought ahead, she realized it was possible that the dirt bike would cross over to Old Blackbird Highway and head north, at which point it would try to get out of town. She hoped it would do so, because that was the only way to get some units in front of it. As of right now, there were no other police cars between the suspect and the Gulf of Mexico, so Regan was on her own. She had now exceeded 100 miles per hour. Even if the nearest unit would try to join in on the pursuit, it would never catch up to her because she'd had such a head start on them.

Trees grew thick along most of the eastern shoulder of Cypress Highway, but there was an area up ahead where the road curved away from the bayou. In that large space between the bayou and the highway, there was a long stretch of bulkhead where a barge crane stayed docked to move shells from several piles that were routinely stored there, and Regan knew this would afford her a look across the bayou.

As soon as Regan reached the open area, she was able to see between the piles of shells to the opposite side of Bayou Tail, and she gasped when she saw a long line of north-bound vehicles stopped on Old Blackbird Highway. Stuck in all of that traffic were dozens upon dozens of box trucks and eighteen-wheelers that were trying to make their way back from the coast. Some of those trucks would be loaded down with supplies that needed to go to various businesses throughout the country, while others were heading back to their home locations to pick up more supplies.

Regan hadn't been to the Mechant Loup Bridge in a few hours, but when she had been there, she had seen a long line of traffic stretching in the opposite direction as people tried to head south into, and through, town.

The opening in the trees suddenly closed up and Regan lost her view of the opposite highway. She shook her head in disgust and cursed the man in front of her. They were about ten miles south of town, so the line was at least that long—extending from the checkpoint to as far as she had been able to see to the south—and this one asshole was responsible for all of it. Not only had he killed three people and injured over a dozen more, but he was also single-handedly responsible for shutting down the day-to-day operations of an entire community.

Regan's siren was blaring now and her lights were flashing as her vehicle approached 130 miles per hour. The dirt bike and rider were growing larger now that she was gaining on them, and she knew it was only a matter of time before she caught up to him. She updated dispatch on their location and speed of travel, and then returned that free hand to the steering wheel. Her heart was pounding, because she knew that it would only take one small mishap for everything to go wrong at that rate of speed. Something as trivial as a flat tire could be the death of her.

Finally, she had come to within a few hundred yards of the suspect, so she eased off of the accelerator. She quickly closed the remaining gap and began pacing him at ninety-two miles per hour. The rider was crouched low on the seat. He turned his head once to see if she was still there, and then he seemed to be looking for a place to hide.

Regan realized he was slowing down, but he still wasn't going slow. They were clipping along at eighty-plus now, and it looked like he was considering turning down one of the many cane roads that were blurring past them. He even stood high in the saddle once, scanning the road ahead of him. After traveling another couple of miles, he down-shifted and his bike slowed considerably.

Thankfully, Regan had maintained some distance between them and hadn't collided with him when he dropped gears. Her siren was still screaming, but it had no effect on the man. He seemed to be completely ignoring her as he searched for a suitable road upon which to turn.

Holding onto the steering wheel with one hand, Regan let dispatch know that they had slowed and he was looking for a place to go. As she secured the mic on its holder, she remained wary, ready for anything. If he decided to turn around in the roadway and head north, that would be the best thing for her backup. However, if he took one of the many muddy roads they were passing, he would surely lose her in that slop. His tires were built for mud, hers were built for roads.

As the dirt bike slowed even more, Regan became increasingly wary. She allowed the distance between them to increase. She removed her seatbelt and shifted in her seat to make sure she had easy access to her pistol. The rider was zigzagging from the right lane to the left lane and then back to the right lane. Suddenly, he hit the brakes, whipped the bike around, and gunned the engine, heading straight for Regan.

She was traveling at a speed of forty-five when she hit the brakes and skidded to a stop. She didn't swerve out of his way—she only stopped in her lane of traffic and braced herself. If he chose to crash into her vehicle, that was his prerogative. At least the chase would be over.

The dirt bike was closing fast and picking up speed. Regan was about to duck under the dash at the moment of impact, when the rider suddenly swerved at the last second and zipped past her, racing to the north. Without wasting a second, Regan shifted to reverse, whipped the car around, and then punched it in drive and continued the chase.

This time around, there seemed to be something different about the man on the dirt bike. He seemed to be riding with a purpose now, as though he had made up his mind about something. He was also driving faster, and Regan had to remain at 135 for a few minutes before she could catch up to him again, and then hovered around 100 miles per hour as they continued northbound on Cypress.

After Regan gave her latest update to dispatch, Baylor radioed to say he was about five miles away from her location, and that he would set up a roadblock. Spike strips were out of the question for this scenario, because they would almost certainly result in the suspect's death. Despite the fact that this man had probably been the one who had plowed through Main Street and killed several people, his only sin at the moment was speeding and resisting arrest by flight. Had he produced a gun and started shooting, that would've changed things, but so far, he was only trying to escape.

Regan started to slow down a little, because they were quickly approaching the bend in the road where the shell piles were located, and she knew Baylor was somewhere on the other side of the curve. However, while she had reduced her speed, the rider on the dirt bike had leaned over the tank and revved his engine even louder. He was pulling away from her at a good clip, even as the curve loomed ahead.

"Baylor, watch out," Regan called over the radio. "The suspect's picking up speed around the curve and heading straight—oh, *shit!*"

Regan took her foot off the gas and watched with her mouth

agape as the suspect drove his dirt bike right off the road and straight for the tallest of the three piles of shells. He was surely going in excess of 100 miles per hour, and it was obvious he intended to try and jump the bayou.

Regan had ridden a dirt bike as a young girl growing up in the mountains of East Tennessee, and she had even jumped some hills from time to time. After landing in the hospital with a broken leg and a fractured collarbone from trying to jump the creek at her house, her dad had forbidden her from jumping any more bodies of water—and for good reason.

As the scene played out before her, it felt like her windshield had been transformed into a movie screen, and all she could do was watch in awe as the dirt bike hit the shell pile and climbed rapidly. The rear tire began kicking up shells almost immediately, and it was obviously losing speed as it ascended to the top of the hill. However, it was still traveling insanely fast when it reached the top, and the momentum carried it far into the air.

Regan was starting to think he had hit the shell pile hard enough to make it to the other side of the bayou, when something happened that neither the suspect nor she foresaw. The loss of torque from his rear tire spinning in the loose shells had changed the course of the bike, and the rider now found himself heading straight for the cables that operated the clamshell bucket on the barge crane.

When the dirt bike made contact with the cables, it did so with such force that the bike seemed to explode in pieces. The mangled body of the suspect squirted through the cables and splattered onto the top portion of the boom, where it seemed to hang suspended for a slow moment, before losing its grips and dripping down to the barge below.

"Um, dispatch," Regan said slowly, "the suspect is down."

CHAPTER 41

Near the suspect's tent

When I joined Shade and peered into the dome tent, I grunted. These were definitely our suspects. On the ground near a bunched-up blanket were several plastic zipper-seal bags, and even from where we stood, we could see that there was blood and pieces of flesh and fabric inside the bags.

"That's how they transferred the blood and tissue evidence from Wesley's truck to Max's truck," I said. "These are some really sick bastards. They've watched way too many crime scene shows for their own good. They learned just enough to be dangerous."

"Yeah." Shade scowled. "But what did they do with the truck? Why can't we find it?"

I was about to say I didn't know, but stopped when I heard Regan Steed come on the radio to say she was in pursuit of the suspect's dirt bike.

"Come on," I said, "let's take some pictures of the outside and inside of the tent and then tear it down. We'll bundle everything up inside and bring the whole thing with us. I'm sure Vanessa would prefer to come here to process it, but we don't have enough people to spare and I don't want to leave it unguarded in case the other suspect doubles back."

Shade nodded and went to work. He and I both took pictures of the outlaw camp and exterior of the tent from different angles with our cell phones, and then we unzipped the flaps of the tent and photographed the interior. We did a quick search of the inside, but only found two blankets, three zipper-seal bags containing remnants of blood and tissue, and two pairs of discarded latex gloves.

Once we had accounted for everything, we cut the tent strings, removed the poles, and carefully rolled up the fabric. It bundled up nicely, and I hoisted it onto my left shoulder, and we trudged off down the muddy road.

We each kept our hands near our pistols as we walked—half expecting to encounter the other suspect on the road—but we made it to the camp without incident. Just as we reached the end of the road, which happened to dump out into the large front yard of the campground where the oak trees grew huge, I heard Regan come over the radio to say the suspect was down.

I stopped walking and listened for more traffic.

"Do you need an ambulance?" Lindsey asked.

"Negative," Regan called back. "He's *very* Code One."

Code One was dead, so I guess that meant our suspect was *very* dead.

"Well," I muttered, "I guess he won't be answering any questions—at least not on this side of the grave."

Shade and I headed to my Tahoe and had almost reached it when Takecia came walking from the main house. She waved and approached us. I opened the lift gate on my Tahoe and stowed the tent inside while she talked.

"The owner let me search every camp, every shed, every barn, and everywhere else you could hide a truck," she said, "but it's nowhere on this property. It's just not here."

I sighed and lowered the gate. I pulled out my cell phone and scrolled to Melvin's name.

"Melvin, you can break down your checkpoint," I said when my friend answered. "The truck's gone, so I'm pretty sure they found a way to get it out of here."

"No one got through us," he said, "and there's no way he drove a truck through the woods. You can get a dirt bike through there, but not a vehicle. Even a four-wheeler or UTV wouldn't fit through those trees."

I considered that, and knew it could only mean one thing—the first suspect had slipped away before we had arrived.

"Come check out those shoe impressions that lead away from the outlaw camp and tell me what you think," I suggested. "They were definitely made after the rain, but compared to the tire tracks from the dirt bike we just saw, they don't look very fresh. I think he walked away from the camp before we arrived and took Wesley's truck out of here."

"But we've been crawling all over this area," Melvin countered. "Surely, we would've seen that truck if it was on the road. And there's no way he made it through the checkpoint, so he's got to be in town somewhere."

I rubbed my head and nodded. I agreed with most of what he had said, but I was pretty sure the truck had been here at some point, and now it was gone.

"I don't know how he did it, but he got out of here somehow," I said. "He probably did it when we were moving in on Max's truck. In fact, that's probably *exactly* why he planted the truck and made that call. It wasn't just to make us think we had the right vehicle, it was to distract us." I shook my head. "We need to focus our efforts somewhere else. This place is a waste of time now."

"Ten-four, I'm on my way," Melvin said. "Oh, and Amy wants you to call her. She left in Shade's truck to go check on Regan."

I nodded and made the call. She didn't even let me utter a word before she began talking.

"Hey, Clint, I stole Shade's truck and I'm headed to where the suspect got dead," she said. "I just talked to Regan and she said he's in pieces."

"In *pieces*?" I asked. "What do you mean?"

"He tried to use one of the shell piles as a ramp to jump the bayou, but he hit the operating cables on the crane claw thingy instead," she explained. "He squirted through those cables and then hit the boom. Somewhere along the way, he lost his head, an arm, and one foot. Regan said it looked like someone dumped a pot of spaghetti on the barge. She said she's never eating sloppy joe again. Oh, and we might not be able to identify this fool."

"Why?" I asked. "Just because he got decapitated?"

I saw Shade whip his head around to stare at me.

"Not just because he got decapitated, but because he lost his head," she explained. "His head's *gone*. It flew right off of him and into the bayou somewhere and, thanks to the helmet, it sank to the bottom like a brick."

"Shit!"

"You can say that again."

"Shit!" I looked up when I heard Melvin's truck barreling down the road toward the campground. While Shade seemed eager to hear what had happened in the police chase, he had overheard my conversation with Melvin, so he walked over and showed Melvin where we'd seen the boot impressions in the mud.

"Are we processing the scene or do we want Vanessa to do it?"

Amy asked, bringing my attention back to the chase between Regan and the suspect. “She’s probably getting tired of doing our dirty work.”

“Vanessa loves this stuff,” I said. “Besides, I need you with me. When you reach Regan, take some photos of the scene and body and see if the suspect’s got a driver’s license. I’ll give Vanessa a call now. She might still be close to town.”

After hanging up with Amy, I called Vanessa. I was relieved to learn that she was at a restaurant north of Rupe’s Dealership called Seafood Sarah. I knew the place well. Not long after I’d first moved into Mechant Loup, I had knocked out a man in that place.

“We’ve got another crime scene and I was wondering if you wouldn’t mind processing it,” I began slowly, almost cautiously. Although I’d sounded confident when I’d spoken with Amy, I was starting to think I was asking a lot of the young scientist. “Unless you’re worn out. I know we’ve been asking a lot of you and your team.”

“Nonsense!” she said. “The sheriff said I can see this one through to the end. Where is it and what happened?”

I explained about the pursuit and what had happened to the suspect, and I gave her the location.

“Oh, this’ll be interesting! I’ve never worked a decapitation before.” She almost sounded eager. She muffled the phone and told her team what was going on. I heard excited chatter in the background. “Okay, we’re wrapping up our meal right now. We’ll pay and get out of here right away. It might take us a little while to get through town because of the traffic, so please bear with us.”

I nodded and thanked her.

CHAPTER 42

After ending the call with Vanessa, I headed to where Shade and Melvin had disappeared down the muddy path. I walked toward where Shade and I had encountered the dirt bike, and I didn't have to travel far before I found them. Melvin was squatting beside a set of boot tracks, and he was testing the edges of one of them with his fingers. He looked up when I approached.

"You're right, it's more than a few hours old." He straightened. "If this suspect left out of here with the truck, he would've been gone before we set up the checkpoint. I still don't see how he got it out of the area without someone seeing it. Even if we were distracted with Max's truck, someone would've noticed that eyesore of a truck driving around. Everyone knows we're looking for it."

I couldn't argue with him, so I didn't. Instead, I turned to Shade and changed the subject.

"Oh, by the way," I said, "Amy stole your truck. When we leave here, I'll bring you to the Evel Knievel scene and you can reclaim it."

It appeared he liked the sound of that—not the part about the truck, but the part about visiting the crime scene.

I glanced over at Melvin, and it seemed as though he was still bothered by something. "What is it, Mel?"

He stabbed a finger in Shade's direction. "Shade, are you sure you didn't see Wesley's truck out here last night during that party?"

"I'm positive." Shade shook his head. "It definitely wasn't here. There were a lot of trucks here, but only two black Chevy trucks, and one of them ended up belonging to Max Broussard. The second one didn't have the dull black paint job Baylor described. It was shiny and new. Other than pickups, there were a lot of cars, that tractor over there, a ton of motorcycles and…"

Shade's voice trailed off and he grunted as he began to survey the giant front yard of the main house. He walked away from Melvin and me and did a complete circle, taking in the entire area.

"What is it?" I asked.

"There was a white box truck parked right there," he said, pointing toward a spot in the mud, "but it's gone now. It was big enough to fit a pickup."

Melvin and I immediately exchanged glances, and then we both nodded.

"Let's go!" I said, and headed for the main house. When we hurried up the steps, I knocked on the screen door and waited impatiently until Daisy's face appeared. She cracked a nervous smile.

"Someone said the killer was here." She stood there wringing her hands. "Is that true?"

"Yeah," I said, wanting to get straight to the point. "Look, do you remember seeing a box truck out here this morning?"

"A *box* truck?" her nose scrunched up. "What's that?"

"It's a delivery truck with a big closed-in cargo area," I explained, turning to point where Shade said it had been parked. "It was white and it was parked right over there."

"Oh, yeah, it was here this morning," she said. "It's actually been here all week."

"When did it leave?"

"Um, right after Lucille left for the store this morning, and before y'all came over here."

I squeezed my fists. "What time did Lucille leave this morning?"

"Hold on, let me get her." Daisy disappeared inside the kitchen. When she returned, she had Lucille Cheramie in tow.

"I hear we're having a bit of excitement around here," Lucille said. "What can I help y'all with? Do y'all need to search some other places? I thought Officer Gayle covered everything."

"What time did you leave for the store this morning?" I asked hurriedly.

"Well, it was about seven o'clock," she said. "After I finished cooking breakfast. I had run out of dough for beignets, so I went to the store to get more."

I nodded impatiently. "The men who came here in that box truck, do you know who they were?"

"I should have it written down," she said, turning to go back into the house. "Come on in the kitchen while I get my book."

I shot a glance at Melvin. He was fidgeting like I was. We could feel the suspect slipping away. Daisy stood there looking embarrassed while we waited in the kitchen for Lucille to return. I caught her glancing at Shade from time to time, but he didn't seem to notice.

When Lucille returned, her nose was already in her notebook. "Let's see…they arrived on Monday and they rented one of the tent pads. Number twelve."

"We walked by that tent pad," Shade said. "It was empty."

I nodded. It either meant the people at number twelve had nothing to do with our case and had simply left the campground, or they were our suspects and had set up the outlaw camp to avoid being observed by other guests.

"Do you have their names?" I pressed.

"Only one of them," she said. "He was the one who paid for everything. Of course, he paid with cash, so I have no way of verifying who he was, but he gave his name as Keith Collins."

I blinked. Who the hell was Keith Collins? I glanced at Shade and Melvin, but they both shrugged. The name meant nothing to them.

"Does it say where he's from?" I asked.

"Now, that's something we do ask, because we like to get a sense for where our guests originated." She glanced back down at the notepad. "It says here that he was from Lake Charles, and he paid for one week, so he doesn't have to leave until Monday at noon."

"Would there have been any reason for you to get their addresses or cell phone numbers?" I asked.

"Yeah, I did get his phone number." She glanced up. "Are you ready for it?"

I pulled out my pen and nodded. As she called it out, I copied it on the palm of my hand. I then fished out my cell phone and pulled up the picture we'd retrieved from the surveillance cameras at M & P Grill. I showed it to Lucille.

"Do you recognize this man?" I asked, feeling confident that she would say yes. She didn't.

"I've never seen him before."

I looked at the picture and then turned it back to Lucille. "Look again," I said. "Are you sure this wasn't one of those men?"

"Look, the man who came up to the house to pay wore sunglasses and a baseball cap, so I don't know what he looks like. The other man stayed by the truck, so I never got a look at him." She tapped my phone screen. "I've never seen this man, unless he was the one wearing sunglasses, but I don't think so. His nose is shaped differently."

I cursed under my breath and then asked if she'd seen anyone on a dirt bike.

"No, and I would've killed them if I could've gotten my hands on them!" Her face twisted in anger. "They were running around at all hours, disturbing my guests and probably tearing up the trails. I don't allow dirt bikes on my property for that—

"Wait just a minute!" Lucille caught her breath and then scowled. "Was this Keith Collins the one who was on that dirt bike? Is he the one who was disturbing my guests?"

I wasn't positive, so I told her I didn't know.

"If I find out it's him, I'll throw him out of here and not refund his deposit." She grunted. "I don't play around like that. They sign an agreement to keep things peaceful, and I expect them to live up to that agreement, or there will be consequences."

I couldn't think of anything else to ask her, so I thanked her and headed for my Tahoe. I stopped outside the driver's door and turned to Shade first.

"How big was that box truck?"

"It was at least a twenty-two-footer," Shade said.

"Okay, get on your phone and research the dimensions of the cargo area, and also the outer dimensions of a Chevy Silverado." I then turned to Melvin. "Call the checkpoint and tell them to be on the lookout for a white box truck that's at least twenty-two feet long."

They both grabbed their phones and sprang into action. While they did that, I grabbed my own phone and dialed the number for Keith Collins.

I held my breath as the phone began to ring. It rang once, twice, three times…and on and on, until it went to voicemail. A recording told me that my suspect hadn't set up his voicemail yet. I cursed.

Shade looked up, and I nodded to let him know I could listen to him.

"The inner dimensions of a standard twenty-two-foot box truck is a little less than twenty-two feet long, right about eight feet high, and about eight feet wide," he said. "A Silverado would fit right in there. They might have to crawl through the window to get out, but it would work."

I shook my head. While these suspects had made some mistakes, they had done a decent job of hiding Wesley's pickup from us. If they had loaded it into that box truck and already driven it through the checkpoint north of the Mechant Loup Bridge, we might never recover it.

I lifted my phone and dialed Keith's number again. It rang

several more times and was about to go to voicemail again, when I heard a click. I held my breath and waited.

"Clint?" the voice on the other end said. "Why in the hell are you calling a dead guy's phone?"

CHAPTER 43

Abby Bruce's Residence

Susan was just parking in Abby Bruce's driveway when she heard Regan call in on the radio that she was in pursuit of the suspect's dirt bike. She wanted desperately to speed off in that direction and get in on the chase, but she knew better than to do that right now. Instead, she just sat there in her Tahoe and listened to the updates on the radio, feeling nauseous and useless.

Finally, she heard Regan call out that the suspect was down and the chase was over. She breathed a long sigh of relief and stepped out of her Tahoe. She ignored the rumbling in her belly and made her way to the front steps of the Bruce home. It was well past lunch and neither she nor any of her officers had eaten yet, and none of them would as long as they were on the heels of their suspects. She felt as though they were close, and they couldn't let up now. Their persistence had paid off and they'd gotten one of the bad guys, but the second suspect and the truck were still out there somewhere. She was hoping this visit might lead to more answers.

Moments after Susan knocked on the door, a woman with a quick smile answered, and her appearance shocked Susan. Although the woman appeared pregnant and had more curves than Malory, she bore a striking resemblance to the victim.

As for Abby Bruce, her smile quickly faded when she saw Susan's uniform. Susan wore her BDUs like she always did when working parades, but it was a police uniform nonetheless, and she could tell the woman was equally as shocked as she had been.

"Oh, no, Chuck," Abby hollered over her shoulder, "it's true! It was my truck!"

Susan cocked her head to the side as footsteps pounded from the back of the house and a man approached the front door. The couple just stood wide-eyed, staring at her in disbelief.

"Is it okay if I come inside?" Susan asked. "I don't want to have this conversation where the neighbors might be able to hear us."

Abby nodded and ushered Susan through the doorway. She and her husband led the way to a tiny living room furnished with a love seat, a rocker, and a box for a coffee table. Abby pointed to the rocker.

"Please, take it," she said, dropping nervously to the love seat with Chuck. "It's really comfortable. My grandpa made it."

Susan took her seat and leaned forward. "What did you mean when you told Chuck it was your truck?"

"Well, we got a call from some friends of ours this morning, and they said someone killed a bunch of people last night," Abby explained. "They, um, they said it was the guy who bought my old truck that did it. They said he used the truck to kill them."

Susan frowned. She hadn't considered such a rumor spreading around town. Poor Wesley Chouest was lying on a cold slab at the morgue, a victim of this heinous act, and people were blaming him for the murders.

"No," Susan corrected. "Wesley Chouest was a victim. Someone stole his truck and ran right over him and his wife. That's why I'm here."

Abby clutched at her neck. "But...but why? Is the truck still registered in my name? I sold it, but am I still responsible for it? Am I in some kind of trouble?"

"No, not at all, but I have some questions about the spare key," Susan explained.

Abby let out a sigh. "Oh, my, I thought I was in trouble."

"No, you can't be responsible for someone else's actions," Susan explained with a shake of her head. "The reason I'm here is because Wesley's father told me he never got a spare key for the truck when he bought it. When I went by the dealership, they said you only turned in one key with the trade-in."

"Yeah, because that's all I had."

Susan groaned inwardly. She had at least hoped for another direction in which to go, like maybe the woman had bought it from someone else who had held onto the spare key and possibly used it to commit the crime. But now, they might be back to operating under the belief that the truck had been stolen, which would greatly increase their suspect pool and complicate matters. Susan did wonder at the identity of the man Regan had chased. She would need that name as soon as possible to see if it meant anything to the couple she was now interviewing. She asked them to excuse her while she sent a text message asking Clint to provide her the information right away, and then she glanced back up.

"Did you ever have the spare key?" Susan asked.

Abby hesitated. "No, the one I gave to the dealership was the only one I ever had."

Susan sensed there was a lot more to the story of the truck. She settled into the rocker and asked Abby how it was that she had come to be in possession of the truck.

"Um, well, I was married before. His name was Norris Mills. It was his truck. He got it from his dad when he graduated high school. It was his dad's most prized possession and he promised it to Norris if he would finish school." Abby paused to shake her head in disgust. "I swear he loved that truck more than he loved me. Anyway, I won it in the divorce and he didn't like it, so he refused to give me the spare key. I spoke with the original dealership and they said I could have one made, but I never did. After I moved down here, I decided I didn't want it anymore, so I just traded it in."

"So, Norris has the spare key?"

"As far as I know. I haven't spoken to him or any of his family since we got divorced—and I prefer it that way."

Rather than jumping around, Susan decided to start from the beginning. "How long were you married to Norris?" she asked.

"A little over three years," Abby said. "I was going to college to be a lawyer when we met, but he talked me into quitting school to stay home and have a family. He ran his own business, so he said I would never have to work a day in my life. As a young girl struggling in college, that sounded great to me at the time. It was like a fantasy come true. And things were okay for a few years, but then they went downhill."

Susan hadn't noticed any pictures of kids around the small living room in which she sat, so she asked Abby if she had any. The woman smiled and touched her belly.

"We've got one on the way," she said, "but I didn't have any with Norris. His whole idea was to keep me home and pregnant, but that never worked out. He blamed me for being barren, but I think he was sterile. Well, at least I know now that it wasn't me. Anyway, I thank God every day that we never had kids together."

"Why's that?" Susan asked.

"Because if we had kids together, I would've never left him," she said with a frown, "and I would've had to live in misery for what he did to me."

"What'd he do to you?"

"Well, after we made our third-year anniversary, he started coming home late at night, claiming he had to work, but he was the boss. The boss doesn't have to work late if he doesn't want to. And besides, he ran a trucking company, so there wasn't much to do while the trucks were on the road." Abby took a breath and exhaled forcefully. "I started getting suspicious when he came home one night smelling like perfume."

"Did you ask him about it?"

"Nope, I pretended I didn't notice," Abby said smugly. "The next morning, I borrowed a friend's car and followed him to work. I parked down the street from the shop and waited. Around lunchtime, I saw his truck leave the shop. I couldn't see who got into it from where I was parked, but I followed him to this cheap motel in town, and that's when I saw his secretary get out with him. What really pissed me off was that I knew her. We were friends—or so I thought—but you know what? She got played, because he owned his own business and had a lot of money, but he was taking her to this sleazy place where they rented by the hour. That should've been a warning sign to her, but she didn't realize she was being used until he dumped her and fired her in an effort to get me back. I wasn't having it. Like that Carrie Underwood song goes, *next time that he cheats, it won't be on me*!"

CHAPTER 44

Susan found herself admiring Abby Bruce's tenacity. She asked Abby what she did when she caught her husband and his secretary at the motel.

"My friend had this dash camera for in case she got in a wreck, and I used it to film them going in and out of the motel room," she explained. "I then followed them back to the office and kept watching. I found a better place to hide where I could film the parking lot and waited for the office to close. A few drivers came and went throughout the day, but when it was time for the shop to close, they were the only two left inside. An hour later, they both came outside and he walked her to her car. They stood by her car for a while and then kissed before he finally went to his truck and left."

"Did you say anything to him that night?" Susan asked curiously.

"Nope." Abby shook her head. "That was a Tuesday. On Wednesday, I called a lawyer and set up a meeting for the next day. On Thursday, I signed the papers with my lawyer to file for divorce. On Friday, I packed up my Suburban and moved back in with my mom and dad. I didn't say a word to Norris. I just put a copy of the dash cam footage on his laptop and taped a message to the screen telling him to play the video."

Susan leaned far back in the rocker and studied this unassuming woman. She then glanced at Chuck.

"You'd better never piss her off," Susan said.

"Oh, I know it." He nodded his head. "That's one of the reason's I love her. She won't let anyone take advantage of her."

"I can't imagine that the divorce went smoothly," Susan said, an image beginning to form in her mind. Abby was pregnant, so she was a little heavier than Malory, but at night, approaching the same truck that Abby used to drive, Malory could've easily been mistaken for Norris' ex-wife.

"No, it didn't go smoothly at all," Abby acknowledged. "It was hard to get him served with the divorce papers. He would lock his shop and refuse to answer when a process server would show up. He was very careful when he came and left the house or the shop, and the deputies didn't have time to sit around stalking him. Finally, my lawyer hired a female private detective to follow him. She got him the first day. She put on a short skirt and a low-cut blouse and he opened the door to his shop right away."

"That must've made him mad."

"It did, so one night, he got one of his friends to sneak onto my parents' property and steal the Suburban right out from under me. I'd never really worked since college, so I was having a hard time finding a job, and it became impossible once they stole the Suburban. I called the police, but they said there was nothing they could do since it was community property. I called my lawyer, but she said the same thing. She said I'd just have to wait it out until the community property settlement hearing."

"Speaking of that, if Norris got his truck before y'all were married, how'd you win it in the divorce?" Susan asked.

"Well, the Suburban was already paid for, so Norris went and sold it right after he took it from me," she explained. "The dummy thought that if he sold it and spent the money he got before the divorce was final, then he wouldn't have to give me any of it. Turns out, he was dead wrong, and he owed me half for the Suburban, half for the business, and half for the house. Only problem was, he had run the business into the ground and he couldn't buy me out, so we were forced to sell off everything, including the house. Instead of money, I got his gun collection and the truck, and he ended up with my credit card bills to Target and Ulta."

"Ouch," Susan said. "That must've really pissed him off."

"Oh, it did. He loved that truck and his gun collection more than anything else in the world."

Susan glanced down at her notes. "So, how long have you been divorced?"

"It's been four years now."

"And where'd you live when you were married to Norris?"

"Lake Charles."

"And how long have you lived here?"

"Two years now," she said. "I met Chuck at an LSU football

game three years ago, when I was finishing up my degree. He told me he loved me that first night, and we hadn't even held hands yet."

Chuck's face turned instantly red. "I mean, when you know, you know."

"So, you got to finish college?"

"Yes, ma'am, but it was rough," she said. "I couldn't afford an apartment in Baton Rouge, so I drove two hours back and forth every day. Now that I live here, I'm still going to Baton Rouge for law school, but it's not as far of a drive."

"Congratulations on pursuing that dream," Susan said. "Did you drive the primer black truck to and from school?"

"Absolutely," Abby said, "and I heard it pissed him off every time he saw it on the road."

Susan was thoughtful. Abby was a long way from home. If she had remained in Lake Charles for two years, why hadn't Norris reclaimed his truck back then? If he was, indeed, the culprit, why had he waited four years and traveled over 200 miles to use his spare key to steal back his truck? And how had he found Abby down here in the swamps?

"When did you and Chuck get married?" Susan asked, an idea coming to her. "I know you've been living here for two years, but did y'all also get married two years ago?"

"No, we got married last June."

Susan could see the newspaper article now: *Abby Mills, of Lake Charles, Louisiana, to wed Chuck Bruce, of Mechant Loup, Louisiana.*

"Did an announcement go out in the papers?" Susan asked.

"Yeah, it did."

"Here and in Lake Charles?"

"Yes, ma'am." Abby cocked her head to the side. "Why do you think that's important?"

"I'm wondering if that's how Norris found you," she explained. "Whoever stole the truck, it appears they had the spare keys to it, so it had to be Norris. And our victim, she looks a lot like you. I hate to break this to you, but it looks like they might've been targeting you."

Abby's mouth fell open. "You really think they thought it was me?"

"Someone got into the truck and waited for the precise moment when Malory and Wesley were approaching it before they sped off," she explained. "And two weeks earlier, someone slashed the tires on the truck. I'm not saying this to alarm you, but we think the spare key has a strong connection to our case. From what you're now telling me, Norris Mills has that spare key."

"Yes, he does," Abby said, still seemingly shocked by the information.

"When was the last time you've seen or heard from him?" Susan asked.

"It's been a long time." She shook her head. "Even when I was still living there, I never ran into him. Lake Charles is a big place, you know. Now, we used to have mutual friends, and I'd run into some of them from time to time. They'd tell me that they saw him in a bar or at the store and that he would always mention still being in love with me and how he wanted me back. One of our old friends said Norris mentioned being pissed when he saw his old truck driving across the city, but that's all hearsay. The last time I saw him myself was the day of the divorce, when we were in the courthouse. My lawyer got the judge to let me walk out first to make sure he didn't start trouble with me outside."

"What happened when he lost the business?" Susan asked. "Did he ever go back to work?"

"I don't know. Someone told my mom that he had started using drugs, and that all he talked about was rebuilding his business and winning me back, or some such nonsense." She shrugged. "I don't know any of this firsthand, because when I divorced him, I moved on and never looked back."

Susan nodded, glanced around the modest home. "What about his gun collection? Do you still have that?"

She shook her head. "I sold the guns and used the cash for a down payment on my Jeep Grand Cherokee. I knew I wouldn't get much for the old Silverado because of all the mileage it had on it, and I didn't want a big car note, so I got rid of the whole gun collection. I'm applying for jobs in New Orleans and La Mort, so I need reliable transportation."

Susan asked a few more follow-up questions before pulling out her cell phone. "We were able to retrieve video footage from the night the truck tires were slashed," she said, accessing the image Amy had disseminated earlier. She didn't know what Norris Mills looked like, but she would've bet money this was him. "Do you recognize this man?"

Abby's eyes widened. "Yeah, that's Norris' best friend! He's the one who stole my Suburban out from under me! Where is this?"

"M & P Grill."

"What on earth is he doing in town?" While Abby had seemed shocked earlier by the thought of someone targeting her, it was nothing compared to the sheer horror that now spread across her face. Seeing the picture had made it very real for her. She glanced toward the door. “Is…is Norris really here with him?”

“Like I told you, we believe he’s involved,” Susan said soothingly. “He had the spare key to the truck, so the only thing that makes sense is that it’s him.”

Abby gulped and grabbed at Chuck’s arm. “I know you said it, but I didn’t believe it. It…it just seems too crazy to be true.”

“Do you need me to put a deputy on your house?” Susan asked, knowing all of her officers were busy and she would have to borrow a deputy from Sheriff Turner. “We can provide around-the-clock protection if necessary.”

“There’s no need for that,” Chuck said quietly. “I’m not gonna let him hurt Abby.”

Chuck seemed to be a man of few words, but the words he did speak carried a lot of weight.

Susan pulled a business card from her left breast pocket and handed it to Abby. “Call me if you need anything at all.”

“Before I go, I’ll need the name of Norris’ best friend.”

“Fred,” Abby said. “Fred Hatton.”

“What’s his cell number?”

CHAPTER 45

Dirt bike crash scene

I saw Amy and Regan huddled over Keith Collins' lifeless body when I drove up to the scene with Shade. Melvin was right behind us, and he was talking excitedly on the phone when he reached me.

"The deputies at the checkpoint said they've been having box trucks come through there all morning long," he said, "and there's a bunch of them in the line right now waiting to leave town. I told them to start asking to search them, but if they say no, there's nothing we can do. If I was one of the drivers, I'd probably tell them to screw off and let me through, especially after sitting there for so long."

As I pondered his question, an idea came to me. Not only would it help in our search for the remaining suspect, but it would help to keep the traffic moving. Of course, if the suspect had already driven the box truck through the checkpoint, we were screwed.

"You still have the key to Wesley's truck, right?" I asked.

Melvin nodded.

"Get to the checkpoint right away and tell them to let the cars go by slowly," I explained. "When a box truck approaches, tell the deputies to stop traffic for a second. When they do, I want you to press the alarm button on the key fob and see if the horn—"

Melvin didn't even let me finish. He whipped around and was gone in a flash.

Amy and Regan both turned when the tires to his truck kicked up shells as he sped off. Once Shade and I reached the barge where pieces of the dead guy had rained down from the cables above, Amy tossed Shade his truck keys.

"Where in the hell is Melvin going in such a hurry?" she asked.

I explained the plan for the checkpoint and then indicated the dead guy. "Did you find his wallet?"

"Yep," she said, holding up a plastic evidence bag that contained his wallet. "Lucille was right. His name is Keith Collins and he's from Lake Charles, but that's all we know about him at the moment. I called Lindsey to do some background work on him, but she's running something for Susan right now, so it'll be a minute."

I nodded absently as I studied my surroundings. It seemed like this Collins fellow had watched too many Evel Knievel stunts. While a professional might've attempted to jump the bayou from one of those shell piles, it would've certainly come with a warning that stated, *Don't try this at home*, and they would've definitely removed the barge crane before the jump.

I had been sorely disappointed earlier when Amy had answered Keith's phone, because I was hoping he would be the suspect who was still at large. If the remaining suspect would've answered, I might've been able to talk him into surrendering or at least find out why he was doing this. If all else would've failed, we could've begun tracking his GPS coordinates and hopefully capture him that way. A search of his cell phone records could've certainly told us his location at the time of my call, but we no longer needed those records—except to find out the identity of his accomplice.

"Did the stuntman receive any other calls on his cell phone?" I asked Amy.

She shook her head. "You're the only one crazy enough to talk to dead people."

"Did you check his calls?"

"Nah, his phone's locked," she said. "The only thing I can do is answer if someone calls, but no one else has."

I pointed to the phone. "Keep it with you in case the other suspect calls."

It was right around then that Vanessa drove up in her Suburban. I turned and joined her in the parking lot. I told her about the campsite we'd discovered and how we'd located plastic bags containing blood and tissue samples. I also explained that I'd wrapped up all of the evidence inside the tent and carried it out that way.

"I know it's not the most ideal method of evidence collection," I conceded, "but we had to get out of the woods in a hurry and I didn't want to leave anything behind in case the other suspect returned to destroy everything."

Vanessa nodded her understanding, but she was barely paying attention to me. Her eyes were fixed on where Amy and Regan were still standing over the body.

"Today has been a different kind of day, that's for sure," she said absently, before telling one of her techs to retrieve the balled-up tent from my Tahoe. She then gave me a courtesy nod and eagerly headed for the scene, followed closely by her other techs.

This was a new scene for me, too. In all of my years working as a detective, both here and in La Mort, I'd never responded to a scene where a rider had died trying to jump a bayou with a dirt bike. I wondered what must've gone through Keith's mind as he saw the cables quickly approaching through the air. Once he went airborne, there was nothing he could do. No course correction, no stopping—no nothing.

I glanced up at the cables and could see pieces of his flesh twisted into the metal cables. I shook my head. Vanessa would have to call the crane operator to come out to the scene and lower the boom, because there was no way she and her team could get up there to gain access to the DNA evidence.

My cell phone rang and I glanced down at the screen. It was my wife.

"Clint, I've been able to identify the man who slashed Wesley's tires." Her words came out in rapid succession. "His name's Fred Hatton and he's best friends with Norris Mills. They're both from Lake Charles."

"Who's Norris Mills?" I asked. The name hadn't come up in our investigation so far, so I had no clue how he factored into the current events.

"He was the original owner of the truck," she explained. "Well, his dad was the original owner, but his dad gave it to him as a graduation gift. He owned a business and he was married to Abby Bruce, only she was Abby Mills at the time. She's since divorced him, because he was cheating on her with his secretary. Anyway, the primer black Silverado truck and his gun collection were his prized possessions, but he lost all of it in the divorce."

"Did he have to sell it?" I asked.

"No, Abby was awarded the items because he took her Suburban when they first separated, sold it, and spent the cash," Susan said. "He actually thought if he spent the money before the divorce was final no one would know about it and he wouldn't have to report it in the settlement. If you ask me, he got what he deserved."

"Sounds like it."

"And get this—Abby Bruce looks just like Malory, except she's pregnant."

I nodded thoughtfully. "So, we're thinking Norris Mills came here to reclaim his truck and kill his wife to avenge his damages during the divorce?"

"No, we're thinking it was Fred Hatton," she said. "Lindsey told me Amy asked her to run Keith Collins through the system. Is he the other suspect?"

I told her he was.

"Good. I checked both names to see if they had any social media accounts. I found a Keith Collins and a Fred Hatton, both from Lake Charles, on this one social media site and they're both friends. I believe Fred's working with Keith, and he's gonna be the one driving the box truck."

"But what about Norris?" I asked. "Wouldn't the ex-husband be the most likely of all suspects?"

"He would," she conceded, "if he was still alive."

"Wait…he's dead?"

"Yep. When I ran his name online, I found an obituary from two weeks ago."

"How'd he die?"

"It didn't say."

"Two weeks ago…" I was thoughtful. "Wesley's tires were slashed two weeks ago. That can't be a coincidence. We need to find out how he died. Did the obituary list any family members?"

"Yeah, he was survived by his dad, one sister, a brother, three uncles, two aunts, and thirteen cousins who weren't named," she said. "He was preceded in death by his mom, four grandparents, a brother, and an aunt. I've got some addresses and numbers for a few of them, and I'm about to start making contact. I'll let you know as soon as I find out how he died."

"Okay," I said, and then asked, "What do we know about Fred?"

"There's not a lot to know. He's a plumber from Lake Charles. It says here that he's married. He's got pictures of himself with three different kids throughout the page. It doesn't list their names, but they're obviously his kids or his wife's kids. I'm sending his picture out in a group message so all of y'all will get it. This has got to be our guy, Clint."

"If he has a wife and kids, why would he risk it all to come down here, steal a truck, and run down a bunch of people for a friend who's already dead?"

"What about vengeance?" she offered. "He came all the way

down here from Lake Charles two weeks ago to cut Wesley's tires, so why not come back and steal the truck? Besides, he was the one who stole Abby's Suburban for Norris during the divorce, only it wasn't considered theft because it was community property."

I couldn't think of a feasible argument, so I just asked if he had a criminal record.

"Nope, they're all clean."

"I just don't get it, Sue," I said. "Why would he go from nothing to murder just like that—especially if he has a wife and kids?"

"We could ask the same thing of Keith Collins," she said. "He's got a wife and kids, too, but we know for a fact that he just tried to jump Bayou Tail on a dirt bike. And look, it could be that they really thought Malory was Abby, and Wesley was her lover."

"So, you think they killed them intentionally?"

"I think so," she said, "and I think they blame Abby for Norris' death. She said Norris started using drugs heavily after the divorce, so it's possible he overdosed. Although his actions were the reason for the divorce, I'm sure his friends blamed her for leaving him and taking everything."

"Well, it's all we've got," I said, pulling my phone away from my ear to study Fred's picture. I could see the resemblance between him and the man in the surveillance footage. "Okay, put out the BOLO. If nothing else, we've got him for slashing tires to the tune of a few thousand dollars."

While I had been talking to Susan, Shade had been walking around the parking lot surveying the ground. I had noticed him drop to his knees a few times and he even took pictures of something he saw near one of the shell piles. It was the shortest of the piles, and the top of it was flat across the top, while the others were tall and rounded.

The plateau was about thirty yards across, and it appeared to have been used as a work area, because there was a welding machine and some other pieces of equipment positioned off to one side. Shade had inspected this area carefully, and was now making his way across the top of the plateau. He suddenly stopped and looked up in my direction. When we made eye contact, he waved excitedly for me to join him up on the plateau.

"I've got to go," I told Susan. "Shade's calling me. Thanks for running this down. That's some amazing work. If you weren't the chief of police, I'd try to steal you from the patrol section and bring you over to the detective side."

"Shut up," she said with a laugh, but then grew serious. "Oh, and don't think I'm not aware of what you're up to, you little thief."

"What do you mean?" I asked innocently. "Who're you talking about?"

"You just mentioned his name," she said. "I see how you're showing him all the ropes and filling his head with all of your investigative stories and lessons. At first, I thought you just wanted to help him be a safe and productive patrol officer, but I now realize you're trying to groom him to be the next detective. You already know Baylor and Melvin are patrol dogs for life, so you're trying to win the new guy over before he comes to the dark side and gets a taste of real police work."

"I love you, but I have to go," I said with a laugh. "My detective just found something."

CHAPTER 46

"Look at these tire tracks and gouges in the shells," Shade said when I was standing beside him on the plateau. "It looks like a truck backed up to this pile of shells, and another truck drove right up against it."

I stared in awe at the marks at our feet. The top of the plateau was about five feet high, and the tire tracks along the top of the plateau went up one side and disappeared on the other side, seemingly into nothingness—or, as we now knew, into the cargo area of a box truck that had been backed up against it.

"This is how they loaded the pickup into the box truck," I said, studying the rest of the parking lot. "Keith knew what he was doing. He was familiar with this area, because he had already been here. He knew he would have to be heading north to jump the shell pile, so that's why he hauled ass to the south before turning around and coming back this way."

I stared across the bayou and scowled. Why was he trying to jump to the other side? Of course, there was the obvious reason, which was that he was trying to escape Regan's pursuit. I then glanced to the south before swiveling my head back around to face the bayou again.

"They were driving around here scouting the area before the parade even started," I mused aloud, "so they knew about this place. They had planned ahead to use this spot to load up the truck. I bet one suspect was waiting here in the box truck while the other suspect stole Wesley's pickup and headed south on Old Blackbird. When he reached the bridge south of town, he crossed onto Cypress Highway and headed right to this location. As soon as they loaded the pickup into the box truck, it was over. Y'all were flooding the area, but the pickup was already gone—hidden in plain sight."

Shade nodded. "We probably drove right by them and never gave them a second look."

He was right. It had taken some time for our officers to break through the parade lines and start searching for Wesley's pickup, and that would've given the suspects enough time to load up the truck and hit the road. The easiest thing would've been for them to file into traffic and try to make their way out of town, but people had died, so they knew we would never stop looking for that pickup. The only way they would be free to drive Wesley's truck in public without fear of there being a BOLO on it would be to leave behind a fall truck. And if they went through that much trouble, they meant to keep Wesley's truck for themselves.

It was a brilliant plan, and it might've worked had Baylor not gotten a good look at the paint job. A discrepancy in a lay witness' description could be explained away, because witnesses make mistakes all the time, especially at night and during times of extreme stress. However, I knew Baylor would never make such a mistake. He was battle-tested and he was excellent under pressure.

I turned and pointed south along Cypress Highway.

"I'm betting the box truck headed south this morning when it left the campground," I said. "Once it crossed the bridge south of here and merged into traffic on Old Blackbird Highway, it would've blended right in and looked like any other delivery truck heading back from the coast. Depending on how much the traffic has moved in the last few hours, he could be anywhere from Lafayette to Lake Charles by now. At least we have a name to go on."

I stopped talking for a second and considered everything I knew so far. I was rubbing my chin when it hit me.

"Wait a minute," I said. "He's got to still be here! When we ran into Keith, he was leaving the campground to meet up with the box truck. Fred wouldn't leave Keith behind."

I paced back and forth, trying to think like our two suspects. "They're supposed to meet up on Old Blackbird," I finally said. "That's why Keith was trying to jump the bayou. Fred isn't in line—he's somewhere on the other side waiting for Keith to show up."

I hollered for Amy and Regan to join us, and I quickly called Melvin.

"What's up?" he asked when he answered.

"I don't think the truck's in line," I said. "I think he's parked somewhere waiting for Keith. He won't leave town without his accomplice."

"Roger that," Melvin said. "Do you want me to head south or wait here? So far, we've had about ten box trucks come through, and I'm not getting a response from the key alarm."

"Start heading south," I said. "Stop and press the panic button on the key fob near every box truck you see. We're gonna start working the line from this end, looking for any box trucks that are pulled over."

When Amy and Regan had walked up to Shade and me, I told Shade to head north on Cypress Highway and start searching the back side of town. He was gone before I turned to Regan.

"Cross the bridge and head south on Old Blackbird," I said. "Amy and I will cross the bridge and head north."

"Won't we get bogged down in traffic?" Amy asked as we headed for my Tahoe.

"We'll run lights and siren," I said. "If we can't make it down the left lane, we'll take the shoulder of the road."

I quickly got onto the road and raced behind Regan, heading south on Cypress Highway. I indicated her car with a nod of my head.

"How's she doing?"

"Good."

"She was okay with the crash?"

"Regan's got her head screwed on tight," Amy said. "That kind of shit doesn't bother her. She wishes it wouldn't have happened, but she knows it was his choice."

"Indeed, it was his choice, and a stupid one." I slowed as a box truck approached us heading north. When it was still a few yards away, I got a good look at the driver and saw that it wasn't Fred.

"What if Fred isn't the driver?" Amy asked, twisting around to follow the truck with her eyes as it drove by. "What if there were three suspects?"

I had been worrying about that myself, and I was hoping Susan would be able to provide more answers.

We encountered a few more cars heading north on the highway. Some of them were probably locals trying to get home, while others were no doubt trying to use Cypress as a detour to bypass the long line on Old Blackbird Highway. They probably figured if they could pop out onto Main Street farther to the north, they would get to cut the line. It might or might not work for these drivers and I didn't care either way. What I did care about were the box trucks. If enough of them did the same thing, it would be impossible to keep track of them.

Fred—if he was indeed the driver—could have easily gotten lost in town or on some back road. He could've secreted the box truck in a garage of a vacant home or a tractor barn out in the fields. While it seemed the original goal had been to reclaim Norris' truck, it was possible that he had left by some other means to avoid being captured. Or, he could be sitting inside the truck right now waiting for the heat to die down so he could escape.

Although I'd seen a number of sheriff's office patrol cars in the area helping us in our search efforts, we didn't have the personnel to send into every cane field and cow pasture or down every street. Hell, we didn't even have the authority to start searching barns out in the pastures and fields. Such was one of the advantages of being a criminal. He could go anywhere without a warrant and hide.

I had just reached the bridge and cursed out loud when I saw the traffic backed up on it. Regan was blasting her siren and trying to force the cars that were already on the bridge onto our side of the bayou, while trying to keep more cars from clogging the artery. She wasn't having much luck. Amy jumped out and began hollering at drivers to get their asses out of the way. Within a minute, she had the left lane of the bridge clear and Regan was able to squeeze through. Amy held the traffic at bay while I crossed the bridge, and then I waited for her to rejoin me.

I shook my head when we crossed over to the left shoulder of Old Blackbird Highway and began heading north. The cars stretched for as far as I could see to the front and rear. If the killer wasn't in line waiting to cross the Mechant Loup Bridge, or parked along the highway, I didn't know how we would ever find him.

CHAPTER 47

Mechant Loup Police Department

Susan was itching to be out on the road with her officers, but she knew it was best for her to stay off the road for the moment. Besides, someone had to do the digging while the others were searching for the killers. Lindsey could run anything they asked her to run and she was capable of doing whatever digging they needed her to do, but she simply didn't have the time. At the moment, she was handling radio traffic for all of their officers, plus a dozen or more sheriff's office deputies, not to mention communicating with two helicopters that had flown in to help find the killers.

After running criminal background checks and social media searches on both suspects, Susan had decided to focus her efforts on Norris Mills. She needed to know how the man had died, and she needed to know if it had anything at all to do with their case. She had located addresses and numbers for several family members, but none of them were current.

Finally, by cross-referencing names she'd found at an old address for Norris, she decided that a woman named Taylor Brown was his sister. Taylor was now married and it appeared she was living just outside of Lake Charles with her husband, Mike. After a little more digging, she located three possible phone numbers for the Browns. She called all three, but none were operable.

"Shit!" she said, turning back to her search page and deciding to focus on Mike. Through his name, she found another number that appeared to be for a landline, and it appeared to be more current than the others. Holding her breath and saying a silent prayer that someone would answer, she dialed the number from her desk phone. She exhaled when a woman answered, and quickly introduced herself.

"I was trying to get in touch with Taylor Brown," she said, "the sister of Norris Mills."

"Um, I'm Taylor." There was hesitation in the woman's voice. "What's this about?"

"First, I want to say how sorry I am to hear about Norris' passing," Susan began in all sincerity. Before she could say another word, the woman interrupted her.

"You knew Norris?"

"No, ma'am, I didn't know him," Susan quickly said. "I'm working a case here in town and his name came up."

"He's dead," Taylor said. "How can his name come up?"

"It's about his old truck." Susan kept her voice soothing, because she recognized the hurt that was still present in the woman's voice. "His ex-wife, Abby—"

"That whore is the reason my brother's laying in the ground right now," Taylor said bitterly. "The selfish bitch refused to let my brother pay installments for the community property settlement. Because of her, he was forced to sell off his business and his house. How in the hell is he supposed to work if he ain't got a business? Where in the hell is he supposed to live without a house? She didn't give a shit about any of it. Just as long as she got her money, that's all she cared about. And you know what else? That no-good slut took his truck and his guns, because she knew how much they meant to him. She wasn't happy just divorcing him. Oh, no, she set out to ruin him. Well, I bet she's happy now. I hope his ghost finds her and strangles her to death."

Susan was tempted to ask Taylor for her whereabouts last night, but she resisted the urge. Besides, she had called the woman on a landline, so she was in Lake Charles at the moment.

"I'm very sorry about all of it," Susan said. "I can't begin to imagine what your family has gone through."

"No, you can't. My father had to watch his own child waste away to nothingness. Do you know how hard it is for a father to go through that?"

"No, ma'am, I don't," Susan said, although she'd seen the anguish that had befallen Clint in the years after he'd lost his first daughter and wife in an armed robbery.

"I…I don't know if my dad can survive losing Norris." Taylor took a quivering breath. "He was the youngest—my dad's baby boy.

First, he lost my mom, and now this? It's just too much for him."

Susan paused for a moment. She felt bad asking Taylor for help, considering everything her family had gone through, but she needed to find Fred. She was also curious why Taylor had called Abby a whore. From what Abby had said, Norris was the one who had been unfaithful in their marriage.

"Ma'am, do you know any of Norris' friends?" Susan finally asked.

"I know all of them."

"Well, I've been trying to get in touch with Fred Hatton," Susan said, trying to sound nonchalant about everything. "He was down here last night and I need to get a message to him."

"Where are you calling from again?"

"Mechant Loup."

"Where's that?"

When Susan explained the location in relation to Lake Charles, Taylor scoffed.

"It wasn't Fred who was down there," she said. "Fred was here last night. I saw him at the parade."

"Y'all had a parade last night?" Susan felt deflated for a brief moment, but then realized that Taylor could be in on the crime.

"Yeah, it started at seven," Taylor said. "Fred was here with his wife and kids. He stopped to talk to us. We hugged and cried for a good five minutes. He misses my brother as much as I do. They might not have been blood related, but they were definitely brothers."

"Does that mean he would have done anything for your brother?"

"Absolutely. Wait a minute…" Taylor's tone became cautious. "What's this about?"

"What do you know about Fred slashing the tires on Norris' old truck a couple of weeks ago?"

Taylor was quiet for a long moment. So long, in fact, that Susan thought she'd hung up the phone.

"Judging by your silence, I'm guessing you knew something about it," Susan said, taking a shot in the dark. "At this point, we're not interested in filing charges against anyone. I just need to speak with him—and you—about the incident."

"I wasn't there, so I don't know nothing about it."

"Well, what did Fred say about it?"

"I didn't talk to Fred."

"What did Norris say about it?" Throughout the back-and-forth, Susan had remained patient. The woman had lost her brother, so she didn't want to cause her or her family any more grief.

"All he said was that Fred mentioned seeing his truck somewhere," Taylor finally said. "I don't remember what town it was in, but it was far away. I think Fred was down there fishing or something."

"What else did Norris say about Fred's visit?"

"Nothing much, really."

Susan nodded to herself. Taylor definitely knew more than she was saying, and a picture was starting to form in her mind. She wasn't sure how close she was to the truth, so she'd have to approach this carefully.

"Did Fred also mention seeing Abby during his trip?" Susan asked.

"Um…I guess so."

"Did he mention her having a boyfriend?"

"Fred told Norris something about Abby letting another guy drive his truck," she conceded. "Fred said it looked like they were much more than friends, but I don't know anything about it."

Susan sank into her chair. As she had feared, this might be a case of mistaken identity. Good for Abby and Chuck, but horrible for Malory and Wesley. She also now understood why Taylor had called Abby a whore and a slut, and she knew that nothing would change the woman's mind. She had lost her brother and she blamed Abby—plain and simple.

"What kind of impact did this news have on Norris?" Susan asked, deciding to use some of what she'd learned from Abby. "I mean, considering he was trying to win Abby back. That must've been a blow to him."

"It killed him." Taylor was sniffling now. "I wish Fred would never have told him anything about it. Norris was okay as long as he had his dreams, you know? But once he found out she was with another man, he realized his dreams of getting her back were over. I think that's when he decided he had nothing left to live for."

"What happened to him?" Susan asked softly.

"He overdosed." Taylor took a breath and blew it out forcefully. "The night Fred told him about Abby, Norris went to my dad's house, locked himself in the shed, drank a bottle of vodka, and took enough fentanyl to kill everyone in the Super Dome. At least, that's what the detectives said. I don't know anything about that drug except a lot of people are dying from it. I see it on the news. I just can't believe my brother got his hands on some."

"Oh, God, I'm so sorry," Susan said. "I feel really bad for you and your family."

"I feel even worse for my dad," Taylor said through sobs. "He left for work the next morning and didn't get home until about six o'clock. He started making supper and went to Norris' room to check on him, but he wasn't there. He looked all over the house but couldn't find him. He called me and my other brother, but we hadn't seen him. He even called Fred to see if Norris was with him, but Fred said he hadn't seen him. And that's when he found him in the shed."

Taylor stopped talking for about a minute and just sat on the other end of the phone crying. When she continued, it was hard for Susan to understand her.

"When my dad found him, he was laying on his face on the floor and there was vomit everywhere," she said through bawls. "He died on the dirty floor like a rat, and I blame that little whore bitch for taking my baby brother from me. If she would've just left his business alone, he would've been okay. He could've bought another truck and some more guns and kept on with his life, but she had to take everything away from him for some stupid mistake. She ruined him, and I hope she dies and goes straight to hell!"

Susan sat there listening as Taylor cried hysterically on the other end. She had more questions for the woman, but she knew she wouldn't be getting any more answers from her now, so she thanked her and hung up the phone. She wasn't convinced that Fred had been at the parade last night, so she began searching for some contact information on him.

If Taylor *was* telling the truth and Fred had been in Lake Charles last night, he might still be able to help. If he was best friends with Norris, he would know all of Norris' other friends and family members, and he might know who out of the bunch would be the most likely to involve themselves in something like this. He was definitely friends with Keith Collins, and Collins was definitely involved in the murders, so he should be of some use to her. Hopefully, he could identify the other suspect and help bring an end to this manhunt—unless, of course, he was that other suspect.

CHAPTER 48

Old Blackbird Highway, south of Mechant Loup

As I drove my Tahoe the wrong way down the eastern shoulder of the road, Amy and I kept a sharp eye out for a box truck with a driver who looked like Fred Hatton. When we'd come upon a stretch of tractor trailers stopped in traffic, it would be almost impossible to see to the western shoulder, so I'd have to park my Tahoe and one of us would slip between two of the trucks and scan the north-bound shoulder.

So far, we hadn't found anything. I even left the highway a few times to peruse the neighborhoods we'd come across, but we kept coming up dry. Regan had headed south along Old Blackbird, and she radioed a few times to let dispatch know she was out with a box truck. Each time she did, she came back on to say she was clear of the vehicle and continuing south.

The possibility did cross my mind that Fred might have headed south to meet up with a boat along the coast. It would be easy to conceal a pickup truck in a shipping container, load it onto a barge, and then push that barge to Lake Charles via the Intracoastal Waterway. The mere thought of that possibility had my head spinning. We were already searching by ground and air. Would we have to now put someone on the water?

I was still pondering this when Amy pointed up ahead.

"Did you see that?" she asked.

The left lane was clear for about a mile, so I had been cruising along in that lane instead of the shoulder and hadn't seen anything noteworthy. Of course, I had been paying more attention to the right lane and beyond that to the shoulder.

"No," I said. "What's up?"

"A box truck just turned in the area of Rooster Drive." She slapped the dashboard. "Let's go! I think he saw us coming and he's making a run for it."

I didn't hesitate. When I stomped my foot, the Tahoe shot forward and we cleared the distance in mere seconds. I heard Amy groan when the Rooster Drive neighborhood came into view and we saw the box truck stopped at the front of the street.

"Okay," she acknowledged, "he's not making a run for it, but he still got off the road when he saw us approaching. I'm going check it out."

I nodded and parked on the shoulder of the road just south of Rooster Drive. I could see the driver, and he looked nothing like Fred Hatton. Amy waited for an eighteen-wheeler to pass and then she stepped out of my Tahoe and approached the box truck. I glanced at the long line of vehicles to my right. They hadn't moved in a while, but as I watched, a vehicle far to the north pulled forward just a bit, and the rest of the vehicles in the line filled in the space that had been vacated in front of them.

A tanker truck was one of the vehicles that moved forward, and when it did, I caught a fleeting glimpse of a vehicle parked on the eastern shoulder of the road. As the truck behind the tanker closed the gap between them, I once again lost sight of the vehicle on the shoulder.

I glanced in Amy's direction. She and the driver were standing on the road, talking cordially. I saw Amy point toward the cargo area, and the man nodded and reached for his pocket. I was about to spring from the Tahoe when his hand produced a ring of keys. I relaxed and watched them head toward the back of the truck.

Knowing she had everything in hand, I dropped from my Tahoe and waited for a motorcycle to drive by before crossing the left lane. I walked around the back of the tanker and moved toward the eastern shoulder. When I glanced to the south, all I saw was the white front portion of a large truck and an open hood. I couldn't tell if it was a small truck or a large truck, but it definitely appeared to be broken down.

I turned to see that Amy was standing to one side while the man removed a padlock from the rear door of the box truck. Knowing she could take care of herself, I strolled toward the disabled truck. As I drew closer, I could see that there was a box on the back end, but I couldn't tell how long it was until I got to within several yards and saw that it was the right length to be the one for which we were searching.

I lowered my hand to my pistol and faded toward the left, closer to the trees. If this was the suspect and he decided to come up shooting, I wanted to be able to use one of the large tree trunks as cover. I still couldn't see a driver, but I figured he had to be close by, because the driver's door had appeared to be open a crack. Had he gone for help, he surely would've closed his door.

When I made it to the front of the truck, I paused long enough to reach up and touch the side quarter panel. It was cool. This truck had been parked here for a while. I didn't see or smell radiator fluid, so I figured it couldn't have overheated. I approached the passenger-side door and placed my left foot on the gas tank stair step. With my right hand close to my pistol, I lifted myself with my left leg and glanced through the window. The passenger compartment was empty.

I lowered myself to the ground and walked around the back of the truck. The roll-up door was closed. The locking mechanism was secured with a padlock. I was about to move toward the driver's side when a voice brought my attention to the road.

"Hey, there, can you help me?"

I looked over to see a man in his mid-sixties walking away from a minivan that was stuck in traffic.

"What's the problem?" I asked.

"I think the battery died," he said. "I'm close to empty, so I pulled over to try and wait for the traffic to clear out. When I tried to crank her up, she wouldn't turn over. If you had some cables, I would appreciate it. It'll only take a minute."

I rubbed my face. I would have to start maneuvering vehicles around in an effort to make an opening big enough for my Tahoe to squeeze through, and that alone would take some time. Not to mention having to dig out my jumper cables and connect them.

I glanced again at the man. "How long have you been sitting here?"

"Most of the day," he said. "I've talked to twenty or thirty people, but none of them would help. One trucker stopped and got out to help, but then the traffic started moving again and he jumped back in his truck."

I heard someone approaching and turned to see Amy.

"What's going on?" she asked.

"This man needs a jump," I said, turning to watch as another box truck eased into view. The driver didn't look anything like Fred.

Amy pointed toward the back door and asked the man, "What's

in there?"

"It's some kind of electronic oilfield equipment that's going to Texas and it's packaged in a large crate," the man said. "They said if I crash the truck it could ruin the equipment, and if that happens, I'm fired. I can't afford to be fired."

"Can we look inside?" she asked.

"I wouldn't care, but I don't have a key to the lock and they put a metal cargo seal on it to make sure the merchandise isn't tampered with." He frowned. "It's also time sensitive, so I really need to get going. There's a job waiting on this equipment and they're losing money by the hour. I would really appreciate that jump so I can get back on the road."

I glanced toward the lock and saw the seal. Movement from the highway caught my eye and I saw that the traffic was beginning to move again.

"We need to go, Ames," I said. "The suspect could be escaping."

"What about my jump?" the man protested. "Come on, aren't y'all the police? Aren't y'all supposed to help stranded motorists?"

I turned and hurried toward my Tahoe. I dug in the cargo area until I found my booster cables. I returned and tossed them toward the man. "You can have these," I said.

"But…"

I waved him off and stepped in front of the next approaching vehicle. When the car stopped, I walked over to the driver and dug forty dollars out of my wallet.

"Here, take this," I said. "All I need for you to do is park next to that truck while he jumps his battery, and then let him out in traffic when he's done. You don't even need to get out of your vehicle."

The driver, a young man wearing a Yellowstone T-shirt, nodded his head excitedly. "Sure thing!"

I then turned to Amy. "Come on, let's get out of here!"

CHAPTER 49

Mechant Loup Police Department

Susan hesitated before dialing Fred Hatton's cell phone number. Taylor hated Abby vehemently, so she would probably lie for anyone who said they killed her. If she was telling the truth and Fred was in Lake Charles, then that meant Clint was looking for the wrong man in the box truck. But how would she know for sure?

Not wanting to waste any more time, she just shook her head and dialed the number.

"Go," said a scratchy voice.

"Is this Fred Hatton?"

There was a moment of brief silence, and then hesitation. "Um…yeah, who's this?"

"Susan Wolf," Susan began, wishing he was sitting in front of her. "I'm the police chief for Mechant Loup. I need to talk to you about Norris Mills."

"Norris." Fred cleared his throat. "What about him?"

"First, I'm really sorry for your loss. I know you two were best friends, and I know how hard it can be to lose a best friend." Susan paused, but he didn't say anything. "I lost my dad when I was young, and it was the worst. Again, I'm very sorry for your loss."

"Thank you," he said hesitantly. "But what's this about?"

"If you're close by, I'd like to speak with you in person," Susan said. "It would be better that way."

"Close to where?"

"Mechant Loup."

"I'm in Lake Charles, lady," he said. "I'm three hours away from

Mechant Loup."

"Wait, what's that? I couldn't hear you."

"I said I'm in Lake Charles."

"Look, I've got some important information about your friend, but I'm having trouble understanding you," Susan bluffed. "Is there a landline near you?"

"I'm sitting inside a restaurant," he said, "but I'm sure they won't let me use the phone."

"What's the name of the restaurant?" Susan asked, turning to her computer. He told her the name and she quickly found the phone number for it. It was definitely in Lake Charles. If he answered, he was not their suspect.

"Wait just a minute." Susan snatched up her cell phone and called the restaurant. When an employee answered, she asked her to bring the phone to a customer named Fred Hatton. The employee resisted for a second, but then relented when Susan said she was a police chief and the message was important.

Within seconds, Fred was on the phone.

"Can you hear me now?" Susan asked.

"I always could hear you," Fred said, probably looking ridiculous with a phone to each ear.

"Oh, there," Susan said, "I can hear you on your phone now. Give the restaurant phone back to the nice lady."

Susan quickly ended the call to the restaurant phone and sent out a text message to Clint telling him that they had the wrong person, and that Fred Hatton was not the driver of the white box truck.

"What in the hell is going on?" Fred asked irritably. "Are you really a cop?"

"You bet your ass I am, son," Susan said. "And if you don't want to go to jail for felony theft and criminal damage to property, you'd better lower that voice."

There was a gulp from the other end, but he didn't say another word until Susan asked him when it was that he'd last been to Mechant Loup.

"Um, it was about a month ago."

"Try again, but this time leave out the bullshit," Susan said. "I don't have time for it."

She glanced down when her cell phone beeped. It was a message from Clint asking for more information.

Working on it now, she texted back.

"I won't ask you again," she said to Fred. "When was it? And keep in mind that I already know the answers to the questions I'm asking."

"It…um, it was a couple of weeks ago. Two weeks ago."

"And what'd you do when you were down here?"

"I went fishing."

"What else did you do?" Susan pressed.

"That's it. I just went fishing."

"Bullshit. Look, I already told you I'm in a hurry, so that means I've got zero patience for lies." Susan took a breath. "If you don't start telling me the truth, I'll swear out a felony warrant for your arrest and have officers storm that restaurant and drag you out in handcuffs. Is that what you want?"

"Look, lady, I know my rights," Fred said, sounding more defiant. "I'm not saying another word without a lawyer being present. That means you can't talk to me anymore. Boom!"

Susan moved the phone away from her ear and stared at it for a brief second, trying to stifle a chuckle.

"The Miranda rights only apply to custodial questioning," she said. "But sure, you can hang up and not talk to me, but I promise you one thing, you will not like what I do next."

She held her breath, half expecting to hear a click on the line as he ended the call. However, that didn't happen.

"What do you mean by that?" he asked, the bravado gone from his voice. "Are you threatening me?"

"I don't care what you call it. If you don't answer my questions, I'm getting a warrant for your arrest. Plain and simple. And if I find out you're involved in the murder, you won't be getting—"

"Whoa, whoa!" Fred hollered. "What are you talking about? I don't know nothing about no murder!"

"I don't know, Fred, you keep lying about slashing the tires on Norris' old truck, so how can I believe you about not murdering anyone?"

"I didn't lie about them tires," he said. "You never asked about the tires."

"You said you were here fishing, and that fishing was all you did," Susan reminded him. "Was that not a lie?"

"I…I guess so."

"Are you ready to start over and tell me the truth about everything?"

"And if I do?" he asked. "Will you still get a warrant?"

"No," she said, and meant it. "I just need answers from you. I don't care about the tires."

"Okay. I'll talk."

CHAPTER 50

Susan asked Fred if he had come to Mechant Loup specifically to slash the tires on Norris' old truck.

"No, I went there to fish," he said. "That part was true. When I was coming back from fishing, I drove by this restaurant and saw Norris' truck parked in the parking lot. I would know Norris' truck anywhere. They don't have another one like it. Anyway, I called Norris to tell him that I knew where Abby was, but he didn't answer his phone."

"Why would you do that?"

"Because he had been trying to find her for years," he explained. "You know how that goes."

"No, I don't know," Susan said. "If she divorced him, why was he trying to find her?"

"He still loved her, so he just wanted to find her and see if she'd give him a second chance." Fred stopped to clear his throat, and then continued. "Anyway, I parked my truck at this gas station and started watching the restaurant. We were there for a long time, because the restaurant stayed open late. Finally, when everyone was gone, Abby and this guy walked out of the restaurant and got in the truck. It looked like Abby was wearing a uniform, so I figured she worked there."

"Wait a minute," Susan said. "You left out the part about you slashing the tires."

"No, that was the next night," he said. "I slashed the tires on Saturday night. After I tried calling Norris and we saw Abby and her man, me and my buddy went back to the motel to sleep. I got a call from Norris late on Friday night and I told him that I'd seen Abby and that she was with this man and she was letting him drive his truck. I, um…"

Fred's voice cracked just a little.

"You what?" Susan prompted. "What'd you do?"

"I wish I would've never said anything to him, that's what." Fred sniffed. "I told him what I saw and he got real mad. He started cursing real loud and saying everything was over and that they would never be able to get back together now. I…I asked him if he wanted me to try and talk to her, to tell her that he loved her and beg her to come back, but he…um, he said no."

"That's not all he said, is it?" Susan asked softly.

"No." Fred took a breath and exhaled long and slow. "He, well, he told me to kill her. He wanted me to kill her and her lover."

"I know you didn't, so what did you do?"

"My buddy and me went fishing again Saturday, and then we drove out to the restaurant later that night. I had my friend act as a look-out while I slashed the tires on the truck," he said. "I'm not gonna lie, Norris told me to cut the brake lines, but I didn't do it. So, if they died because someone cut the brake lines, it wasn't me. I just cut the tires and I left. I figured that would make Norris happy enough, but…"

"But what?"

"I…I never got to talk to him again," Fred said softly. "He killed himself Friday night. His dad found him on Saturday when he got back from work. I didn't find out until I got back home on Sunday. I had tried calling him a few times, but the calls went straight to voicemail. They told me later that he destroyed his phone Friday night, and I was the last one to talk to him."

Susan shook her head. It was sad that Norris had taken his own life over an ex-wife, but it was downright maddening that someone had killed Malory and Wesley in a failed attempt on Abby and Chuck's lives.

"When did you get back to Lake Charles?" Susan asked.

"On Sunday."

"And when did you come back here?"

"Oh, I haven't been back since then," he said. "And I probably never will go back."

"Why not? Did you do something wrong here?"

"I mean, yeah, I cut the tires there," he said slowly, "but if I go back, it'll just bring back those memories of my last call to Norris and how it's my fault that he's dead."

Susan didn't say anything to relieve him of the guilt he felt.

Instead, she focused on the case at hand.

"If you didn't come back to Mechant Loup and try to murder Abby and her new man, then who did?"

"I swear to God, I have no idea!" There was real panic in Fred's voice now. "You can ask anyone around here. I've been here all day. I never left Lake Charles."

Since Fred hadn't tried to claim he was elsewhere last night, which was when the crime had actually occurred, Susan was left to believe that he had nothing to do with the murder. Of course, it was still possible he was trying to play her, so she wasn't letting him off the hook just yet.

"Where were you last night?" she asked.

"At the parade here in the city," he said. "They have it the Friday before Mardi Gras every year and we never miss it."

"When you say *we*, are you referring to your beautiful wife and lovely children?" Susan asked.

"Wait a minute, how do you know about them?"

"I know a lot about a lot of things," Susan said. "But before we get into that, who was with you on your little fishing trip to Mechant Loup?"

"An old friend."

"What's his name?"

"I…I really don't want to get anyone in trouble here."

"Did your friend slash the tires or did you slash the tires?"

"I did," he said.

"What crime did your friend commit?"

"I…I mean, none. He just waited in my truck."

"So why do you feel the need to protect him?" Susan asked.

"I just don't want to involve anyone in my mess," he said. "I did it, and only me. No one told me to do it. I just wanted to do it to make Norris feel better, you know?"

Instead of telling him that she didn't know what he meant, she reminded him of their deal.

"If you don't tell me the truth, I will swear out a warrant for your arrest," she said. "And you know what? It won't be based on anything you've said here today. I've got clear video footage of you at the crime scene."

"I knew it!" he blurted. "I thought I saw a camera."

Susan suddenly leaned forward. "So, you knew about the surveillance cameras, didn't you?"

"Not at first, but when I was leaving, I turned around to see if the coast was clear and I thought I saw cameras," he explained. "There were two of them on the front of the building and I wasn't sure if they were cameras or motion detectors, but now I know."

"And who did you tell about the cameras?"

"No one."

"Your buddy in the truck knew about the cameras, didn't he?" Susan interrupted as he began to answer. "And not another lie, or I'm ending this conversation and sending the police to ruin your meal."

"Okay, yes, my buddy knew about it," he conceded. "I mentioned it when I got back in the truck."

"And what's this buddy's name?"

"You promise me he won't be in trouble?"

"Yes, I promise that no one is going to jail for the tire slashing if you tell me the truth," Susan said. "Like I've already told you, I'm investigating a murder, not a tire slashing."

"I thought you said it was an attempted murder?"

"No, I said someone tried to murder Abby and Chuck Bruce, but they got it wrong."

"What?"

"Yeah, they murdered an innocent couple." Susan leaned a forearm on her desk. "Now, for the last damn time, tell me the name of your friend."

"Um, it's Keith," Fred said. "Keith Collins, but…but there's no way he'd ever…he would never do something like murder."

Susan took a breath and settled back into her chair. Her mind was racing. Of course. It made sense, because Keith would've known how to find the truck and he would've known about the cameras, but what were his ties to Norris?

"Were Keith and Norris friends?" she finally asked.

"No," Fred said, "they were cousins."

"I see." She drummed her fingers on the desk. If Fred hadn't been let in on the plan, they must've kept it amongst family. That would mean the driver of the box truck was related to Norris, so it narrowed things down a little. But who might it be? Was it possible that Taylor was in on it? Susan shifted the phone on her ear. "Fred, how does Keith feel about Norris' death?"

"What do you mean?"

"Does he want Abby dead?"

"No!" Fred said. "Of course not!"

"What about Taylor?"

A moment of hesitation. "What about her?"

"Does she blame Abby for what happened to Norris?"

"Sure," he said. "We all do."

"Does Taylor want her dead?"

"No!" he insisted. "No one wants her dead. We just wish she hadn't done what she did to Norris, and then he'd still be alive."

"Answer me this: if Keith came back to Mechant Loup and attempted to kill Abby and her lover," Susan began slowly, "who would he bring with him?"

"I don't…I…Keith would never do anything like that," he said. "He wouldn't even get out of the truck when I slashed the tires."

"Are you related to Norris?"

"No, we're just friends."

"Well, blood is thicker than friendship," Susan said. "Keith might not do something as trivial as slashing a tire, but if he believed someone was responsible for the death of his kin folk, that might be a different animal. Now, answer my question. Who loved Norris enough to come down here and kill Abby to avenge his death?"

"I swear to you, Keith had nothing to do with it."

"When's the last time you saw Keith?"

"Um, at Norris' funeral."

"Well, the next time you see him, it'll be at *his* funeral," she said flatly, "because he was killed trying to elude our officers after playing a part in murdering two innocent people."

There was a horrifying gasp from the other end of the phone.

"Now, if you won't tell me who else is behind this, I'll have to assume you're involved and you're trying to cover it up," Susan said coolly. "Everyone involved will be tried for first degree murder, found guilty, and then sentenced to either life in prison or death. Unless you want—"

Fred cut her off and spat out a name. "I don't know anything about a murder, but if anyone's involved with Keith, that's who it is. I saw them huddling together at the funeral. It seemed like they were being very secretive…"

He continued talking, but Susan was no longer listening. Her fingers were flying across the keyboard, as she tried as quickly as she could to produce a driver's license picture of their new suspect.

CHAPTER 51

Old Blackbird Highway, south of Mechant Loup

Amy and I were just walking away from the kid in the Yellowstone T-shirt when I heard a siren up ahead. The southbound vehicles began to pull onto the western shoulder of the highway to make a lane for the approaching emergency vehicle. There was a bend in the road to the north, so we weren't able to see who was approaching until a tractor trailer inched over and Melvin's F-250 came into view.

He slowed to a stop when he reached the spot where my Tahoe was parked, and I could see him extend his arm in the direction of the white box truck. I knew instantly that he was using the key fob in an attempt to locate the truck. That he had gotten this far without locating Wesley's pickup was disconcerting. He was running out of vehicles to search.

"Shit, Clint," Amy said, "I thought the suspect would've made it to the bridge by now."

"Me, too."

I was about to cross the open highway when two things happened in rapid succession. First, my phone beeped and I pulled it out to see who had texted me. It was Susan and she had sent along a picture. The image was just coming into view when the second thing happened. A muffled car alarm suddenly began blaring from somewhere nearby. I looked up to see Melvin staring intently at the truck that Amy had checked out, but I knew it wasn't coming from that direction.

I whipped my head around just in time to see the driver of the disabled box truck do the same. He looked first toward the cargo area of his truck, and then turned in my direction, a confused expression on his face. I saw him look past me toward Melvin, and he suddenly understood what was happening.

"Donald Mills!" I said, shooting a finger in the direction of the man that Susan had just identified as Norris' father. "Stop right there! You're under arrest!"

Reacting immediately, and with surprising dexterity, Donald tossed the booster cables to the ground, pulled down the hood on his truck, and sprang into the driver's seat. I instantly realized he had been lying about needing a jump, and that realization came almost too late, as he fired up the engine and shifted into first gear. With a jolt, the truck was suddenly in motion and heading in a direction that would take it straight through Amy and me and toward the open lane that Melvin had created on his approach to our location.

I shoved Amy toward the southbound lane of traffic and just out of danger as the front of the truck reached us. The engine roared like a lion as the truck began to pick up speed. The front tire was just rolling past me when I made a split-second decision. I began running forward as fast as my legs could carry me, trying to match stride with the truck. I knew if I waited too long, it would pull away and become a wrecking ball of death and destruction.

As I felt the truck slipping away, I quickly grabbed onto the side mirror and jumped onto the gas tank stair step. My left arm jerked violently when my hand closed around the mirror, and I almost lost my footing on the step. I had misjudged the speed at which the truck was already traveling, and that could've proven a costly mistake.

Righting myself and gaining a solid footing, I reached into the open window and punched Donald Mills right in the mouth. His head snapped around, which caused him to jerk the steering wheel to the right. It threw me forward, but I was brought up short when the truck sideswiped an eighteen-wheeler that was stuck in traffic.

The alarm on Wesley's truck was still blaring from the cargo area, but I could hear Melvin's siren and his screeching tires as he began to give chase. My keys were still in my Tahoe, and I knew Amy would be joining Melvin in the pursuit.

The truck jerked as Donald shifted roughly into second gear, picking up speed rapidly. I knew I needed to stop him before he reached dangerous speeds, otherwise he might kill someone else—and that someone could be me.

I glanced up to see a long line of vehicles on the southbound shoulder, as well as the long line of vehicles that were in the northbound lane. The left lane was open for as far as I could see, so Donald wouldn't be forced to stop anytime soon. I had to do something.

I threw another punch in his direction. He had been anticipating it, and reacted by jerking the steering wheel to the left and releasing the door handle. The door flung open, the motion nearly throwing me from the vehicle. I held onto the mirror for dear life, while also clutching onto the upper doorframe. My left foot had slipped from the step, and I was trying to keep it from making contact with the ground.

I couldn't see in the direction we were heading, but the line of traffic on the southbound shoulder blurred by, and it was way too close for comfort. I just knew Donald would swerve and send me and the door smacking into a vehicle. Pulling with my left arm, I shifted my body closer to the truck. I had barely made that move when the edge of the door made contact with something. I wasn't sure what it was, but there was a loud crash in my ear as metal banged against metal and the door was suddenly slammed shut.

I winced in pain as the fingers of my right hand became smashed in the door. Ignoring the pain, I regained my footing and let go of the mirror with my left hand. Throwing my body forward, I landed a vicious left punch to Donald's temple, and then another. I knew my actions would probably cause him to crash the truck, but that was inevitable. What I needed was for this truck to crash as soon as possible, before it could reach dangerous speeds.

Donald tried to swipe back at me with his left hand, but I knocked it away and jabbed my thumb in his eye. The man screamed in agony as I fought hard to shove my thumb through his eyeball and into his brain. He had let go of the steering wheel and the truck was starting to sway from left to right on the road. I could feel the weight of Wesley's pickup rocking back and forth, and I knew we were in danger of careening out of control.

I pushed with my feet and got myself higher up on the steps, and I used my weight to drive my thumb deeper into his eye socket. He was clawing at my arm with both of his hands now, trying desperately to remove my thumb from his eye.

"Hit the brakes, you murdering piece of shit," I said through gritted teeth, trying to use my back and shoulder to hold the steering wheel steady. "If you don't, you'll never see out of this eye again!"

"Go to hell!" he bellowed and stomped the gas even harder, equally determined to continue his escape plan.

The top portion of my body was halfway into the cab now, and I shot a glance toward the front windshield. I didn't like what I saw. About a mile to the north, a truck was heading straight for us, trying to pass up the long row of vehicles that were stopped on the shoulder. If something didn't happen quickly, we would be involved in a head-on collision, and we'd probably all die.

I scanned the row of vehicles in the right lane, hoping for something soft to crash into. There was nothing but vehicles. My arms burned from Donald's scratching and clawing, but I didn't remove my thumb from his eye. I cursed as I tried to decide what vehicle to hit. A large tractor trailer with a heavy load would've been the safest thing for me to crash into—well, for the public at large, anyway—but we were approaching a long line of passenger vehicles, many of which were probably occupied by children. The thought of hurting a single innocent person terrified me.

I let out a string of curse words that would've made even the devil blush, as I pushed deeper into Donald's orbital socket in my attempt to compel him to apply the brakes, but it was no use. This man was willing to die, and he didn't care who he dragged to hell with him.

Suddenly, I saw a minivan stopped in the right lane with the blinker on, trying to turn left into a neighborhood. A truck was blocking access to the street and the southbound traffic was at a standstill, so the minivan was just sitting there. The traffic in front of the minivan had continued onward, leaving a gap in the roadway—a gap big enough for me to fit this truck. Three options flashed instantly through my mind, and I didn't like any of them.

First, I could continue on our current course and run head-on into the oncoming truck, possibly killing Donald, me, and the occupants of the truck. Second, I could swerve in front of the minivan and continue onward until I hit the rear end of the last vehicle, possibly killing Donald, me, and everyone in that vehicle. Or third, I could swerve in front of the minivan and head straight for the trees, possibly killing only Donald and me. I took option three.

Removing my thumb from Donald's eye, I grabbed the steering wheel and prepared to make the turn. Donald was screaming in pain and flailing around, striking blindly at my face and arms. I let go of the steering wheel to punch him a dozen times violently in the face. It was enough to disorient him, and he sank into his seat.

I quickly turned my attention back toward the highway. The truck was drifting to the left and was about to sideswipe a vehicle when I took control again and steadied us. The truck that had been barreling toward us had stopped in the roadway and reversed course, trying to create distance between us and it, but it was no use. We would be upon it in seconds.

As soon as we cleared the front of the minivan, I swerved sharply to the right. I felt the back of the truck sway dangerously as Wesley's pickup rocked from side to side, even as I was pulled away from the door of the truck. My right hand kept me married to the truck, and I was able to maintain my hold on the steering wheel and guide us toward the trees that lined the bayou side.

Donald, oblivious to what was happening, was still screaming beneath me, but I ignored him as I braced for impact. A tree loomed directly ahead, and I cut the wheel back to the left to try and avoid it. Although I managed to avoid a direct collision, the right rear panel struck a solid blow against the trunk, and it sent us careening down the embankment and straight toward the bayou.

I tried to pull my right hand free from the truck, but it was no use. I was stuck. I took a deep breath and braced myself as the truck went airborne for a split second, and then plunged headlong into the muddy waters below.

CHAPTER 52

Melvin Saltzman watched in horror as the box truck rocked to the left, swerved violently toward the right, and then glanced off of a large tree on its way to the steep embankment of Bayou Tail. Just as the truck was about to go over the edge, Melvin saw Clint try to jerk away from the runaway vehicle, but his hand appeared to be stuck in the door.

"No!" Melvin bellowed, punching the steering wheel in desperation. "No, damn it!"

Before Melvin's F-250 skidded to a halt in the grass along the highway, the box truck had disappeared between the trees and over the edge of the embankment. He was just dropping from his truck when he heard a loud splash and water exploded into the air.

Not even stopping to remove his gun belt or his boots, Melvin made a mad dash straight for the bayou. He knew the bank was high in this area, but the water was deep, so he could jump in without fear of getting stuck in the mud. However, the fact that it was deep presented another problem—the truck, with Clint attached to it, would be submerged for an extended period of time. Thus, he knew it was imperative that he get to the bottom of the bayou and bring Clint to the surface as fast as he could.

Melvin's legs were thick and strong, and they were built for short, explosive bursts of energy. Making full use of his attributes, he was soaring through the air within seconds of exiting his F-250. As his body rapidly dropped to the water, he searched desperately for the path that the box truck had taken to the bottom. The water was black in south Louisiana, and it would be virtually impossible to locate Clint without some clue as to where he went down.

Luckily, an explosion of bubbles at the center of the rippling waves provided an approximate pathway to the truck, and Melvin twisted his body in that direction as soon as he hit the water. Moving like his friend's life depended on it, he took several long strokes and reached the spot in a flash. He then took a deep breath and dove for the bottom.

Although he knew it was no use, he kept his eyes wide open as he made his way through the murky water. He kicked his feet like pistons and pulled a giant handful of water with every stroke of his arms. A feeling of dread washed over him as he descended deeper and deeper into the water. What if he was on the wrong pathway? What if the truck had entered the water closer to the middle of the bayou?

Melvin's lungs began to scream and he started to panic. Not for himself, but for Clint. His best friend had been in the water for at least ten or fifteen seconds longer than he had, and it wouldn't be long before Clint's body forced him to take a breath.

He didn't know how far he had gone, but he was starting to think he had made a costly mistake. He was about to change direction when his left hand struck a hard, rounded surface. He quickly oriented himself by feeling with both hands, and he realized he had found the box truck. The bad news was that it had landed on its roof.

Grabbing onto the axle, Melvin made his way quickly toward the front of the truck, and then moved to where he thought the driver's door would be. He was about to round the belly of the truck and come up the side when something smacked him in the face. It felt like the heel of a boot, and the blow was a solid one. It snapped his head back and stung his nose.

A surge of hope suddenly coursed through him. Was it Clint? Had he escaped and was now making his way to the surface? Although he was hopeful, he was not leaving the bottom of the bayou without checking. There was still the possibility it was the suspect who had escaped.

Melvin kicked his legs and pulled his way toward the top of the truck, and that's where he made his grim discovery. He found Clint in the soft mud of the bayou, and he wasn't moving. A quick tug on Clint's arm revealed the horrifying truth—he was trapped down there and each passing second brought him that much closer to death.

Melvin had known instantly that Clint's hand was trapped in the door, so he moved quickly to the knob. He pulled on it, but nothing happened. He jerked on it for all he was worth, but still nothing. He pulled himself to the top of the truck and discovered that the roof was buried in the mud, trapping the door.

As his lungs screamed for air and his heart pounded, Melvin tore frantically at the mud along the edge of the roofline. He felt a burning pain as his hand slid over a sharp piece of metal or glass, but he didn't care. He dug harder and faster. He had already made up his mind about one thing: if Clint was going to die down here, he wouldn't die alone.

Melvin moved from the trench he had dug to the door handle again, and this time it budged a little. He then reached for Clint and jerked on him. He was still stuck. Knowing there was no time left to dig—and realizing it was probably already too late for his friend—he braced his boots against what felt like the door, and jerked Clint's arm with all of his might. He fell backward—the water making it feel like slow motion—with Clint's arm still in his firm grasp.

Twisting around, he hooked an arm under Clint's chin and launched himself from the underside of the box truck. He was like a fish in water, but he was in full police uniform, he was trying to bring a friend to the surface, and his lungs were about to collapse. It was an almost impossible feat.

Melvin gritted his teeth so tightly that he was sure he chipped a tooth. He kicked his powerful legs harder than he ever had before. He reached high into the water with his left arm, paddling with every ounce of strength that was left in him. And just when he thought he wasn't going to make it, his hand broke the surface of the water. His head followed immediately afterward and he quickly blinked away the water, trying desperately to get his bearings. The land was to his left, so he began swimming toward it, even as a feeling of dread fell over him. How on earth was he supposed to get Clint up that embankment?

And then, just like that, someone was beside him, pulling Clint from his fading arms. Melvin gratefully let Clint go to someone who was fresh, and that's when he realized it was Baylor who had scooped up Clint. Baylor had apparently stripped down to his BDU pants, and he was able to glide through the water like an Olympic swimmer.

Melvin caught sight of a cable dangling down from the steep embankment, just above the muddy slop at the water's edge. He recognized it to be the cable from his winch, and he saw two straps extending from the cable. Attached to one of the straps was an empty harness, and attached to the other strap was Regan, who also wore a harness and was waiting to receive Clint.

Melvin glanced upward to see Amy staring down from the

embankment, waiting to hoist Clint and Regan to the shore. He could hear sirens in the distance, and knew they were from either an ambulance or a fire department rescue vehicle.

As Melvin watched Baylor's progress, he noticed another movement in the water. It was the suspect, and he was heading straight for the winch, trying to reach it before Baylor did. Baylor was so focused on getting Clint to shore that he hadn't noticed the man.

Feeling a new surge of energy, Melvin lunged into action. The aching in his arms and legs melted away as he raced through the water. There was no way he was going to let this man interfere with Baylor's efforts to get Clint to safety. He popped his head up a couple of times to keep a bead on the man, and he realized he was gaining on him.

When the suspect was about ten feet from reaching the winch, Melvin grabbed a handful of his hair and jerked his head back and down. The man gave a startling cry that turned to chokes and gasps as water filled his mouth and got sucked into his lungs.

Melvin was in no mood to be nice. He dragged the man through the water by his hair, as he swam the last few yards to the water's edge. It was muddy along the bottom of the embankment, and he continued dragging the suspect through the mud until he was completely out of the water. He then jerked the suspect's arms behind his back and cuffed him.

Once the suspect was secure and no longer a problem, Melvin turned to watch Clint's limp body being hoisted toward the shore above them. He could see the worried look on Amy's face as she waited to accept him, and he knew it was bad—really bad. He gritted his teeth and tried to bite back the tears, but it was no use. They flowed freely and mixed with the water that dripped from his face.

Through a blur, he saw where Baylor had dropped to his knees and turned his gaze skyward to watch Clint's body ascend to the heavens. He looked as lost and utterly broken as Melvin felt. The only thing that gave Melvin hope—however slight it might've been—was the sight of Regan with her legs interlocked around Clint's body, and giving him rescue breaths as they were pulled to the top of the embankment.

CHAPTER 53

Chateau General Hospital

I woke up in a hospital bed. My head ached and my right hand was throbbing, but other than that, I felt fine. The last thing I remembered was seeing my first wife and daughter—Abigail and Michele—and thinking that I had died.

Wait a minute…had I died?

I quickly opened my eyes, but winced as a hot searing pain shot through my temple. Yep, I was alive.

"He's awake!" cried a voice I recognized. "Go get the doctor! He's awake!"

I opened my eyes more slowly this time and glanced around the dim room. I was grateful for that. I didn't think I could handle bright lights at this moment. When I shifted my head to the left, I saw the most beautiful face I'd ever seen.

"Sue," I said, smiling weakly. "What happened?"

"You…um…well, Melvin and Baylor pulled you out of the water and Regan breathed life back into you," she said, scrubbing away a line of tears that streamed down her face. "How do you feel?"

"I feel fine," I said, shifting my attention to the door as a doctor entered. I recognized her from being here before. She smiled and approached the bedside, chart in hand. I turned back toward my wife. I kept my eyes on her while I answered the doctor's questions as completely and concisely as possible. There was something different about Susan. Although her face was red from crying, there seemed to be a glow about her. I figured she must've been damned happy to see me.

Once the doctor was done, she informed me that she'd like to keep me overnight for observations, claiming that I had been unconscious for longer than she would've liked.

I didn't argue. I wanted to do whatever I could to make her finish and leave me alone with Susan. I appreciated her looking out for me, but I had questions, and it looked like Susan had some answers.

When we were finally alone, she began talking, her mouth moving a hundred miles a second, telling me about the case, and getting into more details about how Melvin and Baylor had pulled me from the water and Regan had performed rescue breaths until the ambulance arrived to take over. I already knew some of what she told me, but there were parts I was hearing for the first time.

"We've got him, Clint," she said. "Donald Mills was the killer, and Keith Collins was his accomplice. Fred Hatton was the one who initially found Norris' old truck in town, and he thought the woman with Wesley was Abby. Malory does look like Abby, so it's easy to see how someone could've made that mistake—especially in the dark—but this was as bad as a misidentification in a murder trial. His mistake cost Malory her life."

Susan took a quick breath. "Donald said he blamed Abby for his son's death, and he proudly admitted to killing her and her lover. He said he had given the truck to his son, and Abby stole it from him, so he thought it was very fitting that he was able to run her over with it. He said he used the spare key from Norris to gain entry to the truck, and he sat there waiting for Abby and her lover to return from the parade. He said he had been watching them for three days, and he knew the parade would be the perfect time and place to take them out."

The door opened and a nurse walked in with a tray of food, so Susan stopped talking.

"Your wife said you would probably be hungry once you woke up," she said, "so we made you a plate from the cafeteria."

I gratefully reached for the tray. Once it was settled into my lap and I was munching away, Susan continued telling me how Donald had shown little remorse when Amy had asked him about the other victims.

"He called them casualties of war," Susan said. "He said he had come here prepared to die for his cause, but he admitted that dying wasn't part of the plan. He said he had watched this movie once where a man had planned a robbery down to the very last detail, and he said he had done the exact same thing."

"He planned to steal Max's truck to throw us off like we

thought?" I asked around a mouthful of food.

"Yeah." She nodded for emphasis. "He said they parked Max's truck at the campground until they were ready, and then brought it to the cane field road, shot it three times, and then planted the blood and tissue evidence that they had scraped from Norris' truck. He said they were hoping we would find it and pull everyone away from the checkpoint. When we didn't find it right away, he blocked his number and made the anonymous call. He said he was surprised that we didn't abandon the checkpoint."

"Did Amy tell him we weren't fooled?"

"You know Amy," Susan said with a laugh. "She didn't mince words. She let him know what a bungling idiot he had been, and she even showed him a picture of his headless nephew. That really shocked the shit out of him. He thought Keith was still somewhere in town waiting for him. He said Keith helped him plan everything out, because he knew the lay of the town from when he had gone fishing with Fred. Keith was also the one who told him about the surveillance cameras on the restaurant, and Keith recommended Lucille's campground because it was secluded. It's where he and Fred had stayed on their fishing trip. Shade went back to Lucille's campground and found Fred's name in her books from two weeks ago, and Fred's DL picture matched the image from the surveillance video on the night the tires were slashed."

"Did they use the shell pile to load up the pickup?" I asked, pausing to take a sip of the apple juice the nurse had brought me.

"Keith told him about the place. He had seen it when he and Fred were driving down to the coast, and Donald said he had even joked about trying to jump it on his bike some day." She took a breath and rubbed her face. I could see it was flushed a little, but she continued.

"Donald said Keith dropped him off in town on the dirt bike," Susan explained, "and parked the bike at their campsite. He then drove the box truck to the shell pile and backed it into place, waiting for Donald to show up with the pickup. When Donald got there, he drove right up the pile of shells and into the back of the box truck. He said they locked it inside, put the cargo seal on it to make it look legit, and drove it to the party at Lucille's campground."

"Were they able to pull the box truck out of the bayou?" I asked.

"Yeah, they got it out a few minutes ago," she said. "I just got a call from Vanessa. She said they broke the back door open and found Wesley's truck inside. The spare keys are still in the ignition and there's blood evidence on the front bumper and grill. Malory's purse was on the front passenger floorboard, and her car keys were inside the purse. There was a pistol in the glovebox of the box truck, and, as it turns out, the truck was registered to Norris Mills' trucking company."

Susan paused and was thoughtful. "Oh, yeah, and Venessa also found three bullet holes in the lower portion of the windshield, exactly like Baylor described it."

"Thank God we got him, Sue," I said, sighing. "This one could've easily gone unsolved."

"Yep, it's a bit of a miracle. Donald said they drove the Chevy into the box truck and never moved it. The only time they opened the back door was to scrape some blood evidence from the front bumper and grill to put on Max's truck." She shook her head. "If they would've just left town right away and returned to Lake Charles, we might've never gotten the evidence to arrest him."

"Why didn't they? Why didn't they just get in traffic last night and leave town?"

"He told Amy he anticipated us setting up a roadblock and searching every vehicle that drove by," she said. "He didn't realize we couldn't do that. He thought we would stop the search and pull down the roadblocks once we found Max's truck, but when we didn't, he figured they would have to take a chance. He left Lucille's and got in line with the traffic from the coast, and Keith was supposed to check out the roadblock and see if we were searching trucks. If we were, they would regroup and devise another plan. If we weren't, then they would go down a back road, load the dirt bike in the box truck, and drive right through the checkpoint. When Keith didn't show up, he said he pulled to the side of the road and pretended to be broken down to buy time for Keith to get there. That's when you arrived."

I pushed my tray away with my left hand and shifted in the bed. My stomach felt much better, but I still had so many unanswered questions.

"What did he say when he found out he'd killed the wrong person?" I asked. "Did he show remorse at that point?"

"Oh, no," Susan said, "that's when Amy had to knock him out cold."

My jaw dropped. "What?"

"He was pissed when she called him a loser and told him he had killed two innocent people," she said. "Baylor was in the dispatcher's station and he heard the man roaring from the interview room. By the time he got there, the room was a mess and the man was unconscious. Amy had to break the digital recorder across his skull and put him down, because he was hell bent and determined to break out and finish the job. Clint, if this man ever gets out of jail, he's definitely going after Abby and Bruce."

I nodded thoughtfully, recognizing how important it would be to put together an airtight case.

There was movement just outside the hospital room and I suddenly heard a voice calling for me.

"Gracie!" I said, jerking up in bed. The stabbing pain returned and reminded me that I was not well, so I sank into the thin mattress and watched as Regan, Shade, Baylor, Takecia, and Melvin all came rushing into the room with Grace riding on Takecia's shoulders.

It was obvious that my soon-to-be four-year-old daughter didn't fully grasp how serious things could've been, because she was beaming like she was attending a birthday party. She did know enough to recognize when someone was injured, and her little face fell when she saw the cast on my right hand.

"Daddy, what happened to you?" she asked, pointing a small finger in the direction of my injury.

I raised my hand and studied it, remembering my fight with Donald Mills.

"I guess I broke a few fingers when the truck door slammed on my hand," I said, frowning. "I sure wish it would've been my left hand."

"Um, Clint," Melvin said, lowering his head sheepishly and raising a hand in the air. "It was me."

"Huh?" I asked. "What was you?"

"I broke your hand trying to pull you free from the wreckage," he said slowly. "If I could've gotten the door open, you would've been fine. Your hand would've been fine and you would've been able to wipe your—"

He quickly caught himself and glanced at Grace.

"Had I not jerked your hand so hard," he continued, "you would still be able to write your investigative notes. Since it was my fault, I'll go ahead and take notes for you until your hand heals."

I laughed, shook my head, and thanked all of them for everything they had done. "We've had a rough couple of days," I said, "but it could've been a whole lot worse."

"You had a rough day, Daddy?" Grace asked, cocking her little head to the side.

"Yeah, Pumpkin, I did."

"Aw, do you want me to let you drive my Barbie Jeep?" she asked. "That will make you happy again!"

The room roared in laughter and no one heard the door burst open until Amy shouted, "Congratulations, old man!"

Everyone stopped and turned to stare at her, their mouths open. I glanced from Susan to Amy and thought I detected something between them, but I wasn't sure what was going on.

"Wait," Amy asked slowly, "did you tell him yet?"

"Tell me what?"

Susan turned to me and smiled. She handed me a little blue stick.

"What's this?" I turned the little blue stick over and saw a small indicator window with two vertical red lines displayed. I suddenly caught my breath. "Oh, shit, I get it!"

Susan smiled warmly. "We're gonna have another baby."

CHAPTER 54

One month later…

"Be careful," I said to Susan as she stepped out of my truck. "Don't slip on the running board."

She turned to me and glared. "I'm not a chicken egg, and neither is this baby. Even if I were to fall, we'd both be fine."

"I know, I know," I said, still beaming with excitement. Although we were a long way from finding out if it was a boy or girl, Grace and I had already picked out names.

"If it's a boy, we're naming him Baretta," I had said when we'd all returned home from the hospital.

"We're not naming our son after a pistol," Susan had said with a roll of her eyes.

"Not Beretta," I had responded. "*Baretta*…after the main character on that old detective show—the one with the bird."

"How would you know about that? It was before your time."

"I watched all the reruns when I was a kid," I said. "It's a great television show."

"And if it's a little sister," Grace had chimed in, "I'm naming her Little Sister!"

We had all laughed.

Now, though, it was time to posthumously honor Cole Peterson for his sacrifice from a month ago. The events that had transpired on that horrible night were still burned into the minds of everyone in town, and I was sure no one would ever forget about Cole and how he had given his own life for a small boy. I knew I never would.

Donald Mills might have been formally charged with three counts of first degree murder—one each for Wesley, Malory, and Cole—and twenty-three counts of attempted first degree murder—one each for the twenty-one injured, as well as for attempting to run over Baylor and Benny—but that had provided little consolation to anyone.

Amy, Vanessa, and I had met with newly-elected District Attorney Britt Lucas two weeks earlier to present our evidence against Mills and his nephew, Keith Collins. Through her excellent work, Vanessa had been able to match the fingerprint she had recovered from the delivery van at M & P Grill to Donald. She had also matched his DNA to swabs she'd recovered from Wesley's truck, Max Broussard's truck, and the box truck.

Blood and tissue from the plastic bags that Shade and I had found in the tent matched the DNA from the blood and tissue Vanessa had recovered from the two trucks, the blood and tissue from the busted down gate, and the blood that Regan had located on the shoulder of Cypress Highway. Vanessa's team had been able to trace all of that DNA evidence to eleven of our victims, one of them being Cole. Donald's fingerprints were also found on the plastic bags and on the insides of the latex gloves that Shade and I had recovered at the outlaw campsite.

The gun that was found in the box truck had been purchased by Donald some thirty years ago, and the bullets pulled from Max's truck were determined to have been fired from Donald's pistol. Additionally, the ballistics team had been able to match the bullets that were pulled from Wesley's truck to Baylor's pistol.

There was other evidence, though not as compelling, but Vanessa had presented the findings anyway. Danny Kiger had been shown a photo lineup that included Donald Mills' mug shot, and he tentatively picked Donald out as the man he saw in the M & P Grill parking lot on the night of the murder. Donald's boots were a presumptive match to the shoe impressions we had recovered from the outlaw campsite and from near where we had recovered Max's truck. The results of the tire tracks comparison from the dirt bike were inconclusive, but it didn't matter. We had Keith Collins' DNA all over the bike, and when the divers had pulled his head out of the water, we had been able to positively match his helmet to the one from the driver who had driven past Max's house, thanks to a unique sticker on the side. Donald's helmet was found in the box truck, but it didn't amount to much in the way of evidence.

After a long and detailed presentation, Britt had assured us that she would not only prosecute Donald for multiple counts of first degree murder, but she would seek the death penalty. She warned us that we were in for a long and exhaustive legal battle, but she was pleased with the job that had been done and was confident that we would be successful.

"Are you ready to go inside?" Susan asked.

I had stopped at the door to the fire department to read a plaque that had been mounted to the wall near the entrance. I nodded and we entered the large meeting hall.

The service was a beautiful one that culminated in Mayor Pauline Cane presenting a posthumous life-saving award to Cole's mother on his behalf. Mrs. Peterson tried to put on a brave face, but she fell apart when she heard the way Mayor Cane spoke of her son. There wasn't a dry eye in the house after that point. When it was over, everyone in the room lined up to hug her. Members of the fire department shared brief stories about Cole—stories that would make any mother proud.

After the last person had spent a brief moment with Mrs. Peterson, everyone moved out back, where tables, chairs, and trays of food had been set up. Susan and I moved to a table where Melvin, Takecia, Amy, Baylor, Shade and Regan were already sitting. There were two spaces between Baylor and Shade, and this was where Susan and I headed.

Amy was talking about her upcoming marriage to Baylor, but she stopped when she saw us.

"I'm so sorry, Clint," she said, a frown tugging at the corners of her mouth.

"About?" I asked, waiting for it.

"I'm sorry you'll be eighty when your new baby graduates." She shook her head. "It's so sad."

I just laughed.

"How's your hand?" Melvin asked. He must've apologized a thousand times over the past month for breaking my fingers. No matter how many times I told him he could break my fingers any day to keep me alive, he still felt bad.

"My hand's great," I said, making a fist. Although I hadn't regained all of my strength, the splints had come off and I had full mobility again. "It's as good as new, and I'm damned glad to be alive."

As I had also done a thousand times over the past month, I thanked Melvin, Baylor, and Regan for saving my life. The doctors said I would've definitely suffered irreparable brain damage, and probably died, had Regan not immediately begun performing rescue breaths while I was being hoisted to the top of the embankment.

"Had she waited until you were on the bank," the doctor had said, "you wouldn't have survived."

Instead of letting that bit of news get me down, I was thankful to have been given another shot at life, and a chance to meet our new child and watch him or her and Grace grow up.

I was staring across the grounds where a group of people were huddled around a fire truck when Shade leaned close.

"Hey, Clint," he began, fidgeting a little, "if I met someone while I was working, would it be unethical of me to ask her out on a date?"

"You graduate from the police academy next week, don't you?" I asked, ignoring his question.

"Yeah, finally."

"Are you getting any awards?"

"I don't know," he said, stammering a little. "They didn't say anything about any awards."

I smiled inwardly. He was getting the Top Cadet Award for excelling in all aspects of the academy, which included physical fitness, firearms, and academics. Brandon Berger had sworn me to secrecy, so I kept my mouth shut.

"This girl," I said, "is she a victim?"

"Um, not on any case I worked." Shade shuffled his feet under the table. "But, um, she was a victim in the past on a different case, back before I came to work here."

"Is she blonde and has blue eyes?" I asked, trying hard to stifle a grin.

Shade's face lost some of its color. "Yeah, how'd—?"

"I don't know, Shade," I said in as serious a tone as I could muster. "I don't think it's a good idea. She's not the right person for you."

He seemed to mull it over. "Really?"

"I mean, look at them." I indicated Amy and Baylor. "She looks really happy with Baylor and they're planning a wedding—"

"No!" he quickly said, trying to keep his voice low. "I don't like Amy!"

Every head at the table jerked around.

"What'd you say?" Amy asked, putting a hand on her hip. "You don't like me?"

"No, I didn't mean it like that." His face was burning red now. "I was asking about someone else who had blonde hair and blue eyes. I like you as a person, but—"

We all began laughing and I slapped his shoulder.

"Alice Pierce is a wonderful girl," I said. "I think y'all would make a nice couple."

He was even more confused than ever now. "But…but how'd you know I was talking about her?"

"Please." I waved a dismissive hand. "When I invited you to go meet her the other night you acted like you were headed for the electric chair. I've never seen you act so unsure of yourself before."

"Don't let him fool you," Amy said to Shade. "Clint didn't have a clue what was going on. I had to tell him that sparks were flying."

They continued talking, but their voices faded away in the background. I was watching one of the firefighters help a young boy up to the driver's seat of a fire truck. He gripped the steering wheel in wide-eyed awe. It was Benny, the boy Cole had saved. I smiled as I imagined all the things he might go on to do in his life. Perhaps he would play basketball in middle school, or join the marching band. He might play varsity football in high school and write for the school newspaper. He could go to college or learn a trade. Maybe even join the military or become a cop. Some day, he might become a father, and when they had kids, a grandfather.

I nodded to myself. Everything he would do from here on out—everything he would become—was only possible because one selfless young man had jumped in front of a truck. I remembered my mom quoting some Bible scripture saying that there was no greater love than for a man to lay down his life for his friends. Well, Cole had done one better—he had laid down his life for a perfect stranger.

Like BJ Bourg on Facebook

BJ Bourg

BJ Bourg is a former professional boxer and a lifelong martial artist who retired as the chief investigator for a district attorney's office. A thirty-year veteran of law enforcement, he has worked as a patrol cop, detective, detective sergeant and police academy instructor. He has investigated thousands of felony cases and trained hundreds of law enforcement officers in self-defense, firearms, and criminal operations.

Throughout his career, Bourg has served on many specialized units such as SWAT, Explosives Search Team, and Homicide Response Team. He founded his agency's sniper program and served as its leader and trainer for nearly a decade. A graduate of seven basic and advanced sniper schools, he deployed as the primary sniper on dozens of call-outs, including barricaded subjects, hostage rescue operations, and fugitive apprehensions. He also served as the sniper instructor for the 2001 Louisiana Tactical Police Officers Association's Conference.

Bourg has been the recipient of numerous awards, including Top Shooter at an FBI Sniper School, the Distinguished Service Medal, and Certificates of Commendation for his work as a homicide detective. In addition to speaking at numerous law enforcement and writer's conferences, he has written dozens of articles for leading law enforcement and tactical magazines covering a wide range of topics such as defensive tactics, sniper deployment, suspect interrogation, report writing, no-knock search warrants, and more.

Above all else, Bourg is a father and a husband. The highlight of his life is spending time with his beautiful wife and wonderful children. Originally from Louisiana, he now proudly calls Tellico Plains, Tennessee home.

www.bjbourg.com

Made in the USA
Columbia, SC
29 March 2024